CYBER QUEST

CARVER CHRISTIAN HIGH SCHOOL
7650 SAPPERTON AVE.
BURNABY, BC
V3N 4E1
604-523-1580

SIGMUND BROUWER

Tommy
NELSON

Thomas Nelson, Inc.
Nashville

Copyright © 2000
by Sigmund Brouwer

All rights reserved. No portion of this book may be
reproduced in any form without the written
permission of the publisher, with the exception
of brief excerpts in reviews.

Published in Nashville, Tennessee,
by Tommy Nelson™, a division of Thomas Nelson, Inc.

Cover illustration: Kevin Burke

Library of Congress Cataloging-in-Publication Data

Brouwer, Sigmund, 1959–
    CyberQuest / Sigmund Brouwer.
        p. cm.
    Contents: Pharoh's tomb—Knight's honor—Pirate's cross—
Outlaw's gold—Soldier's aim—Galilee Man.
    ISBN 0-8499-7577-8
    [1. Science fiction.   2. Virtual reality—Fiction.
3. Christian life—Fiction.]   I. Title.

PZ7.B79984 Cy   2000
[Fic]—dc21   00-020019
                                                    CIP

Printed in the United States of America
00 01 02 03 04 05 QPV 9 8 7 6 5 4 3 2 1

Dedicated to Michael Kooman,
a perpetual villain on
number eighteen.

CYBERQUEST TERMS

BODYWRAP — a sheet of cloth that serves as clothing.

THE COMMITTEE — a group of people dedicated to making the world a better place.

MAINSIDE — any part of North America other than Old Newyork.

MINI-VIDCAM — a hidden video camera.

NETPHONE — a public telephone with a computer keypad. For a minimum charge, users can send e-mail through the Internet.

OLD NEWYORK — the bombed-out island of Manhattan, transformed into a colony for convicts and the poorest of the poor.

TECHNOCRAT — an upper-class person who can read, operate computers, and make much more money than a Welfaro.

'TRIC SHOOTER — an electric gun that fires enough voltage to stun its target.

VIDTRANS — a video transmitter.

VIDWATCH — a watch with a mini television screen.

WATERMAN — a person who sells pure water.

WELFARO — a person living in the slums of Old Newyork.

THE GREAT WATER WARS

In the year A.D. 2031 came the great Water Wars. The world's population had tripled during the previous thirty years. Worldwide demand for fresh, unpolluted water grew so strong that countries fought for control of water supplies. The war was longer and worse than any of the previous world wars. When it ended, there was a new world government, called the World United. The government was set up to distribute water among the world's countries and to prevent any future wars. But it took its control too far.

World United began to see itself as all-important. After all, it had complete control of the world's limited water supplies. It began to make choices about who was "worthy" to receive water.

Very few people dared to object when World United denied water to criminals, the poor, and others it saw as undesirable. People were afraid of losing their own water if they spoke up.

One group, however, saw that the government's actions were wrong. These people—Christians— dared to speak.

They knew that only God should have control

of their lives. They knew that they needed to stand up to the government for those who could not. Because of this, the government began to persecute the Christians and outlawed the Christian church. Some people gave up their beliefs to continue to receive an allotment of government water. Others refused and either joined underground churches or became hunted rebels, getting their water on the black market.

In North America, only one place was safe for the rebel Christians. The island of Old Newyork. The bombings of the great Water Wars had destroyed much of it, and the government used the entire island as a prison. The government did not care who else fled to the slums of those ancient street canyons.

Old Newyork grew in population. While most newcomers were criminals, some were these rebel Christians. Desperate for freedom, they entered this lion's den of lawlessness.

Limited water and supplies were sent from Mainside to Old Newyork, but some on Mainside said that any was too much to waste on the slums. When the issue came up at a World Senate meeting in 2049, it was decided that Old Newyork must be treated like a small country. It would have to provide something to the world in return for water and food.

When this new law went into effect, two things happened in the economy of this giant slum. First, work gangs began stripping steel from the sky-scrapers. Antipollution laws on Mainside made it expensive to manufacture new steel. Old steel, then, was traded for food and water.

Second, when a certain Mainside business genius got caught evading taxes in 2053, he was sent to Old Newyork. There he quickly saw a new business opportunity—slave labor.

Old Newyork was run by criminals and had no laws. Who was there to stop him from forcing people to work for him?

Within a couple of years, the giant slum was filled with bosses who made men, women, and children work for almost no pay. They produced clothing on giant sewing machines and assembled cheap computer products. Even boys and girls as young as ten worked up to twelve hours a day.

Christians in Old Newyork, of course, fought against this. But it was a battle the Christians lost over the years. Criminals and factory bosses used ruthless violence to control the slums.

Christianity was forced to become an underground movement in the slums. Education, too, disappeared. As did any medical care.

Into this world, Mok was born.

BACKSTORY 1

MAINSIDE, A.D. 2076. From the top of the cliff, giant searchlights slashed swords of white at the shoreline below. The black river released ghosts of fog that rose like gray smoke through the shafts of light. At the dock, where the ferries arrived and departed every four hours, soldiers patrolled the shoreline from behind electric fences. Their dogs pulled them along by straining against their leashes.

Two men stood beneath the lights on the dock, waiting for the next ferry. They faced the river. Searchlight circles danced across their backs, throwing flashes of long, eerie shadows onto the water. The old man wore a long coat against the cold. A small suitcase rested near his feet. Standing beside him, a much younger man shivered in a light jacket.

"Manhattan, Manhattan," the old man said. He coughed and spit red into a handkerchief. "Who would have thought it would come to this?"

"Manhattan?"

The older man smiled in apology. "Sorry," he said. "I was lost in thought. Before the great Water Wars, the island of Old Newyork was called Manhattan."

"Oh, yes," the younger man said. "I've seen photos on multimeed disks. Bridges once connected it to Mainside, right? Then the Water War bombs destroyed them."

"Bridges and tunnels." The old man pointed downriver. "A half mile away was the entrance to the tunnel called Lincoln. It went beneath the river and came up on the other side of the island. In the gasoline era. They used it for automobiles."

"You remember that?"

The old man laughed at himself. "I *am* old, aren't I?"

He paused.

They both stared across the water. Each for different reasons. The older man had memories. The younger one had doubts.

The ghosts of fog were like shapeless soldiers, rising from the black deep. Past them, on the far shore, flickers of small fires appeared.

A coughing fit took the old man. It bent him almost to his waist.

The younger man waited until the other had regained his breath. Both pretended the coughing had not happened.

"There was once a time you could see the lights of Manhattan across the horizon," the old man said, searching for a way to break the awkward silence. "Lights of skyscrapers standing on the most expensive real estate in the world."

"And now," the young man said, "it's worse than worthless. A giant slum."

The young man needed to voice his earlier doubts. "Why should you offer them your help?"

As he spoke, a wide, flat-bottomed boat broke from the darkness into the spotlight circles. A bell rang on top of the hill. Within seconds, a dozen more spotlights burned through the night sky, bathing the ferry in a bright glare. The scene silenced both men on the dock.

In the boat's wake, three heads bobbed.

A sentry spotted the swimmers and blew a shrill whistle of warning. Soldiers shouted and dogs barked as all of the patrols moved toward the shore. Two dozen soldiers and dogs were waiting as the three swimmers staggered out of the water to be roped and marched toward the dock. They were barely more than boys, soaked and shivering, skinny and limping.

Both men on the dock remained silent as they watched the soldiers approach. The ferry was secured against the dock. The soldiers marched the three boys past the men and held them at rifle point near the end of the dock.

A large truck backed to the dock. Workers jumped out, pushed a ramp up to the side of the ferry, and began to unload large crates. Then they loaded food supplies onto the ferry for its return trip.

"Those three will be put on the ferry and returned to Old Newyork," the younger man said. "And you'll go with them, Benjamin. Are you sure this is what you must do?"

"As you grow older," Benjamin Rufus said, "you grow less certain of what the right course of action is and rely more on God's grace. Pray for me."

"Why must you go?" the younger man said with some impatience. "They are criminals and steel scavengers. They are the enemy. Surely there are better places to—"

"Think of the Cross," the old man said quietly.

The young man bowed his head.

"Cambridge," the old man said gently after a few moments. "You are not afraid to face difficult questions. That has been as important to me as your faith and intelligence."

The old man coughed again. He wiped his mouth and shook away his pain. "Your strength will make you the leader of the Committee when I am gone. Use the resources wisely."

Workers carried off the last of the crates. The soldiers prodded the three swimmers onto the ferry and handcuffed them to its rails.

"I want you to continue what I began here. Give the children hope." Benjamin Rufus leaned over and picked up his suitcase in his left hand. With his right, he reached out to shake Cambridge's hand.

"I'll be fine," Benjamin said. "By the time the ferry reaches the other side, I'll be dressed to move among them. I can make a difference there. And my illness won't kill me too soon. I'm a stubborn man. I'll send reports as long as I can."

"For the last time, sir, let me go. Take your money and return to the hospital. More treatment will—"

"Delay my death a year or two? No, Cambridge. Besides, I'm the only one on the Committee who can travel among them. I've been there before."

"You've been in Old Newyork?" Cambridge could not hide his shock.

Benjamin smiled. A passing searchlight showed the tired lines on his face. "Now, as I leave, I feel safe in telling you something I've kept hidden, even from the Committee. I was once sent there."

He paused and smiled sadly. "And that, of course, is why I must return."

With those last words, Benjamin Rufus left Cambridge standing alone.

Long after the ferry had slipped back into the darkness, Cambridge remained on the dock, staring at the water.

The old man had once been sent there! Yet only criminals were ever sent to Old Newyork.

And he knows he will die among them, Cambridge thought. *Otherwise he wouldn't have told me his secret.*

Cambridge also knew that getting into Old Newyork was simple. But once there, it was almost impossible to escape.

CHAPTER 1

MAINSIDE, A.D. 2096. The twelve Committee members chose a Friday early in February of 2096 as the day to kidnap Mok. They scheduled his trip to begin shortly after noon. The field ops had reported it was Mok's daily habit to nap at that time. They would find him in a crumbled portion of the abandoned subway tunnel that ran beneath Broadway.

By 9:00 A.M. on that Friday in February, eleven of the Committee members were seated in a luxury high-rise. The Committee owned the building, which sat on the west side of the Hudson River. All eleven sipped on imported water as they safely watched a vidtrans monitor Mok's last three hours in Old Newyork.

The twelfth Committee member was missing. He said he had a bad case of the flu. It was a lie.

Besides those twelve, two others knew Mok's destination. They were level-five field ops. Both were in far more danger than the Committee in the high-rise. The field ops were stuck in the center of Old Newyork. They were doing their best to keep their mini-vidcams on Mok.

Mok, of course, knew nothing of this.

CHAPTER 2

OLD NEWYORK, A.D. 2096. The field ops, Miles Steward and Lee D'Amico, had been waiting in the building shadows for five minutes, watching Mok.

Just down the street, Mok stood at the edge of a small crowd around a waterman. Sunlight glinted diamonds through the flasks of water on a rack behind the waterman. No pretty diamonds, however, glinted from the ugly machine guns the guards on each side of the waterman carried.

Mok did not move. He stood taller than most in the crowd around him. He might have been a big fifteen-year-old. Or smaller at age twenty. Mok probably didn't know his age either. No hospitals meant no birth certificates. And bad nutrition meant slow growth.

The only thing certain about Mok was that his face—framed by dark, curly hair—showed a mixed background, a mongrel nobility of high cheekbones and faintly Asian eyes.

"Heat bomb," Miles said to the younger field op.

Miles was the taller of the two. Height was all that distinguished him from Lee at the moment, as both were dressed in formless bodywraps. They were as filthy and ragged as any of the Welfaros who

2

passed them in the crowds. Their faces were lost in the unkempt beards they had grown for this assignment; not a single one of their Mainside friends would have recognized them.

"Huh?" Lee replied. The mini-vidcam in his sleeve was directed at Mok and the waterman. But Lee's attention was on a rat that nosed the pants cuff of an old man nearby on the cracked pavement.

"Hit 'em with a heat bomb," Miles said, half indignant his junior partner didn't hang on his every word. "I tell you, kid, we should nuke 'em. Zap! Fuse all these Welfaros and their cockroach hotels into a puddle of glass. No more smell. No more garbage. No more food riots. And best of all, more water for the rest of us. I'll bet Mainside could save a couple million gallons a day."

Miles scratched his side. The old clothes were itchy. Or maybe it was fleas. He hoped it was the clothes.

Lee hardly heard his partner. He had just watched the rat crawl up the old man's pants leg. Head, body, then tail of the rat disappeared.

"Miles?"

"Yeah?"

"I think that guy's dead."

"What guy?" Miles didn't like it when his younger partner ignored his great ideas.

Lee pointed. "That guy. See the bump moving up his pants leg? It's a rat."

"No big deal," Miles said. "This is Old Newyork."

Not that either needed a reminder. Every breath

they took filled their nostrils with the stench of sewage from the gutters. Up and down the street, as far as they could see, rickety shacks filled the street canyons. Some shacks were lost in the shadows of the taller buildings. Other shacks were warmed by the morning's sunlight.

Miles softened his tough-guy voice. He told himself to remember this was only Lee's second time across the river. "Look, kid, you'll get used to it. Welfaros live different from Technocrats."

"They die different too." Lee couldn't take his eyes off the rat crawling beneath the man's clothes.

"Don't get bleeding heart on me," Miles said. "At least we haven't cut off their water. And—"

He broke off. "Your vidcam better be getting this. Look!"

Mok had moved to the stands and grabbed a water flask. He shouted at the waterman, waving the flask. Then Mok threw the water flask high and hard toward a nearby shack.

The waterman's guards, filled with horror at the possibility of seeing the flask shatter, dived to catch it. In that brief moment, Mok plucked another water flask from the stand and dashed back into the crowd.

Before the guards could raise their machine guns, the crowd broke into a stream of shouting, panicking people. Through the confusion, the waterman stared at the fleeing figure of Mok as he ducked and weaved his getaway.

"Did your vidcam get that?" Miles asked.

"All of it," Lee said. "Do we follow?"

"Of course. But not in a hurry. That's why you brushed up against him to plant that velcrotrak a half-hour ago."

Miles paused. He let his voice get tough again. "Earlier you wondered if this was right. How do you feel now that you've seen he's low enough to steal pure water?"

CHAPTER 3

AS THEY MOVED through the throngs of Welfaros, Miles and Lee were forced to be careful about several things. First of all, they didn't dare smile. Their teeth—white, straight, complete—would have given them away as Technocrats. Welfaros had stained and rotted teeth because Old Newyork did not have dentists.

Miles was also careful not to let anyone see him check the vidwatch on his wrist. The street grid on the watchface showed a pulsing red dot, which gave Mok's location. It should be easy to track Mok's movement. But if a Welfaro discovered technostuff could be had for the taking, Miles and Lee would be mobbed and killed. Their 'tric shooters might save them from a dozen Welfaros, but not from hundreds. So each time he looked at the vidwatch, Miles pretended to scratch his arm as he pulled back his bodywrap.

Because of their need to be careful, it took them half an hour to finally catch up with Mok. They passed Welfaros cooking chunks of meat over oil drums filled with burning garbage. They once stopped to let a work gang drag a steel girder past them down the street. They kept their heads down as a ganglord passed them, surrounded by guards armed with swords.

Finally, Miles and Lee turned down a side street, guided by the velcrotrak stuck to Mok's bodywrap.

"Here?" Lee whispered when Miles stopped and frowned at the broken-down entrance of a tall building.

"Here. Inside."

"Do we go in?" Lee asked.

"Are you nuts?" Miles replied. "There are thirty levels. He could be anywhere." Nothing, not even the invisible watching eyes of the Committee, could get Miles to step inside an unfamiliar Welfaro building. You never knew when or where the steel support girders had been thieved.

"Yatt Hote," Lee said as he craned his head to look at the entrance arches. "What kind of name is that to put on a building?"

Miles sighed. Ten years ago, when he'd gone through the Academy, pre–Water War history was as required as basic computer programming. This new generation of agents knew nothing.

"Hyatt Hotel," Miles said.

"Hotel?"

"Before the Water Wars, Technocrats used to visit here."

"From Mainside?"

"Where else? No one's come back from Mars yet."

"I mean—"

"Shhh!" Miles adjusted his earphone. "The velcrotrak's hit voice activation."

"Send it on to Mainside?"

"Of course."

7

Lee pushed a switch on the vidcam strapped to his forearm. They both listened. The words were also sent on to the Committee in the luxury high-rise on the other side of the Hudson River.

"Water?" a reedy, wavering voice asked Mok, somewhere in the thirty levels of building above the field ops.

"You need it, don't you?" Miles and Lee recognized Mok's voice. Low, calm, and unhurried. They had yet to hear him speak differently.

"But this is pure!" she said. "Where did you get the credits?"

"It doesn't matter," Mok told her. "This should last you a few days."

"But nobody gives away pure water." The reedy voice broke into sobs. "And nobody cares about old women close to death."

"I've got to go," Mok said. "Hide the water. Make it last. I don't know when I can be back again."

Several moments of silence. Then the woman's voice reached them again. Faintly, as if Mok had already stepped into a hallway.

"Why have you done this for me?" she asked. "I can't pay you back."

More silence. Had Mok moved down the hallway? Or was he returning to answer the woman's question?

"All right." Mok's voice came in clearly. "I'll tell you why. But if you laugh, I'll leave."

"I won't laugh." The old woman's voice was a whisper. Mok must be right beside her.

"The Galilee Man. His Father's house has many rooms. He went there to prepare a place for us."

"I won't laugh, boy. But I don't understand."

"He said his followers who give the little ones a cup of cold water will truly get their reward."

"The Galilee Man? Who is he? Where did you hear this?"

"From an audiobook. I memorized it before it was stolen from me."

"Audiobook? Where did you get an—"

"Hush. Sip on some water. This book had wonderful tales about the man who walked in Galilee. I want to believe they are true. But no one I've asked can tell me if Galilee is a place or a legend."

"I surely cannot," the old woman said. "An audiobook! To think—"

"I listened to it again and again while I had it. There was a man in this audiobook. He gathered twelve men to follow him. Some were fishermen and—"

Mok's voice stopped abruptly. "What is this?"

"Looks like a spider without legs," the woman said moments later.

Miles and Lee shot glances at each other.

"He's found the velcrotrak," Miles said.

A loud snap nearly pierced their ears.

"He's *stepped* on the velcrotrak," Lee said. "Now what do we do?"

"Not a problem." Miles grinned. "We'll be waiting for him when he gets to his hiding hole."

CHAPTER 4

MAINSIDE. The Committee member who had called in sick was not at home. He was hundreds of miles south of Old Newyork.

He stepped into a private suite in the main office of the World United government, where a man waited for him. This man's face was stretched tight in the highly fashionable manner of reconstructive surgery. He was the president of the World United—the most powerful person among the billions who had survived the Water Wars.

The Committee member bowed as he entered the room. Then he lifted his arms as if he were about to fly.

The president waved a detecto-wand around the man's body, searching for weapons and recording devices. Usually an assistant would do this, but no one else must know the Committee member was there. The detecto-wand remained silent.

Finally satisfied, the president nodded to allow the other to speak.

"I am here to tell you that the Committee is ready to test another candidate, Your Worldship."

"And?" the leader of the World United prompted. He wore the black silk toga that signified a high-status

Technocrat. He was a bulky man with white hair and pale skin flushed slightly pink.

"I doubt you need fear," the Committee member said. "The latest candidate is a male Welfaro. One named Mok. Born in the slums of Old Newyork. He can't even read. Who knows what Cambridge was thinking? As I said, we have nothing to fear."

"Don't tell me what I need or need not fear," His Worldship said. Although he barely spoke above a whisper, his anger was obvious. "I have a billion dollars' worth of investors ready—investors who will kill me in the blink of an eye if I lose their money. And I have a hundred million of my own dollars at stake. This candidate must fail. We *must* take Old Newyork."

The Committee member stared at the wall, too afraid to make eye contact. "Yes, Your Worldship. We both know in one month the Senate will vote on your proposal to drop a heat bomb on Old Newyork. This candidate will fail, and Cambridge will have nothing to convince the Senate to vote otherwise. Then—"

"I know what will happen then, fool. That is why I've promised you a Senate post and a share of the investment. You know full well that the stakes are too high to risk any mistakes. Return to Cambridge. Watch the proceedings closely. Report as needed."

"I shall keep you informed, Your Worldship," the first man said.

"Of course you will. You are too far into this to go any direction but where I order."

CHAPTER 5

OLD NEWYORK. Miles and Lee hid behind a wide collapsed beam, hoping the tunnel walls would not cave in farther. Dust dotted a shaft of sunlight that dropped into the subway tunnel through a grate. Rats squeaked and rustled in the semidarkness beyond the shaft of light.

Miles and Lee were not enjoying their wait.

"You want to tell me that Technocrats actually came down here?" Lee asked. "Rode with Welfaros in cars along those tracks?"

"They called it the subway," Miles whispered. "They rode in the hundreds, all packed together. Before the Water Wars, fool. You know, after the dawn of the computer age. I wish they'd teach you rookies something about history."

Lee opened his mouth to protest, but Miles elbowed him into silence. "In case you haven't noticed, I've kept my voice to a whisper. And that's only to answer your stupid questions. I'd rather not speak at all."

"Stupid questions? I—"

"Quiet." Miles elbowed Lee again. "If he hears us, it might take us days to find him again. This guy is fast and smart. How much longer do *you* want to stay in Old Newyork?"

Lee wisely shut his mouth. He didn't believe Miles's story anyway. As if Technocrats would travel with Welfaros. Miles thought he knew everything, but Lee was sure that what he didn't know, he made up.

Lee just wanted to get back to Mainside. Real food. Real beds. And, of course, a real shower. He wanted to shower so badly that he had already decided to take some of his risk pay and buy an extra five minutes of warm, wonderful water. No, make that twenty minutes. He deserved it after days in Old Newyork. And it would be a real shower. Not one of the disinfecting showers they'd face before they were allowed back Mainside. He'd sing in the shower and . . .

Miles was elbowing him again.

Footsteps approached.

Mok moved into the shaft of sunlight. It showed him for the mongrel he was. Any fool could look at him and see there'd been no clear bloodlines in his genetics since before the Water Wars.

"Stop," Miles ordered, stepping out from behind the beam.

Lee remained hidden. It was standard field op policy. Never let the enemy understand your full force. Not that it made a difference here. Miles held the 'tric shooter chest high in both hands, training it on Mok.

Mok stopped.

"Good," Miles said. "You're making my job easy."

"Job? Are you with a work gang?"

"Nope. And before you say another word, I'm

going to stun you." Miles smiled. "It's that simple."

Miles squeezed the trigger. A high-volt beam crackled from the 'tric shooter and arced the short distance into Mok's chest.

CHAPTER 6

MAINSIDE. It was a large room on the tenth floor of the luxury high-rise. The Committee kept it mainly empty. That made security much easier. No one could disturb or monitor the activities on the tenth floor.

Cambridge stood near the door, waiting. At the far side of the room, the nitrogen cooling system of the supercomputer hummed quietly. Two comtechs stood nearby, waiting too.

Five minutes later, the elevator bells rang. Cambridge did not relax until a doctor entered, followed by three medtechs who wheeled a high, narrow cot into the room. Mok's body, on top of the cot, was covered with a blanket. Cambridge knew what route the field ops had taken to bring Mok to Mainside. Seeing the covered body briefly turned Cambridge's thoughts back in time.

Nearly twenty years earlier, Cambridge had stood on the dock and watched the old man leave for Old Newyork. Only rebels, outcasts, and criminals lost themselves in Old Newyork, so the World United government never stopped anyone from going there. In fact, Old Newyork was such a convenient dumping ground, all criminals were sent there.

Getting to Old Newyork, as Cambridge had seen,

was as simple as stepping onto the next ferry. But that was the last simple thing any passenger faced. Since the World United had abandoned Old Newyork to the poor, the desperate, the dying, and the criminals, there were no hospitals, no police, and no electrical power. There, among the slums, ganglords ruled like kings.

No one was ever allowed back to Mainside for any reason.

One look at a map showed how easy it was for the World United government to transform the island into a prison. The East and Hudson Rivers formed the arms of a Y on both sides. At the north, the Harlem River was a channel between the other two rivers and served as a lid of the Y.

The Mainside shores of all three rivers were zoned with a wide no-cross zone dotted with explosive mines. Beyond the mines were high electric fences, and behind those deadly fences, soldiers endlessly patrolled with guard dogs. Upstream and downstream, patrol boats waited for anyone who tried to swim, drift, or boat to freedom.

None of that had changed since the night Cambridge had watched the old man go, never to return.

What had changed was Cambridge.

Inspired by the old man's faith and sacrifice, Cambridge had vowed to set up a safe passage route from Old Newyork, much like the underground railroad that had freed slaves centuries earlier.

So, armed with the almost limitless Committee funds, Cambridge found an old map that showed the site of the Lincoln Tunnel. He had purchased land close to the original entrance. The Committee had built its high-rise building within a hundred yards of the river. Millions of dollars later, they had a tunnel from the basement of the building to the old Lincoln Tunnel entrance. More millions of dollars had gone into running a six-foot plastic tube through the length of the old tunnel, coming up in a hidden entrance on the other side of the river. Now the Committee literally had a pipeline into Old Newyork.

The passage had been finished too late to bring the old man back; his reports had ended years before. But the tunnel served a purpose. It was through this passage that the Committee shipped medical supplies for relief efforts in Old Newyork. It was through this passage that field ops went back and forth at will. It was through this passage that they had smuggled Mok back to Mainside.

"He is ready, sir."

It was the doctor, taking Cambridge's mind off the past. The comtechs were busy at the supercomputer. Cambridge gave the young doctor—short and red-headed—his full attention.

"Sir, we ran the required tests on him. Despite a lifetime of poor nutrition, he has a healthy body. It should be no problem to keep him on life-support."

"Good," Cambridge said to the doctor. "And brain-wave activity?"

The doctor dropped his head, as if trying to find courage to continue.

"Yes?" Cambridge said more softly. Cambridge

was tall, almost thin. He dressed as casually as he could—soft brown sweater and blue jeans—but he knew that his hawklike appearance, the intensity in his eyes, and his reputation all served to frighten people who did not know him. Cambridge reminded himself as often as he could—indeed prayed over it as a weakness—that he needed to be more focused on others and less wrapped up in the world of his own thoughts.

"Well . . . ," the doctor nearly stammered.

Cambridge forced himself to wait. The poor man was obviously nervous—something unusual for doctors. Cambridge did not want to make it worse for him.

"It's just that his inner-core brain waves scanned extremely high, sir."

"Is that a problem?" Cambridge asked. "I thought high inner-core readings were a sign of intelligence."

"That's just it, sir. We find it hard to believe that a slum child would show this kind of intelligence."

Cambridge smiled. "It's not a surprise to me."

"Sir?"

"Nothing, doctor. Please proceed with hooking him up to the computer. For what he is about to face, we should thank God that at least he has one thing going for him."

"Yes sir."

As the doctor walked away, Cambridge let out a deep breath. Less than a month to go. Cambridge did not want to think about what would happen if this final candidate failed.

CHAPTER 7

CYBERSPACE—EGYPT. Mok screamed in his nightmare. He saw a man step out from behind a concrete beam, a man who promised to stun him. The man pointed a strange object at Mok. A crackling arc of blue light reached into Mok's chest, tearing his consciousness away in a surge of exploding pain.

Mok woke in total darkness, trembling at the vivid memory of his nightmare. It had been years since he'd cried out in his sleep. There was too much danger that the noise would give away his hiding spot. Only once had the work gangs found him. Without parents to claim him at night, he'd been a prisoner of the factory for a month before he'd escaped. Mok had vowed never to be taken again.

Mok drew deep breaths, and tried to quiet the heaving of his chest. *Calm,* he told himself, *reach for calm.* Night was never safe for those who gave away their hiding spots. He must remain silent.

Yet as awareness returned, Mok became edgier and edgier. Why did he feel so strange?

He realized he could hear an unfamiliar sound. A sighing, the way wind sometimes pushed its way through the street canyons of Old Newyork. Sighing was not the sound he fell asleep to each night. No, he fell asleep to the steady dripping of seepage from above. He strained his ears to hear water. Nothing.

Where was the plop of water drops so familiar to him over the years?

Mok shifted and almost sat bolt upright with surprise. Long habit stopped him though. The crevice he used each night as a bed was hardly bigger than himself. Once, when he was younger, another bad dream had brought him to a sitting position. He had smacked his head against the concrete directly above. Then he had fallen back onto the collection of rags that served as his mattress and blankets.

Only now he wasn't on his rags!

His back was on something rougher and flatter than rags. A mat, perhaps. And it seemed he was wrapped in soft cloth. He reached above and to both sides. *His groping hands could not find the walls of concrete that usually surrounded him.*

As his eyes adjusted to the darkness, Mok also noticed faint details above him, lines of lesser darkness against black. Then pinpricks of light. Stars?

Impossible! Mok crawled into his hiding hole every night. Without fail he piled up rocks at the low, narrow entrance to keep the rats out. How could any light reach him?

The air!

It was dry. Hot. Not damp and cold.

How could he not be where he always slept? He tried to remember crawling into the crevice as he did at the end of the day. With a lurch of sickness, he discovered he couldn't remember. The crackling arc of blue light came back to him not as a dream, but as something that had actually happened.

Fear washed over him. Mok hated fear. It was an enemy.

"Our Father who art in heaven," he whispered in slow rhythm, "hallowed be thy name."

He knew it was ridiculous to behave like the little boy who had escaped into the wonderful tales of a precious audiobook. Yet Mok continued whispering into the darkness until he finished his favorite speech given by the Galilee Man. Mok didn't know why whispering it soothed him when he felt lonely, but it always did. Maybe, Mok thought, he liked to think about having a father of his own. The place the Galilee Man called heaven sounded nice, and Mok wanted to believe such a place could some day be home.

When Mok finished his whispering, part of the fear dissolved. His confusion, though, remained.

On his back, Mok stared at the stars that appeared through the outlines above him. He stared and waited. He had no idea how much time passed, but eventually his patience was rewarded. The gray of dawn arrived to show that the outline was a window carved into a limestone wall.

Only then did he rise. He was dressed in a strange white tunic that he could not remember putting on.

Mok stepped toward a large doorway in the opposite wall and to the light outside.

CHAPTER 8

THE SAND and rocks will shred your feet. Instead of admiring the early sun, you should go back and get your sandals. You will find them beside the water jug in your room of sleep."

Mok spun around to face the unexpected voice. He saw a wizened dwarf wearing the same kind of white tunic he wore, leaning on a cane.

The dwarf laughed. "If only you could see your face! A man would think you had no idea where you are."

The dwarf whacked Mok's leg with the cane. "Which you don't, do you? Admit it. You're lost."

Mok was glad for the whack. It gave him a place to release his anger. Anger at his confusion. How had he gotten here? Where was he?

Standing outside this strange flat building, Mok had never before felt air so dry and hot. He had never before seen sand—endless in all directions. Nor a sky without buildings. Nor a wide ribbon of water. He looked up the road from the water and saw an immense pile of square stones tapering to a point high in the sky. Never had he seen such a thing.

But Mok had seen damaged and mutilated Welfaros. There were plenty of them in Old Newyork,

22

including dwarfs. This was something he could handle.

Mok grabbed the dwarf by the shoulders, and lifted and shook him.

"Set me down," the dwarf said, keeping his grip on his cane but not striking back. "Or I won't offer you any help."

Mok stopped his shaking, but did not set the dwarf down. He spoke between clenched teeth. "Give me help or I'll choke you."

"Choke away," the dwarf said. If he was impressed with Mok's strength, it did not show. "With me gone, you'll face execution by sunset."

Mok dropped the dwarf, who promptly whacked Mok with his cane again.

"I said *set me down*," the dwarf said angrily. "Not *drop me*."

"Where am I?" Mok asked, equally angry. He refused to rub his stinging leg; the dwarf had whacked him with great enthusiasm.

"Egypt," the dwarf answered. "Thousands of years before you were born. If you had any education at all, you would recognize that as a pyramid."

"Pyramid?" echoed Mok. He decided he was still in a dream. That could be the only explanation for this. How could he be somewhere thousands of years before he was born?

Another whack from the dwarf. "Pay attention. I don't like to repeat myself. What you see is a pyramid. A burial place for pharaohs."

"Pharaohs?" Mok asked.

The dwarf took another swing with his cane, but this time Mok was ready and grabbed it. The dwarf simply let go and grinned, leaving Mok with the short piece of wood in his hand, feeling a little silly.

"Ignorance, allow for the ignorance," the dwarf said, more to himself than to Mok. "Pharaohs are kings. Rulers of many people. They realize one great truth. No matter how rich and powerful you are, death arrives in the same way it does for the poor. These kings want a place to safeguard their bodies for eternity. They believe that as long as their bodies remain intact they will enjoy life beyond."

Mok nodded. His brain felt numb as he tried to think through this unreal situation.

"It's disgusting, actually," the dwarf said. "Once the pharaoh is dead, the royal undertaker and his assistants cut open the body. They remove all the organs and brain to store in sealed clay jars. The pharaoh's body is dried out, preserved, wrapped in linen. Then it's forever hidden in a secret burial chamber deep in the great pyramid."

The dwarf shook his head to emphasize his disgust. "Stupid idea. If that were how you really lived eternally, wouldn't you want something nicer than dried leather for a body?"

Mok suddenly laughed. "I know what's happening!"

"You do?" The dwarf scrunched his face in puzzlement, something that, given his extensive wrinkles, was a remarkable sight.

"Glo-glo water," Mok said. "Somewhere during the

day, I must have drunk water with glo-glo phar-maceuds. Serves me right for robbing the water barons. I'll wake up in a gutter somewhere with a terrible headache. No wonder I've always refused the stuff before. And there's no way I'll touch it again. This is enough to twist my brain."

Mok snapped his fingers. "Hey, why don't I give you a name? Like . . . like Stinko. It seems to suit you."

"You can't name me." The dwarf stamped his left foot. "I already have a name. Blake."

"This is my dream. I can name you what I want."

"Blake," the dwarf insisted. "Call me anything else and I won't listen. And if it makes you feel better, go ahead and think this is a dream. Later in the day, just remember I warned you."

Mok kept laughing. "Oh really?"

"Really," the dwarf said without humor. "You see, yesterday Pharaoh Cheops died."

"So," Mok said, "even if this isn't a dream, I never knew him. What do I care?"

"You should. There's a reason you are here to inspect the pyramid. You're the royal undertaker."

CHAPTER 9

MOK STOOD IN THE CENTER of a long, narrow boat, looking at the red desert hills and wide skies on both sides of him. He was leaving behind the valley of the pyramids, and leaving behind the dumb dwarf.

He stood at the prow. Behind him, a team of rowers pulled to the rhythm of a drum. A full sail on a single mast helped push the boat upstream.

Not only did he enjoy being important enough to have all these men working so hard for him, but Mok also enjoyed the sway of the water and the breeze against his face. What a nice dream. The street canyons of Old Newyork were dirty and crowded in comparison. Here irrigated fields lined both sides of the river. Tall green plants, three times the height of a man, grew along its edge. The boatsman at the steering rudder had called the plants papyrus and then had frowned at Mok because of his question.

Mok didn't care. He was entertained by this dream and proud of his imagination, something he had never known could be this rich.

Stinko had told him the wide ribbon of water was the river Nile, uncontaminated water that flowed for thousands of miles. Stinko had told him the pyramid took tens of thousands of men more than ten years to build. Hundreds upon hundreds of ten-ton blocks of stone had been hauled across the desert and set on top of each other to form the pyramid. Stinko told him again it had been built for the sake of one man, someone who wanted a safe place to hide his body when he died.

It's remarkable, Mok thought, *that my mind was able to come up with all of this, including a bad-tempered, smelly dwarf.* It was so ridiculous it confirmed for Mok this could only be a dream. As if clear water could flow for thousands of miles without armies fighting for it. It was so ridiculous it made him want to laugh. Perhaps when the glo-glo pharmaceuds wore off, he should become a corner storyteller, earning water instead of stealing it to give to others.

Ahead, Mok saw clusters of low, square white buildings on the west bank of the river. As the boat drew nearer, he saw clusters of the buildings stretch for a considerable distance.

"Boatsman," Mok called.

"Yes, royal undertaker." The boatsman wore a pale cotton skirt, bound in a knot at the front. Mok had kept his laughter to himself, thinking that even in a dream a man had a right to dress as he pleased.

"Tell me, does the town have a name?"

The boatsman frowned again at Mok. "Memphis, the capital. Your destination. Where the royal court lies."

"Watch your attitude," Mok growled. "I'll have you whipped."

The man bowed in instant fright.

"It was a joke," Mok said quickly. Didn't anyone in this dream have a sense of humor?

The boatsman straightened but did not dare look Mok in the face again. Mok walked to the front of the boat and thought about the work he had given himself in his dream. Royal undertaker. If the rest of his dream was as rich as this, it would be fun to find out what lay ahead.

CHAPTER 10

HIS NEW GUIDE was a girl—dark-haired, brown-eyed, and wearing a simple wrap much like Mok's. As he stepped off the boat, she waited to show him the way. Mok wanted to wander the busy streets. But she was firm in leading him to a two-wheeled vehicle attached by long, thin leather straps to large beasts.

"In the chariot, sir," she said. "We have the fastest horses possible."

Chariot. Horses. Mok made a note to remember. Yes, he would tell this story on a street corner. What a crowd of Welfaros it would draw. Of course, they wouldn't believe it either, but it might earn him a couple of days' worth of water.

With a crack of the whips, the charioteer drove the horses ahead, scattering a flock of geese that a boy was herding down the road ahead of them. They quickly left behind the squawking birds and the shouting boy. Within minutes, they arrived at the temple gates.

It was an impressive building, guarded by a statue of a giant cat with a man's head. Beyond the giant columns, Mok saw a courtyard filled with dozens of wailing women.

He didn't have time to comment.

His guide stepped down from the chariot. When he joined her, she took his arm again and led him into the courtyard.

Mok watched in amazement as the women around him howled and threw dust over their heads. His guide saw his face.

"Many are professional mourners, of course," she said, as if agreeing with him. "Yet it is amazing how truly sad they are. We all deeply grieve the pharaoh's death."

He opened his mouth to ask for more explanation, but she cut him off.

"Come," she said, "your assistants await you."

She led him into the shade of a hallway at the end of the courtyard. He followed her into the depths of the temple.

There were close to two dozen men in the stone-walled room, all wearing the silly white skirts, all silent, all intent on the tables before them.

Mok put his hands on his hips and tried to make sense of the scene. Body-sized baskets. Large clay jars. Piles of white powder. A horrible smell. And—

Mok jumped back. One of the men was pushing wax up the nose of a body!

"What are you doing!" Mok could not help but blurt out his question.

The man stepped back from the table and bowed. "You have my apologies, sir. It's just that—"

Another man moved beside Mok. This one had a hooknose and was slightly cross-eyed. "As your chief assistant, I took it upon myself to order him to begin with the beeswax. With you inspecting the pyramid, I had no idea when you might return. I did not want to delay the process."

Mok remembered what the dwarf had told him about preparing a body for the tomb. "Oh yes," Mok said. He breathed through his mouth as he spoke. *What a stench!* "I'm glad you decided not to wait for me."

Mok turned his head and rolled his eyes. This dream was hilarious.

"Continue your work," Mok said when he felt he had stifled his laughter enough to speak again. He deepened his voice for melodramatic authority. "Let's get him all wrapped up by evening."

Mok wondered if anyone in the room would chuckle. On the different tables, other bodies were in various stages of preparation. Many bodies were wrapped in linen, and Mok was pleased with his little pun.

"Sir! This is the pharaoh! Joke if you will about the common noblemen, but the pharaoh . . ."

The chief assistant clasped his hands together. His voice rose, almost in panic. "It will take hours to fill him with the white natron powder. Then forty days if we want the powder to dry him properly. And after that—"

"Whatever you say." Mok was not interested in more details. Still, he thought dreams were great.

In dreams, Mok didn't have to take death so seriously. "Go ahead. Don't keep the pharaoh waiting."

"Undertaker," a voice said from the doorway.

Mok turned to see a soldier standing at the entrance. The soldier was a giant, armed with a spear and shield.

"Yes?"

"I have orders to take you to the inner chamber." The soldier pointed the spear at Mok's chest. "At once."

MOK HAD NOT MINDED when the soldier had pushed him
at spear point to a small room hidden in the far corner of the temple. After all, Mok thought, not knowing what would happen next just added to his
entertainment.

Waiting in the stillness of the small room, however, was less amusing. Especially since the soldier
had refused to tell Mok anything about who he
waited for.

Mok killed time by studying the strange symbols
carved into the walls. There were women with six
arms each. Men with dogs' heads. Coiled cobras.
Dancing figures. Fighting figures. Figures in boats.

He stepped forward to run his fingers over the
carvings but stopped as he heard a rustling of soft
cloth and the light flip-flop of sandaled footsteps.
Perfume filled the air.

A woman had stepped into the chamber behind
him. Without turning, Mok grinned. *Naturally,* he
told himself, *if this is going to be a decent dream, somewhere along the way there should be a woman in it.*
Now that he thought about it, Mok was disappointed
he had taken so long to do the obvious. He should
have dreamed her into sitting beside his sleeping

mat. Then, as he woke, she could have been there, offering to feed him grapes, something he'd never tasted but had heard were wonderful.

He kept grinning straight ahead. Oh well, better late than never. Before turning around, he ordered himself to make her beautiful.

He finally turned.

The woman wore a long, formless dress. She was tall and slim. Her hair, shoulder length and cropped to a blunt edge, gleamed black in the sunlight provided by openings high in the chamber wall. A gold band circled her forehead. A coiling gold cobra on the band gleamed in the light from a shaft above.

And she was beautiful, far beyond what he believed his imagination to be capable of creating.

"I am Raha, daughter of the pharaoh Cheops."

Mok would have been happy with just beautiful. But to make her wealthy and royal too? What a masterpiece of a dream.

"I am Mok," he said. Mok hoped he wouldn't wake up too soon. But, in case he was about to wake, he wanted to get to the good part right away.

"Any time now," he said, "I give you permission to declare your love for me."

She clapped her hands three times, the sound hollow and loud in the stone chamber.

"What insolence," she said. Three large men armed with spears entered the room. "All the more reason to have you arrested."

Mok laughed. "Arrested? You can't do that."

The guards rushed forward and grabbed him.

"During the night, three golden necklaces were taken from my father's body," Raha said. "As royal undertaker, you are responsible for the actions of your assistants. Accordingly, you will all be executed."

Mok grinned more. This was his world, and he could do what he wanted. He thought briefly. He decided he would defeat the guards and let her swoon over his bravery. After that, he would find the guilty assistant, return the necklaces, accept her gratitude, and let the dream continue where it might.

He hoped all of this would last as long as possible. This was a much better world than Old Newyork and his cramped hiding hole in the damp cold tunnels below the streets.

Keeping his plan in mind, Mok slammed his heel down on a guard's toes.

He waited for the guard to hop around and look like an idiot.

Instead, the guard punched a heavy fist into Mok's face. Mok felt his head snap back and blood begin to pour from his nose. *What is wrong with this dream?*

Mok held his bleeding nose with one hand and brought his other arm back to punch the guard. The other two soldiers jabbed their spears at his face, stopping just below his chin.

He froze. Blood ran through his fingers.

"Enough," Raha said. "Take him away. No need to punish him now. He'll be dead by sunset."

CHAPTER 12

MAINSIDE. The Committee members followed Mok's activities on the large vidscreen in the conference room. One man excused himself to use the washroom. He followed the hallway, but strode past the clearly marked washroom door.

Hidden in a stairwell, he pulled a satellite-phone from his suit pocket and flipped it open to the tiny vidscreen. He dialed a number and waited for the screen to come to life.

"This better be a scrambled signal," the president's face in the vidscreen snarled as greeting. "And it better be important."

The screen was too small to show any background, and the man was smart enough not to ask what he had interrupted.

"We will not be overheard," the man answered. "I am calling about the Welfaro."

"Make it quick."

"The Welfaro is well into the first cyberstage. His body is responding well to the life-support machine. His brain-wave activities show high intelligence."

"I am disturbed. As I recall from your reports," the president said, "the other candidates went into a panic as soon as they woke up in ancient Egypt."

"That is true, Your Worldship. Even with training. And this one did not have any training to help him . . ."

"I am uneasy."

"Your Worldship?"

"Cambridge knows there is little time. Each of the other Committee members chose a highly educated Technocrat. When Cambridge finally had his turn, why did he choose a mere Welfaro when all the Technocrats had failed?"

"Your Worldship, truly there is nothing to fear. Had you hired me earlier, during the testing of the other candidates, you would know that the virtual reality of cyberspace has constraints."

"Explain."

"At the precise moment of death in cybertime, the brain monitors in realtime show total stoppage of all wave activity." The second man grinned. "Total, permanent stoppage. His brain will literally fry. If he believes he dies in cyberspace, he will die here."

"And?"

"This one is about to face a grave test, which I am sure he will fail. He faces either execution or a prison riot. None of the others found a way to avoid either."

The president smiled. "Report to me when this one is dead."

CHAPTER 13

CYBERSPACE—EGYPT. Execution. At sunset.

Mok looked around the large underground prison. Smoky oil torches gave uncertain light. He was unable to see the expressions on the faces of his fellow prisoners. Most, like Mok, sat silently against the stone walls.

There were twenty altogether. Assistants to the royal undertaker. *His* assistants, if he were to believe the events of the day.

Mok half expected to wake from his dream at any moment. How could he now be a royal undertaker in a faraway country thousands of years before his own birth? How could he be facing execution because one of these twenty assistants had stolen gold necklaces from the pharaoh's body?

It must *be a dream,* he told himself.

Yet, it could not be a dream. How could a Welfaro of the slums of Old Newyork have imagined this world, down to the last details of smoking, flickering oil torches? Mok touched his swelling face. It showed even more reality. The guard had punched him. Didn't one wake up from a dream instead of bleed and suffer?

He heard muttering from the other men. He looked at the far end of the prison, where the chimney of a cooking firepit was set into the wall. A tiny man stepped from the ashes.

As if he didn't face enough trouble, Mok thought, there was also the matter of this nasty little dwarf.

Blake dusted himself with great dignity, sending ashes in all directions. He marched across the prison to stand in front of Mok.

A few prisoners began to gather around the dwarf, mumbling questions.

"Leave us," Mok commanded. He was still the royal undertaker. Even in prison, he had command. The prisoners walked away.

"You can't say I didn't warn you," the dwarf said to Mok. "*Now* are you ready to ask for my help?"

"Stinko . . ." Mok began to stand.

The dwarf pushed him back down to a sitting position. "Two things, you foolish puppy. One, I advise you to whisper. This will not be a conversation you'll want overheard. Do you think I crawled down that filthy chimney because I like the taste of charcoal?"

"And the second thing?" Mok managed to whisper. Sitting down, he was almost at face level with the dwarf.

"My name is Blake. Not Stinko." Blake stamped his foot to make his point.

"Stinko suits you. Blake does not. Do you have any idea how ridiculous you look?" Mok remembered metal barrels of burning garbage in the street canyons of Old Newyork. Families cooked pots of food over their flames. "Your face and hands are as black as a pot's bottom."

"Insults instead of gratitude. I should turn around and climb back up that rope."

"Rope? Is it still there?"

"Put escape out of your mind. You're too large and clumsy to climb out through the chimney. Now lean forward."

Blake pulled a dagger from under his tunic. He flashed it at Mok quickly so that none of the other prisoners could see.

"Lean forward, I said!" Blake hissed. "Are you deaf? Or just stupid?"

Mok leaned forward. The dwarf stepped closer to Mok and pretended to pat his shoulders. He let the dagger fall unseen behind Mok's back.

"You are now armed," the dwarf said, stepping away. "Choose your moment carefully."

"One dagger against swords of a battalion of guards? If you think I'll do that, you're as crazy as you look."

"Fool," the dwarf said. "Not the guards. One of your assistants. Carefully choose a moment to plunge it into his chest."

"Kill one of the assistants? I don't understand."

"The pharaoh's daughter knows that one man in this prison is truly guilty. Kill one of them and blame him. Tell Raha that the man confessed and killed himself. Without him to speak his innocence, you and all the others will be freed."

"Why should she believe the story if the man is dead?"

"Because she wants to," Blake said. "She badly

wants someone to blame. If she can show the people she found the guilty man, they'll believe she can be a good ruler. In other words, she is more concerned about the appearance of justice than justice itself."

Mok thought about it. With every passing moment, the dream seemed more and more real. He wasn't sure if he wanted to find out how real an execution felt. Not with his nose so sore from the earlier punch.

"No," Mok said. "It's not right."

"You're such a child. What does justice matter against all the evils of the world? Or against your own life? Deliver her a thief—even if it isn't the real thief—and she will be grateful to you. Wealth and fame will be yours."

Mok let his mind wander to what it might be like to be rich. Even in a dream.

"No," he finally said. "I will not be part of murdering an innocent man."

"What do you care?" the dwarf asked. "What does it matter?"

Mok thought of his boyhood and the audiobook that had comforted him again and again. He thought of a man from Galilee and his teachings.

"It matters," Mok said. "I will not do this great wrong."

"For one guilty man's crime, all twenty-one of you will be executed. Yet twenty of you are innocent. What is better, one dead innocent man? Or twenty?"

"Unless by chance it happens that I stab the

guilty man, he, too, would be set free," Mok said angrily. "Should an innocent man die to save the guilty?"

The dwarf shrugged. "Do you have some way to make the thief confess? Is there a mark of guilt on him, as plain to see as this soot on my own face? No, young fool, if the thief hasn't confessed by now, don't expect him to do so by sunset. And at sunset, I remind you, you will die."

Without a backward glance, but with a grin spreading across his face, Blake the dwarf marched away from Mok. The young man from Old Newyork had passed the Committee's first test. Blake was pleased. He stepped into the firepit, jumped upward, and disappeared.

CHAPTER 14

MOK STARED THOUGHTFULLY at the empty firepit.

He would not murder anyone. He had seen plenty of cruel deaths in Old Newyork, but he would not consider killing a man. Not even to save his own life.

He thought longer. If only there *were* some way to mark the guilty man like the soot on the dwarf's face.

Like the soot on the dwarf's face! Black as a pot's bottom! Just like the cooking pots in Old Newyork!

"Guard!" Mok suddenly shouted. He rose and stepped toward the door of the prison. "Guard! I wish to speak to Raha, the pharaoh's daughter!"

"There is the rooster you requested," Raha said, pointing at a servant who held the squawking bird upside down by its feet. "And a well-used cooking pot. Remember our agreement. If this fails, *you* shall be executed instead of the guilty man."

Mok remembered. It was the only way he'd been able to convince Raha to agree. Of course, what did it matter to him if they were all to be executed anyway?

"Anything else?" she asked. They were standing just outside the prison door.

"After I go back into the prison, you will remain here," Mok reminded her. "When I call for it, send the guards in with torches."

"That sounds close to an order," she said. "Must I have you again punished?"

She was unable to hide her smile completely. Was she proud of Mok and his idea? Mok began to really hope this wasn't a dream. If this worked, perhaps he could spend more time with the pharaoh's daughter. Beautiful, wealthy, royal . . .

"Enough wasting of time." She clapped her hands. "Guards, open the prison door."

Mok took the feet of the flapping rooster in one hand, the handle of the cooking pot in the other. He stepped back inside the prison.

All twenty of his assistants stared at him in puzzlement.

Mok waited until the prison door shut behind him.

"There is a custom to determine a man's guilt," Mok began with as much authority as he could force into his voice. "Not once has this custom failed."

He had their full attention.

Mok lifted the rooster higher. He shook it until it squawked with rage.

"This is the sound of guilt," Mok said.

The assistants began to speak among themselves.

"Yes," Mok said, silencing them. He moved to the center of the room. In full view of all the prisoners, he overturned the pot. With quick movements, he stuffed the rooster beneath the upside-down pot. It stopped squawking immediately.

"And this silence," Mok said, pointing at the now quiet pot, "is the sound of innocence."

He looked at all the men. "You see, a rooster covered in complete darkness knows the presence of a guilty man."

He let them speak for a few moments, then lifted his hand for silence.

"*Complete* darkness," Mok said. "We will form a line. The torches will be extinguished. One by one, each will step past this pot. One by one, each will place his hands squarely on the bottom of this pot and press hard. When the guilty man touches the pot, the rooster beneath it will crow. The guilty man shall take his punishment. The rest of us will live."

Mok let them speak as he moved along the prison walls. One by one he lifted the torches and stubbed out their flames on the hard ground. When he held the final torch, he turned to the men.

The prisoners had formed their line before the overturned pot. Mok extinguished the torch and the room became totally dark.

"Begin," Mok commanded.

Slow shuffling in the darkness filled the silence.

Mok wondered if they could hear his heart pound out its fear. Surely the rooster would help him find the guilty man . . .

The rooster did not crow. The last of the prisoners touched the pot and called out to Mok.

"Guard!" Mok shouted. This was the moment. If his plan had worked, he would live. If not . . .

CHAPTER 15

NOT ONE, BUT FIVE GUARDS immediately entered the prison. Their torches gave new light and new shadows.

Raha followed them. She stopped and folded her arms.

"Form a line," Raha commanded the prisoners. "Walk past me and show me the palms of your hands."

Mok stood close to her. He, too, wanted to see the palms of each prisoner's hands.

The first prisoner showed palms covered with black smudges—as sooty as the dwarf's hands and face had been. Each of the next ten prisoners also showed soot from the pot's bottom, a result of its years over cooking fires.

Then came the eleventh prisoner, the chief assistant. He showed no fear. But when he showed his palms, they were clean.

Raha nodded, and the guards descended on the man, holding his arms as Raha faced him.

"Where are the necklaces?" Raha demanded.

"Your Highness?" The chief assistant sagged in fear. The guards held him upright. "I do not understand. Why accuse me?"

"Because your palms are clean," she said. "Why

did you not touch the pot? Did you fear the rooster might actually crow and declare your guilt? Instead, you have declared it upon yourself."

The man looked stunned.

"Take him away," she told the guards. "If he tells us where to find the necklaces, his death will be fast and merciful."

She turned to Mok, no longer hiding the smile on her face. "As for you," she said, "you will dine with me."

She stepped toward him and offered the back of her hand.

Mok took it, amazed at the softness of her skin. He lifted it to his mouth and kissed it. Perfume filled his nostrils. He kissed it again and lifted his eyes to hers.

"Raha," he began.

But he was not able to finish. The room suddenly turned black. It began spinning. Spinning. Spinning . . .

CHAPTER 16

MAINSIDE. There was only one Committee member who did not take joy in the news that Mok had become the first candidate to move to the second cyberspace test.

This Committee member secretly hurried to a netphone in the main-floor lobby of the building. Unless someone was there to look over his shoulder as he typed, this was the safest and fastest way to send a message.

When the lobby was empty, the Committee member entered the private dotcom number of the president of the World United. When the system prompted him for his e-mail message, the Committee member typed a few hurried sentences:

> **Warning. Candidate has passed first test. Nothing to fear. Failure at next stage is certain. Will confirm this with face-to-face vidconference at first opportunity.**

The Committee member checked over his message. He was satisfied it said enough . . . for now.

He hit the send button on the netphone keypad.

CHAPTER 17

CYBERSPACE—THE HOLY LAND, A.D. 1296. Night. Stars above. A breeze on his face. Hundreds of small scattered fires flickered below.

Raha? Mok wondered. Where was Raha? And where was the linen tunic he had worn?

His clothes were rough, heavy. He seemed to be standing on the edge of a great building. What madness was this?

"I see you've come to join us. Pray tell, how did you escape execution?"

"Stinko!" Mok was almost glad for a familiar voice.

The dwarf's cane whacked at him from the darkness.

"How many times must I tell you not to call me that—"

"Where am I?" Mok said. "Why do you follow me?"

The dwarf sighed. "We are on the ramparts of a castle. In the Holy Land of Jesus Christ. You are part of a great crusade in his name and—"

"Blake!" Mok was so excited he forgot to insult the dwarf. "Did you say Jesus Christ?"

"Yes . . ." The dwarf's voice was puzzled.

"That's the Galilee Man! From the audiobook I had as a boy!"

"The Galilee Man . . . I suppose a person could call him that. He did come from that region."

"'Let the little children come to me,'" Mok recited from memory. "You see? He loved children. He made promises I've always wanted to believe. Can I find him and speak to him?"

For the first time Mok could recall, the dwarf spoke gently.

"He died more than a thousand years before this castle was built," Blake said. "You will not find him walking this land."

The dwarf paused. "Sleep now. Tomorrow, daylight will show you that those fires belong to a great army surrounding this castle. You are in the middle of a siege. It will not end until every man, woman, and child within the castle walls has died. Including you."

BACKSTORY II

OLD NEWYORK, A.D. 2076. A few hours earlier, the old man had stepped into Old Newyork off the ferry from Mainside. Then it had been dark, with only scattered fires glowing in the night. Now, with dawn fully upon the slums, hazy sunlight gave thin shadows to weeds that sprouted in the cracks of buckled street pavement. Many of the abandoned buildings were black from long-past fires. And ahead, ancient skyscrapers filled the skyline. Their shattered windows showed broken-toothed gaps across the concrete faces.

Few people walked the streets yet. Those who did either darted quick, hungry glances in all directions or kept their heads down. The choice was simple in Old Newyork. Hunt—or be hunted.

Rotting garbage made the air sour. Occasional distant screams echoed through the street canyons, haunting the otherwise grim silence.

It filled the old man with sadness. He had expected decay since his last sight of Old Newyork many years earlier, but nothing this bad.

To return to Old Newyork, the old man had given up his name, his wealth, and his freedom. Less than twenty-four hours earlier—before he had stepped onto the steel ferry—he had been the single largest shareholder of Benjamin Rufus Holdings. The giant Internet corporation had assets in the billions.

Mainside, his name—Benjamin Rufus—commanded respect and sometimes fear. It would mean nothing here in Old Newyork. Welfaros did not read newspapers or get daily newsclips on multivid screens.

Mainside, his income was so great he could not hope to spend in a year the interest it earned in a single day. Here, where computer ID credit chips were worthless, the only currency he could carry was cash. He could not reach any of his wealth through bank machines or electronic transfers. In days or a week or a month, he would be as poor as any Welfaro. And have as little hope.

Most costly of all was the freedom that Benjamin Rufus had given up by leaving his Mainside mansion and crossing the Hudson River. He knew that his ride on the ferry had been a one-way trip.

As Benjamin Rufus walked and gazed at the horror of the slums, he fought despair. Dwelling on hopelessness would serve no purpose. He had much to do in the next days. So he squared his shoulders, forcing himself to pretend strength with every painful step.

Shuffling shoe leather alerted Rufus to people behind him. He moved to the side of the street to let them pass. It was a family—father, mother, son, and daughter—all in ragged dark clothing. They huddled together in fright as they walked slowly toward the center of the slums.

"Where will we stay tonight?" Rufus heard the boy ask. "What will we eat?"

The family moved on before he heard the father's reply.

Benjamin Rufus pulled his long coat tighter around himself. He decided to follow them. He knew too well about the work gangs in Old Newyork. If this family had just stepped off the ferry, they, too, would soon find out how . . .

Even before Rufus finished his thought, three men stepped into the street, blocking the family's progress. The lead man—with dark greasy hair to his shoulders—carried a loaded crossbow. He pointed it at the father's chest. The other two—both shaved bald—carried spears made of knives strapped to short poles. All three wore black leather jackets and black leather pants.

"Far enough," the lead man grunted. He caught sight of Benjamin close behind the family. "You, old man, join this pitiful group."

Rufus stepped forward. The girl began to cry quietly. Her father put his arm around her. One of the bald men jabbed the father with his spear and forced him to move his arm.

"You'll be coming with us," the leader said laughing. "We need you to work as slaves in our factories."

"Slaves? Factories?" The father's voice was strained. "We did not come here to work as slaves."

The leader raised his crossbow to the father's head. "Slaves. You'll wear our tattoos and be our slaves."

Benjamin Rufus stepped through the small family and stood in front of the father. The leader pointed the crossbow at Benjamin's neck.

"Explain," Rufus said, showing no fear. "Tattoos?"

The leader laughed. Breath as horrid as sewer waste blew across Benjamin's face. "You newbies are so dumb. You're always surprised to learn that most people become slaves here. Like Old Newyork is actually going to be better than Mainside for people without money."

He turned his head to show a tattoo on his cheek. It was a crudely drawn scorpion. "See this? We mark you to make you one of ours. Stay in our territory, and you're safe. You get food stamps as long as you keep working for us. We keep you safe from gangs in other territories."

"No," the father said. "We're here to get away from government control. We came here to live our own lives. We'll make our own way."

The leader snorted. "That was your dream? Well it just ended. Here's how it is in Old Newyork. Five gangs. Five territories. We found you first, you take our tattoo. Not many people make it without tattoos."

It had been years since Benjamin Rufus had needed to respond to a physical threat. But here, in Old Newyork, he was a world away from conference rooms and business deals. Here, in Old Newyork, he had to depend on the reactions of his old, illness-weakened body.

Rufus uttered a silent prayer and pressed his right

elbow against his side. It released a 'tric shooter from a strap attached to his forearm, hidden beneath the sleeve of his coat. The shooter slid down into his hand.

With a calm smile, Rufus lifted his arm and pulled the trigger.

An arc of blue light crossed between him and the leader. It hit the leader in the chest and froze him. Rufus snapped off two more quick shots, volting the spearman on the left and then the one on the right. All three stood rigid for a few more seconds, then fell.

"'Tric shooter!" the boy said, his voice filled with awe.

Rufus looked up and down the street to see if anyone else had noticed. It appeared safe.

Rufus stooped and went through the pockets of the fallen men. He stood up holding folded sheets of food stamps. Rufus gave them all to the wide-eyed father.

"Take these," Rufus told him, "and the crossbow and spears. With the stamps and weapons and God's grace, you'll find a way to support yourselves before you get desperate enough for the factories."

He accepted their thanks and strode as quickly as he could toward the skyscraper street canyons. He did not have much time. His shooter would only be effective as long as it held its electrical charge. He couldn't fight these human wolves forever.

As he walked, Benjamin Rufus noticed the despair had been lifted from him. Helping this family had given faces to his goal. The children and the poor of Old Newyork were why he'd left Mainside, abandoning his name, money, and freedom.

And these people were why Benjamin had left a secret Committee behind on Mainside to continue his work long after he died in Old Newyork.

CHAPTER 18

MAINSIDE, A.D. 2096. On the tenth floor of a luxury high-rise on the other side of the river, a group of twelve men stood before a cot in a large room.

On that cot lay Mok's motionless body, draped with a sheet. Two nurses tended to the body. Monitor lines ran from the young man's head to the computer. Other lines from various parts of his body ran to the life-support machine. The steady *blip* of his heartbeat echoed in the silence of the room.

"Most of you have seen this young man on our vidscreen in the other room," the man named Cambridge said. "I thought you should see him in real time, not virtual reality."

"I'm glad we had a chance to see this," one Committee member said. "It makes him more real to us when we talk about him."

Some of the Committee members wore business suits. Others wore the latest fashions in training gear even though none actually went to the workout centers. All of them were in their forties or fifties. These were successful, commonsense men who did not need to wear the black silk togas of Technocrats to boost their egos.

"As you can see," Cambridge said to the whole

group, "the monitors show that Mok is in no physical danger."

"And he has passed the first test," another said. "He was not killed in the prison in Egypt."

"He also refused to kill an innocent man."

"An uneducated Welfaro," a member marveled. "Yet he succeeded where all the others have failed."

"Good thing," another said. "The others, at least, knew they were in cyberspace. They were able to yank themselves out before death struck. This one . . ."

"Yes," a doubting voice added. "This one really believes he is now in a castle. He *has* been cybered to the siege, has he not?"

"Yes," Cambridge said. "He is there, sleeping. You all know how the program works. He is in cyberspace. Around him, the characters and situations have been set up to respond to his decisions. Just as if everything were real."

"And he has a guide?"

"Yes, someone to answer only the necessary questions. This is a test he must pass without help. He must make his own decisions." For the first time, emotion crossed Cambridge's face. Troubled emotion. "And let us pray he succeeds. You know as well as I do that if he dies in cyberspace, he'll die here too. We have medtechs watching his progress on the vidscreens, but death in the castle could strike so quickly that . . ."

A Committee member interrupted loudly, "Don't pain yourself by bringing up this issue again. His psych-profile showed he would have accepted these risks had we given him the choice. After all, in Old Newyork he faced death at any time. Here, even with those risks, he is far safer. And his future far more promising. As it is, the test will be much more effective if he does not know he is in cyberspace."

Cambridge sighed. "Yes, I do keep telling myself that."

It was obvious Cambridge would never be at ease with the Committee's decision. "Any other comments before we move back to the conference room?"

"No question, but a prediction," the doubter said. "We should prepare ourselves for failure. If the finest of our recruits couldn't pass with all their knowledge and training, this one is doomed for certain."

"Wait before you pass judgment," Cambridge said. A small smile crossed his face. "After we cybered him to the castle siege, he asked about the Galilee Man."

Understanding crossed the faces in front of him.

"Yes," Cambridge said. "Mok is searching through the ages for Christ."

CHAPTER 19

CYBERSPACE—THE HOLY LAND. *Tap. Tap. Tap. Tap. Tap.*

Mok awoke. He was half sitting, half leaning against one of the turret walls. He was confused by the quiet, persistent tapping sound. The noise worked into his bones. It seemed to come from the very stones of the castle.

Tap. Tap. Tap. Tap. Tap.

"Blake," Mok said, "do you hear that?"

The dwarf did not answer. Mok was not prepared to admit he liked the grumpy little man. Yet Mok knew no one else and had no other place to turn for help.

"Blake? Blake?"

In the land of pharaohs, the little man with a bad temper had appeared from nowhere to offer unrequested advice to Mok. It figured that the first time Mok truly wanted the dwarf nearby, there would be no answer from him.

Mok stood and opened his eyes wide, straining to see in the darkness. The dwarf who had been with him earlier had disappeared.

Tap. Tap. Tap. Tap. Tap.

Mok wrapped himself in his coat and settled back against the wall. Running around in the dark to find Blake would do him little good. There was no sense in looking for trouble. Mok closed his eyes and waited for morning.

Tap. Tap. Tap. Tap. Tap.

No need to look for trouble, Mok repeated to himself with bitter humor. He fully believed that dawn would bring it to him.

"Young sir," a voice awakened him, "your father has called for you."

Mok blinked himself into wakefulness. He stood and faced the man. Earlier, Mok would have laughed at the strangeness. This man was dressed in metal armor of dull silver. On his head, he wore what looked like an upside-down bucket with a slit that revealed his eyes. On his feet, he wore iron shoes. Earlier, Mok would have decided it was another dream brought on by impure glo-glo water.

No longer.

He stood on a great castle wall overlooking hills so distant they faded blue against the early dawn. The land outside the castle walls was dark with massed soldiers. And the dwarf—before he'd disappeared—had told Mok these soldiers planned to take the castle and kill everyone inside.

This was far beyond the dreams caused by glo-glo water in Old Newyork. Mok had been thrust into something beyond his understanding. He was finally prepared to admit it. All he could do was watch and wait and hope it might soon become clear.

Because of that, he did not laugh at the man in front of him. Especially since the man carried a great sword on his belt. Instead, Mok waited for the man to speak. During the brief silence they shared, Mok heard the noise that had followed him into sleep.

Tap. Tap. Tap. Tap. Tap.

"I speak for every knight in this castle," the man said. "We are grateful for how you encourage us. Day by day, our men have died by arrows fired from below. Yet despite the danger, you run boldly from turret to turret, bringing water skins, passing along news, lifting our spirits. Without doubt, you are truly noble. No one could deny you are Count Reynald's son."

Count Reynald? Mok wondered. *And "night"? This man calls himself a "night"? Are there those who call themselves "days"?* Mok reminded himself of his decision to watch and wait. He held his tongue.

The man seemed of great physical power, yet he slumped with worry. This was no moment for Mok to interrupt.

"The castle shall fall soon," the man said. "Leave us here and join your father as he has requested. If you outlive us—as I hope you shall—honor us by remembering how bravely we fought."

Tap. Tap. Tap. Tap. Tap.

"This tapping . . . ," Mok said. He cocked his head as if listening to the castle walls.

"Yes, m'lord. It bothers me too. As if you or I need reminder of pickax against stone. The miners beneath the great castle walls chip at the foundations like a toothache gnaws at our skulls. I almost welcome the final fight when the castle walls will tumble, if it will stop the sound."

The knight pointed at a stone stairway. "Your father waits in the inner courtyard. Please inform him we are prepared to fight to the end. We knights are *his* soldiers, and we will not go gently."

Mok nodded, trying to understand everything he had heard. His father? A count? From these words, could Mok assume the count ruled the castle?

Mok accepted the man's handshake and walked away in silence. At the stairway, he glanced again over the castle walls at the activity below. Deep ditches had been filled with rubble and broken stones. Hundreds of men pushed great wooden machines over the filled ditches and advanced toward the castle. Thousands of soldiers stood behind them in motionless columns, their distant lances tiny upright lines of black.

Tap. Tap. Tap. Tap. Tap.

And below, miners dug at the stones that supported the castle's walls.

Mok took a deep breath and descended the stone stairway.

CHAPTER 20

AFTER HIS LONG DESCENT to the bottom of the stairs, Mok saw two groups of men ahead in the courtyard. One group stood with horses behind them. Some twenty steps away, the smaller group waited. These men were dressed in the same armor as the knights. One of them motioned for Mok to draw closer.

Mok did so. This was much more than a dream. He had accepted that he could not escape from this strange world. And with no escape, he must live by his wits. It was the only possession he'd carried here from Old Newyork. Mok would listen and try to survive. If they believed he was the count's son, he would act in that manner.

"My son," the man said gently as Mok approached. This, then, was Count Reynald. He placed his hands on Mok's shoulders.

Mok looked at the man with cropped dark hair and a tired face. He wore a purple cloak. There was a long sword belted to his side.

Count Reynald took his hands off Mok's shoulders and nodded in the direction of the other group. At the front was a short man, red-faced and bald. He, too, wore a fine robe. His fingers were heavy with gold rings. The sword in his sheath was short and curved.

"This is Tabarie, the sultan's messenger," Count Reynald explained. "A brief truce was arranged. He is here under a safe conduct, which I issued. He shall inform us of the sultan's terms of surrender."

"Not until your wife joins us," Tabarie said in a high-pitched voice. "Your entire family should hear this message."

The count pointed at two approaching figures. "She arrives. Along with her servant."

Mok's eyes followed Count Reynald's gesture. And he nearly fainted. Not at the sight of Count Reynald's wife, a tall woman who walked with dignity. But at the younger woman behind her. The servant was the beautiful Raha—the pharaoh's daughter from the land of Egypt! Here in the castle!

Mok nearly cried out in surprise, but Raha noticed the look on Mok's face. With a grave, gentle shake of her head, she warned against it. Had Mok not been staring at her, he would not have noticed her signal. No one else saw their brief glances of recognition.

Mok had no chance to wonder about the girl.

Tabarie puffed out his chest and spoke with self-importance. "Listen to me carefully. For your lives are in my hands."

CHAPTER 21

TABARIE PAUSED FOR EFFECT. The sun was hot on Mok's shoulders. When his lungs began to hurt, he realized he was holding his breath.

"No," Count Reynald broke the silence. "Our lives are not in your hands. Nor in those of the sultan who commands you. Our lives are in God's hands."

"Bah," Tabarie said and spit. "Because of that stubborn belief, you face death instead of freedom."

Tabarie raised his right hand. With chubby fingers, he pointed behind him. "Outside waits one of the greatest armies of all time."

He spit again. "This castle was thought to be a stronghold that no one could conquer. Yet, it took us less than a week to destroy your outer walls. Your moats? Hah! Filled with the rubble of your outer walls. We are already using your castle against you."

Tabarie paused for breath. He was so fat that just the effort of speaking made him wheeze. "And how long did it take us to kill most of your soldiers? Even though you had boiling oil and arrows raining down on us. Although twenty of our soldiers died for every one of yours, in the end, your efforts were useless against us."

Tabarie sneered. "Your peasants—except for this

foolishly loyal servant girl—have deserted you. All that remain are your inner walls, protecting you and a small miserable group of knights. You are running out of food and water. Could it be worse? Hardly. And below, our miners dig at the—"

"We know our situation," Count Reynald said. "I doubt your sultan sent you here to boast."

Tabarie's eyes turned to dark coals. "No, he sent me here to give you his terms of surrender. Give up your castle and faith. In return, you will receive safe conduct to the harbor. Ships can take you, your family, and your knights to England."

"Why do you want surrender?" Count Reynald asked. "You already claim certain victory despite anything we do."

"Two reasons. When the foundation of this castle gives way and the walls fall in, we will destroy you. But it will take time and many lives. The sultan would prefer to save both."

"And the other reason?"

"You and your family will set an example," Tabarie replied. "Give up your castle. Denounce your faith. The people must know that the Christians can no longer claim this land as their Holy Land."

"This *is* the Holy Land," Count Reynald said. "Even if we deny it, the truth will remain. Christ himself walked these lands. He died on a cross in Jerusalem and rose again. That truth will ring throughout the centuries, regardless of how many small and petty men try to defeat its glorious sound."

Mok felt his heart leap. He thought once more

of the audiobook he had listened to again and again. It had spoken of a man named Christ, the man of Galilee.

Blake, the dwarf now long gone, had also spoken of the man of Galilee. And now the name of Christ again! Others *did* know of him!

Was the man legend? Or real? Mok wanted to step between the men and blurt out his questions. He held himself back and vowed he would approach Count Reynald with these questions later. If later they were still alive.

"You will not publicly deny the man called Christ?" Tabarie asked Count Reynald.

"No," Count Reynald replied.

"Then you will die a horrible death."

Count Reynald smiled. Peace shone from his face. "No matter how horrible the death, it will only be fleeting in the face of eternity. We will all pass through the curtain of death to be welcomed home by him."

Tabarie looked at the others. "And you, servant girl, are you thus prepared? You may still turn your back on these people."

"Because of my loyalty, they treat me as their daughter," she said. "I will stay with them to the end. I am not afraid of death."

Mok listened with intensity. Count Reynald was repeating much of what Mok had heard in the audiobook. Yet how could it be? Living beyond death? A home with the Galilee Man? How could a person believe with such strength that death held no fear?

Tabarie spoke again. "I will give the sultan your foolish answer."

Tabarie turned his back on Count Reynald. The fat man tried to mount his horse. After several clumsy attempts to lift his heavy body, he snapped his fingers. Two of his soldiers helped him into the saddle.

As Tabarie took the reins of his horse, he gave a final backward glance.

"Everything is ready for our final attack," Tabarie said. "In less than two days the sultan's army will be inside this castle. Not one of you will walk out of here alive."

Tabarie settled his cloak over his shoulders. He rode out. After his departure, the clatter of horses' hooves continued to echo in the courtyard.

CHAPTER 22

MAINSIDE. One of the Committee members waited for the chance to disappear from the conference room. As he had done earlier, he found an empty stairwell. Again, he pulled a satellite-phone from his pocket. He flipped to the tiny vidscreen, dialed a number, and waited for the screen to come to life.

It took five rings for His Worldship to answer his private line. The vidscreen in front of the Committee member remained dark—the president had only answered on audio, choosing to leave the visual button alone.

"What is it?" His Worldship spoke with irritation.

The Committee member's own face, then, showed on the vidscreen on His Worldship's end. "This is when you scheduled me to call, Your Worldship. On a scrambled signal of course."

"Wipe that smug look off your face," His Worldship said. "Give me the latest report and then get off this line."

While it was considered rude to take incoming video without returning video during a call, the president of the World United could do what he wanted. He was the most powerful person among the billions who had survived the Water Wars.

"As you know, the candidate is fully awake in a Holy Land castle, Your Worldship. And the castle is about to fall. Everyone inside will die. I doubt the candidate will find a way to survive. So Cambridge loses both ways. If he leaves the candidate in cyberspace, the candidate is dead. If Cambridge brings him back to real time, the test is over. Either way, the final candidate is finished. And you will win. "

"Let me remind you, he did not die in Egypt as you promised he would."

"I am far from worried, Your Worldship. There are many ways for the candidate to die."

"Tell me."

"It takes millions of gigabytes to construct a cyberspace world real enough for the subject to believe he exists within it. Because of that, there are boundaries."

"Boundaries?"

"Think of it as a movie set, Your Worldship. The Welfaro is in a thirteenth-century castle. He sees the people within the castle walls and the army beyond. But a program this complex strains the available memory on the supercomputer. Only enough cyberspace setting is built to make it believable. Beyond the castle walls, there is a cybervacuum. In this program, if Mok actually leaves the castle, he will step into that cybervacuum. The shock will short-circuit his brain."

"In other words," His Worldship said, his voice less harsh and more satisfied, "if he stays in the castle, he will be killed. If he survives and flees the castle, he will die."

"Yes, Your Worldship."

"Good."

His Worldship then hung up on the Committee member.

In the stairwell, the man took several minutes to compose himself before returning to the Committee.

CHAPTER 23

CYBERSPACE—THE HOLY LAND. After the sultan's messenger left, Count Reynald barked out orders for his knights to guard against an attack. In the confusion, Mok was left to wander.

He followed the count's wife and her servant, determined to wait until the servant girl was by herself. If she truly was Raha, the pharaoh's daughter, she could explain to Mok how they both had gotten here from ancient Egypt.

For twenty minutes, Mok did not get the chance to question her. He followed at a slow pace, always staying just out of sight of the two women.

And always, he heard the quiet sound of miners digging at the foundations of the walls, the quiet sound of horror. *Tap. Tap. Tap. Tap. Tap.*

Mok tried not to think what the sound meant. He tried not to think of the sultan's threat and the army beyond the walls. *Tap. Tap. Tap. Tap. Tap.*

Mok found it easier to ignore the sound when he put his mind on the servant girl. How had she followed him through time? Did she know how he had been taken from Old Newyork? And, more important, did she know why?

As the two women walked along the castle's

inner walls, they stopped to encourage knights and soldiers at their various posts. During their wide-ranging stroll, Mok began to understand the defense system of the castle.

The outer walls—which the army had torn down to fill the ditches—were only the first defense. Between the outer walls and the inner walls were some of the town buildings, long since burned to the ground. The inner walls had not fallen yet and formed a large square. It was on one of these walls that Mok had first found himself in this land.

Inside the walls was the large courtyard where Mok had listened to the terms of surrender and had first seen Raha. Placed around the courtyard were different buildings—stables, a carpentry shop, a blacksmith shop, an oven room where bread was baked, a kitchen, and a place for the soldiers to sleep.

Finally, at the far end of the courtyard was a tall, round tower made of stone. Mok compared it to some of the buildings in Old Newyork and decided it was at least four stories tall. It was protected by sharpened poles sticking outward from its base. There was only one entrance into the tower—halfway up the solid face of stone. A set of narrow wood stairs led to that door.

It was not difficult for Mok to figure out the purpose of the building. It was the final defense. A place for all to retreat to when the inner walls fell.

It also became the place where Mok could finally speak to the servant girl. As the count's wife and the girl neared the huge tower, Mok stayed well behind and out of sight. The count's wife continued on toward the stables. The servant girl began to climb the narrow stairs leading to the tower's entrance. As the count's wife stepped into the stables, Mok ran across the open space to the stairs.

He dashed up them. The servant girl waited for him at the top. Her hand was on the key she had just inserted into the lock of the door.

Mok stopped two steps short of the top and looked up at her.

"Yes?" she said. Her frown showed that she found Mok's activity unusual.

"I need to speak to you," he said.

It was her. He knew it. The same slim height. The same shoulder-length black hair. Only now she wore not a luxurious linen wrap but a plain blue dress. Gone was the gold band that had circled her forehead. Gone also were the jewelry and perfume.

"If you want to speak with me, all you need do is command," she said. "You are the count's son."

Mok's chest heaved as he sucked in a breath and pondered what he might say next.

"Then go on inside," he said when his breath returned. "For I have many questions."

"Will you allow me to continue my task as ordered by my lady?"

Mok nodded agreement. The door creaked on leather hinges as she let them both inside.

Without speaking, she entered the shadowed coolness of the tower. Mok followed and said nothing at first. He was too busy looking around as they wound through corridors and climbed more steps. He could see because shafts of sunlight came through square windows cut in the rock. Carpets hung from the walls, decorated with scenes of hunters chasing deer through forests. Open doors to some rooms showed bed chambers with lavish rugs on stone floors. They passed a small kitchen, an oven-room, and a weapons supply room.

Mok was glad that the hallways and rooms were empty of other people. He wanted as much time as possible alone with this servant girl.

She climbed a final set of stairs and stepped out through a small door.

He crouched to get through, then almost gasped when he straightened in the dazzling sunlight. They were on an open walk at the top of the tower, with waist-high walls around the edges.

"What business do you have here?" he asked.

She pointed at a small cage resting on a ledge. It was filled with pigeons.

"I have a message to send," she said, holding out a small strip of white. "Would you like to read it before I tie it to the pigeon's leg?"

Mok could not read. No one in Old Newyork ever learned. But he was not about to tell her that.

"Where will the pigeon go?" As much as Mok wanted to demand other answers, this interested him.

She gave him another frown, as if he had asked a stupid question. "To where it was born. A town along the sea, some forty miles to the north. Our message is sent to let them know we have not given up."

"That is one of the matters I want to discuss," Mok said, "why we do not surrender. But first, the other matter . . ."

He stepped forward and grabbed her wrists. "Tell me what is going on here. I know you are the pharaoh's daughter!"

Without warning, she stamped her heel down on his toes, crushing the small bones in his foot. Mok hopped backward in pain. He lost his balance, spun around, and fell. The low wall caught him squarely in the stomach.

For a second, he teetered over the wall. Far, far down were the sharpened poles.

She grabbed his hair and yanked him back.

He stood tall, panted, and stared at her.

"You'll get no apology from me," she said. "You may be the count's son, but you have no right to do what you did."

"And you have no right to keep up this mystery," Mok said angrily. "Tell me what game you play."

"The sun has baked your head," she told him. "I play no game."

"You are Raha. A pharaoh's daughter. You tried to execute me."

She laughed. "My name is Rachel. I'm a servant girl. And you are a fool."

Mok glared at her. At that moment, he truly doubted his own sanity. Before he could say another word, however, a whistling scream drew his attention. It ended in a giant roar. And the tower shook beneath them.

CHAPTER 24

MOK ROCKED BACK AND FORTH on his feet. It felt like the entire stone tower had wobbled.

"What was that?" he asked.

Rachel pushed her hair back from her face. She calmly opened the cage, stuck in her hand, and pulled out a pigeon. She tied the message to the bird's leg.

"I expect that was the beginning of the new attack," she said. With a gentle throw, she tossed the pigeon into the air. It circled once on whirring wings, then cut a straight line across the sky.

In Egypt, Mok had believed the events around him to be a wild dream. He had enjoyed the experience then, hoping he might never wake. Now, in confusion and fear, he wished desperately to open his eyes and find himself in his sleep tunnel beneath Old Newyork.

"But what was it? I mean—"

Before he could finish his question, another whistling scream grew louder. A movement caught the corner of his eye. Then seconds later, the roar. Followed by another tremor of the tower.

"A rock," he said with awe. "A rock the size of . . ."

"A chariot," Rachel said. There was no emotion

in her voice. "Fired from a catapult. They are close enough now to hit this tower."

"Anything else?" Mok asked sarcastically, thinking nothing could be worse.

"Oh, they have a rope-wound bow. It takes three men to crank. The giant arrow is released with such force that it will go right through a wooden door. Or a man. And when they get closer, they have giant battering rams. With dozens of men behind them, they can run through a wall. And, of course, the burning buckets of pitch shot from smaller catapults."

She put her hands on her hips. "But why, my young lord, do you pretend to know none of this? You saw it all as they tore away the outer walls."

She was truly not Raha? She was simply, as she said, a servant girl, who fully believed Mok was the son of Count Reynald?

Mok closed his eyes. He wanted to weep in frustration. So many questions. And not even one answer.

Another shrieking whistle. Followed by the explosion and shuddering walls.

"Please," Mok said, "help me."

"My lord? You do not look well."

"Pretend I am a stranger, just dropped inside these castle walls," Mok said. "Explain why the army has attacked. And why Count Reynald would follow the man named Christ into death."

Rachel studied him to see if he were joking.

Mok's face must have showed the anguish and confusion he felt. Her frown relented and her own face softened.

"Sit beside me," she said. "Unless a rock lands right on top of us, we will be safe here. These walls should stand for at least a week."

She sat and drew her knees up. "Why has this army attacked? A few hundred years ago, great Crusades were fought to conquer this land. Now, we in turn are being conquered. By Mamelukes. Long ago, they were slaves brought to serve the Turks of this region. They revolted against the Turks, and have begun to lay claim to the entire Holy Land. Our castle is the last stronghold of Christian knights remaining."

"The Holy Land . . . ," Mok whispered. "Tell me about the man from Galilee." Even with the rocks thudding into the walls, Mok had to know. From his childhood, he'd wondered about this man. And here, finally, was someone who might know.

"The man from Galilee," she repeated softly. "He was born nearly 1,300 years ago. This is the year 1296, and history is marked by his birth."

"He was that important," Mok mused. The sunlight warmed his shoulders. All he could see was the line of the low walls and the blue sky beyond. If it weren't for the catapulted rocks, it would have been a peaceful place to talk to a beautiful girl. "This man from Galilee must have been a king. An emperor. Or even more important."

"He was a simple carpenter," she said, smiling. "A man who made his living by working with wood."

"Only a carpenter? But how—"

Her smile broadened. As teacher, she was enjoying

the response of her student as she guided him in his understanding of the Galilee Man.

"He was alive on this earth for only thirty-three years. Yet because of him, we are here in the castle thirteen centuries later. Over the last two hundred years, our armies have fought to protect the Holy Land for pilgrims who wish to visit the land of his birth."

"How could one man have such impact?" Mok asked.

"Because," she said, "he is the Son of God."

"*Is?*" Mok asked. "Not *was?*"

She opened her mouth to reply but stopped as a trumpet blare echoed in long, mournful blasts.

She stood quickly and pulled Mok to his feet.

"That is a signal calling every person to the walls," she said. "We must join them in the battle!"

CHAPTER 25

MOK STOOD ON TOP of the thick stone walls that formed the final protection to the courtyard. He could hardly believe his eyes. Below him, swarms of soldiers advanced in waves.

A few steps away on each side of Mok were knights in full armor. They formed a line up and down all the walls. Mok had counted earlier. Fewer than two hundred men.

And below?

Thousands upon thousands of soldiers.

What frightened Mok the most was their silence. They moved ahead almost grimly. No war cries to give them false courage, just quiet determination to finish their task.

Behind those soldiers were their great war machines. Creaking on wooden wheels were huge catapults. Behind the catapults, men pushed the long battering rams.

The soldiers moved easily over the filled moats.

The knights atop the castle walls were also silent as they waited for the soldiers to near the castle.

Then the first wave of soldiers reached the walls. They began to throw grappling hooks upward. These were like huge fishing hooks, attached to thick rope. The iron hooks clanged over the stone walls and held. Soldiers grabbed the ropes and began to climb.

Still the knights did not move.

Count Reynald waited until the soldiers below had almost reached the top.

"Now!" Count Reynald shouted.

His knights slashed downward with their swords, cutting the ropes. The climbing soldiers fell backward onto soldiers below them.

At the same time, other knights rolled head-sized boulders over the walls. The bottom of the thick walls curved outward. The boulders followed the curve at high speed, bouncing into the ranks of soldiers below.

Yet other knights began firing arrows. And the women who remained in the castle poured buckets of heated oil over the walls.

The sultan's army did not slow the attack.

For every fallen soldier, three others replaced him. More grappling hooks reached the stone walls. More soldiers below fired arrows upward.

And so the grim battle continued for hours.

Whenever Mok could, he looked around. He did not see one fallen knight. Such was the advantage of a position on top of the stone walls.

But how long could their supply of rocks and arrows and oil hold? How long could they continue to cut ropes before exhaustion set in? Even now, Mok was so thirsty he could hardly move. Only desperation kept him fighting.

If the enemy soldiers managed to crest the walls . . .

One hour of fighting. Two. Then three.

Suddenly, it ended. Just as everything looked lost, just as the knights were falling from fatigue, the army below began an orderly retreat.

Mok did not have to wonder long at the reason.

From far away, he saw the single line of horses riding toward the castle. At the lead was Tabarie, the messenger from the sultan. He carried a long pole with a white flag waving at the top.

None of the knights fired arrows at him or the other riders.

At the castle doors, he reined his horse to a stop.

"Open your doors!" Tabarie shouted up. "The sultan has another message!"

"Move your army farther away," Count Reynald shouted down in a ragged voice. He did not want them to pour in through the open doors, not after all the effort to keep them from swarming over the top of the walls.

Tabarie ordered his army back and waited on his horse. Finally, Count Reynald judged it was safe to open the doors.

Mok joined Count Reynald and his wife and Rachel in the courtyard to listen to Tabarie.

CHAPTER 26

IN THE COURTYARD, Tabarie's face was shiny with sweat. It took two servants to help him off his horse. He dusted off his cloak with deliberate slowness, knowing that Count Reynald and the others had no choice but to wait.

Tap. Tap. Tap. Tap. Tap. The miners below continued their work, blind to the events above.

"A valiant fight," Tabarie finally said. His efforts at dignity were lost when he wiped sweat from his face with a small cloth. "The sultan is impressed at your braveness. He would rather not destroy such good men. That is why he called back his soldiers."

"We will not surrender," Count Reynald said, "unless the terms have changed."

Tabarie did not answer. Instead, he snapped his fingers. Sweat had made them greasy, and no noise resulted. With a look of irritation, he turned his head and shouted at his servants.

They began to move as if according to a plan.

One of the servants unrolled a measuring line. Another took the end of the line and trotted away from the inner courtyard toward the castle gates.

After five minutes of positioning and repositioning the line, and after much rapid discussion in a language Mok could not understand, the two servants nodded agreement at their measurements. A third servant produced a piece of chalk and stooped to draw on the round, flat stones of the courtyard floor.

The sun had begun to settle, and long shadows filled the courtyard.

Except for the scratching of chalk and the eerie *tap, tap, tap* that never ceased, it was silent as the servant drew a circle almost half the size of the courtyard. The servant straightened and nodded that his task was complete.

Tabarie spoke again. "Not only have we undermined your outer walls, but we have also dug beneath your inner courts. Below this circle lies the cave our slaves have mined over the last six weeks. By noon tomorrow, it will finally be complete."

Count Reynald looked at the circle. "As you say."

Tabarie smiled. "The cave is propped with wooden beams. We will pile brush inside. Unless you surrender by tomorrow evening, we will light the brush. Once we start the fire below, the courtyard floor and the walls around it will crack in the heat and collapse. Your great tower will topple. And the sultan promises that his soldiers will not leave a single person inside alive."

"Your terms of surrender?" Count Reynald said. "The same as before? If so, we refuse. Our souls are more important to us than our lives."

"The terms have changed," Tabarie said. "Indeed, you will not be asked to deny the Christ Jesus you call Savior."

"Then we accept."

"Not so fast." Tabarie smiled. "*You* need not deny the Christ. Yet the sultan says he still needs a public denial from this family. The sultan has said it will satisfy him if it comes from your son."

Tabarie turned to Mok.

"What do you say?" he asked Mok with a sly grin. "Will you denounce the Christ? Will you tell the people of this land that you do not believe in him or his cause?"

CHAPTER 27

ALL EYES IN THE COURTYARD turned upon Mok. He swallowed, trying to get moisture into his suddenly dry mouth.

"Your father has made a declaration of his beliefs," Tabarie said. "You need not die for his stubbornness. And a simple word from you will save him. Let me ask again. Does he speak for you? Yes or no."

The seconds moved as slowly as the shadows that crept across the courtyard.

Tap. Tap. Tap. Tap. Tap.

Mok swallowed again.

Tap. Tap. Tap. Tap. Tap.

Below them, slaves widened the cave.

Tabarie stepped closer to Mok. "Think carefully before you answer. I now place not only your life in your hands, but also your father's and your mother's. Indeed, speak up against these foolish beliefs, and you shall save every person still alive within these walls."

"Son . . . ," Count Reynald tried.

"Silence," Tabarie snapped. "He has a will of his own. Let him speak for himself. The sultan will take as much satisfaction in the son's denial as in the count's. Across this land, his word will suffice as yours. And we will be freed of the Crusaders and their beliefs."

Tap. Tap. Tap. Tap. Tap.

The pickaxes below sounded much louder in the concentrated silence that fell upon the group. All stared at Mok and waited for his answer.

Mok thought of his audiobook and the man from Galilee. A man who promised a home to lost children.

If the Galilee Man was real—something Mok was determined to discover—would Mok find the home he wanted to believe waited for him? He thought of the lonely, fearful nights he had spent in the concrete caves of Old Newyork, wishing his father and mother had not died. He had had only the audiobook and its promises to comfort him.

Yet . . .

Yet what if the Galilee Man were only legend? What if the stories were only stories, meant simply to comfort small children? By speaking against a man who might only be legend, then, Mok could save these people. What could it hurt to denounce a legend?

Mok remembered something from the audiobook. *Don't be afraid of people. They can only kill the body. They cannot kill the soul.*

Mok saw the determination on Count Reynald's face, on his wife's face. These two were willing to die for what they believed. There must be a good reason for it, he told himself.

A carpenter who lived only thirty-three years.

Yet in the centuries that followed his death, armies had fought for him.

Legend or truth?

Could the man of Galilee truly be the Son of God?

In a flash, Mok realized that was the single greatest decision to be made in any life. Legend or Son of God? For if the man of Galilee was the Son of God, every life must be lived in the light of that great truth. A truth that would echo through the centuries.

"Well," Tabarie said, "answer me. Your life depends on it."

"Son," Count Reynald said, "your soul also depends on it. Which is of more importance? A brief life on earth, no matter how painful? Or an eternity of love beyond this life?"

A strange feeling of peace filled Mok. He remembered, too, as a child listening to the audiobook, there had been times it seemed the Galilee Man had stood right beside him.

"I stand with Count Reynald," Mok said. "I stand beside him with the man from Galilee."

Tabarie glared at them.

"Tomorrow," Tabarie said, "go to the turrets of your castle. Watch for a long line of slaves carrying brush and wood into the depths of the earth below our feet. And tomorrow evening? Prepare for the fire that will bring the walls down so that our soldiers may massacre you."

CHAPTER 28

MAINSIDE. At his Mainside home, the Committee member sat in his private office. Here, not even his family dared interrupt his work or thoughts.

The office was lined with dark-oak wall panels. The desk in it was large, almost empty except for a vidphone. The phone itself was small, but the vidscreen was the size of a television. The Committee member stared at it, biting his nails as he waited.

When the phone rang, he punched the receive button, cutting the ring to silence.

"You answered quickly," the face on the vidscreen said.

"Your Worldship!"

"You were expecting someone else?" the president of the World United asked. The large screen clearly showed the man's sneer. The man's face was obviously reconstructed, which did little to help hide his age or his distress

"I've been paged to expect a conference call with all of the Committee members," he replied, forcing his own face not to show nervousness. As clearly as he could see the president, the president could see him.

"Then my call is timely. Something has happened. Correct?"

"Correct, Your Worldship. The Welfaro candidate

is well into the cyberstage. He was given two choices: denying Christ or facing death when the castle falls. He chose death."

"This is not a good thing," the president said. He stroked his chin as he spoke.

"There is nothing to fear. If the candidate dies in cyberspace he dies in—"

"You've explained that to me a dozen times. No, you fool, I am disturbed for another reason. Have you no concept of history?"

"Your Worldship?"

"David and Goliath. Joan of Arc. Billy Graham. All it takes is one to turn the tide of history. Something about deep childlike faith arms them against overwhelming odds. I will not underestimate our opponent."

"Is it time to send someone in, Your Worldship? We have a sequence code for emergencies. Perhaps an assassin in cyberspace . . ."

"Let me think on that," the president said. "For now, I believe it will serve our purpose if the Committee thinks it is safe from interference. On the other hand—"

An urgent beeping interrupted.

"Your Worldship, the conference call has arrived."

"I am not finished with you."

"Your Worldship, if I do not answer, Cambridge will wonder what was more important than a Committee gathering."

"Fine. I will talk to you later," the president said and hung up.

The Committee member punched another button on the phone and the vidscreen immediately divided into twelve rectangles. Each was filled with a face, including his own.

"Welcome," Cambridge said. His was the face in the top right of the screen.

All the Committee members greeted each other.

"Let's not waste time," Cambridge said. His voice sounded hollow on the speaker phone. "As you know, Mok has passed this second test. With the help of the Living Spirit, he has made a public profession of his faith, even against the threat of death."

Murmurs filled the speaker phone. The one Committee member who had predicted failure had the grace to bow his head.

"Yet," Cambridge continued, "in private conversations with some of you, a serious matter has been brought up. Some of you believe it is a faith untested, for the walls have not fallen. Some of you say he must actually have a sword to his throat for the threat of death to be real."

The murmurs grew as all began to voice their opinions.

"Enough," Cambridge said. "Time here is also time in cyberspace. We must come to a decision soon. Do we let this cybersegment continue until Mok is at the verge of death? Or do we send him to the next stage immediately?"

The voices grew louder.

"Gentlemen," Cambridge called.

In the new silence, Cambridge spoke quietly.

93

"There is a third option. This candidate has proved himself to be resourceful. What if he finds a way to escape the siege? You all know that if he moves into a cybervacuum beyond the boundaries of this program his brain will be scrambled."

"Escape is impossible," the doubting Committee member snorted. "You know we built this model on an actual siege in the Holy Lands of the thirteenth century—every detail is the same, right down to the sultan's messenger drawing a chalk line of the cave below. No one escaped then. He will not escape now. I say leave him there until he is tested at sword point."

"If we miscalculate by a single second," Cambridge said, "the sword might take his life. And then our final candidate is gone forever. And with him, all our hope."

"This stage was meant to test our candidate's faith to the utmost," the doubter said. "Why move him to the next stage unless we have done exactly that?"

"It is not my role to answer," Cambridge replied. "Instead, I put it to all of you in a vote."

They voted.

Six to five, the other members decided to leave Mok in the castle about to fall to thousands of soldiers.

CHAPTER 29

CYBERSPACE—THE HOLY LAND. In the castle courtyard, four stood in a circle holding hands—Count Reynald, his wife, Mok, and the servant girl Rachel. Two hours had passed since the sultan's messenger had promised that all would be dead by the next evening.

Tap. Tap. Tap. Tap. Tap.

Night and day, as Mok knew, the tapping below the castle had continued for weeks. Daily it had only stopped—briefly—when one shift of slaves left and another shift replaced them.

Tap. Tap. Tap. Tap. Tap.

Mok knew, too, that past the inner courtyard, past the castle walls, an army of thousands waited to flood the castle, engaging the knights in a screaming, raging battle of spears and swords.

At this moment, however, with the sun just about to set, a soft golden light filled the courtyard with a deceptive promise of continued life. The air was still and cool. Except for the echoes of the pickaxes tapping against the stone foundations of the castle, it might have been as peaceful as a cathedral.

The four stood, about to pray as if the courtyard truly were a cathedral. Three of them—Count Reynald, the countess, and the servant girl—stood with heads bowed and eyes closed in reverent contemplation. Mok, copying them, stood with bowed head. He was unfamiliar with prayer, however, and did not know it was the custom to close his eyes against distractions.

"Almighty Father," Count Reynald spoke in his low voice. "Our lives are in your hands. When our time arrives, please take us quickly through the curtain of death to the light of your love on the other side."

Mok furrowed his eyebrows. He was beyond wondering how he'd been thrust here from the street canyons and work gangs and rats in Old Newyork. He was beyond believing this was a troubled dream caused by glo-glo pharmaceuds in his water. He was even beyond the perplexing mystery of the girl opposite him, a girl who was playing the part of a servant even as Mok himself had been put into the role of the count's son.

Mok's puzzlement was more basic.

The count prayed to a father. *Was not the man from Galilee called the Son?*

The count also spoke as if this father could actually hear his pleas. *How could this be? And could the man from Galilee also hear whenever one spoke? Could it be this simple?*

Mok nearly spoke his doubts aloud, but the others were so earnest in their prayer that Mok did not dare interrupt.

The count and his wife began to sing softly, a majestic tune Mok did not recognize. Mok remained silent, staring at the stonework of the courtyard.

Tap. Tap. Tap. Tap. Tap.

Not even the hymn could hide the sound of pick-axes digging closer to their deaths.

Still staring downward, Mok smiled grimly. He needed no more reminder of his impending death than the markings of chalk just beyond his feet. It was a large circle, showing the size of the hole already dug beneath the castle.

Tap. Tap. Tap. Tap. Tap.

It filled Mok with great sadness to think of these people meekly waiting for the invading horde. Wasn't there something to be done?

Tap. Tap. Tap. Tap. Tap.

Below his feet, slaves patiently kept digging.

Tap. Tap. Tap. Tap. Tap.

How far below? Mok wondered idly. How dark and horrid it must be to work as a slave miner.

Then Mok smiled again. Much less grimly than before. Perhaps Tabarie had given them the answer.

When Count Reynald and his wife finished singing, Mok raised a quiet question.

"Tell me," he said, "in what manner do slaves in this land dress themselves?"

CHAPTER 30

FIVE HOURS LATER—in the middle of the night—they were gathered again in the courtyard. Had there been light of day, the count would no longer have been recognizable as the nobleman ruler of the castle. Gone were his fine robes. Instead, he wore sweat-stained rags. His head was shaved; his face and arms were covered with smudged grease and dirt.

The countess, too, had a shaved head and was equally filthy. Hidden beneath their rags, both wore pouches filled with gold. Mok and the girl matched the count and his wife. Mok's scalp, now stubbled, tingled from the earlier scraping of the razor.

"It was kind of the general's messengers to show us the outline of the cave," Count Reynald murmured. "I pray that what was meant to be a show of force proves instead to be a means of life."

"Shall I go first?" Mok said. "I am ready."

At their feet was a pile of flat stones, pried from the courtyard floor. In the opening in the stonework was a hole just big enough to pass through. The end of a thick rope was coiled near the hole. The other end of the rope was tied to a post at the far end of the courtyard.

"No, my son," Count Reynald replied. "Even

though you devised this escape, I shall go first. There is the possibility I might land among the slaves of the next shift. If so, let me take the fight to them. If it is safe, you must help the women follow me down."

Tap. Tap. Tap. Tap. Tap.

Three knights stood behind them. Count Reynald addressed them with matching softness. "You are certain, my friends, you will not join us?"

"We are certain, m'lord," one answered. "Although the fire will begin tomorrow, the stone may not fall through for hours. And we shall fight hard. Tomorrow night, if the castle still stands and we have a chance to escape in the darkness, we will follow. As for now, we will return to our fellow knights upon the ramparts to help create the diversion. And before dawn, we will cover this hole so the light is not visible below."

"God be with you," Count Reynald said. "May we meet in the seaport as planned."

"And God be with you." The three knights bowed, a motion barely seen in the darkness. They hurried away.

Tap. Tap. Tap. Tap.

Minute followed long minute.

Tap. Tap. Tap. Tap.

Silence. The shift had ended.

"Now," Count Reynald ordered. "We must go now. We have little time."

He did not hesitate. He took the end of the rope and tied it around his waist. He handed a portion of the rope to Mok.

"If it is safe once I have landed below," Count Reynald said, "I will tug twice on the rope."

Count Reynald lowered himself into the hole without further instructions. None were needed. Mok braced himself and played the rope out through his hands. When the weight eased, they waited anxiously. Finally came two quick tugs on the rope. Mok's rapid heartbeat increased in a surge of added adrenaline.

The plan was working. They would join the slaves below as they filed out of the cave. From there, they would find an opportunity to escape. And to the people of the land, it would be seen as a miracle.

All that was left was to get the countess and the girl safely down the rope. Mok would then follow.

Mok helped the countess lower herself into the hole.

"Thank you," she said. "You found a way for us to leave and still keep our honor and our vows. I know now that we will be safe."

Mok nodded with dignity.

He turned to the girl.

"Please," Mok said, "let me ask one final time. Were you not the pharaoh's daughter in the land of endless sand? Help me understand . . ."

He allowed his voice to trail away, for in the near dark of the courtyard, he could see her move toward him.

"Embrace me," she said. "Tightly."

He had no chance to refuse, for she was in his

arms and pulling him against her. She hugged him, then pulled back.

"Breathe deeply," she commanded.

He was puzzled, but already she was pressing a cloth into his mouth and nose. A sweet, cloying smell seemed to fill the cavern of his brain. He tried to protest. Dizziness, however, sucked the air from his lungs and drove him to his knees.

He felt himself begin to topple. He sank to his knees, then fell, eyes closed.

She must have believed him already unconscious.

"I'm sorry," he heard her whisper, "but this was done to save you."

It was the final sound he heard in the castle.

CHAPTER 31

MAINSIDE. When the comtechs finished reporting all the details of Mok's cybertest, one Committee member inwardly squirmed with disbelief, anger, and fear. Outwardly, of course, he showed the same growing joy expressed by the rest of the Committee.

This Committee member managed to exchange congratulations with a few others before excusing himself from the room on the tenth floor. The entire time his face was a mask, although his thoughts were on a netphone in the main-floor lobby of the building.

He had been forced to use it once before in a similar emergency—when Mok had passed the first stage of the test. Then, the Committee member had never dreamed he might have to use it again in the same kind of emergency.

There was one small difference. When Mok passed the first cyberstage, the Committee member had raced to the netphone. This time, he walked as if his feet were encased in concrete blocks. He was not looking forward to the message he had to send.

It seemed as if it took him an hour to reach the lobby and cross the marble floor to the public netphone. He wished the trip had taken twice as long.

Although others were leaving the building through the lobby, the Committee member began to type on the netphone's keyboard. For all they knew, he was checking to see if his family had e-mailed him a message regarding a dinner meeting. If someone came close enough to see otherwise, he would hit the delete key and erase everything from the screen.

The Committee member punched in the private dotcom number of the president of the World United. The system prompted him for his e-mail message. The Committee member's fingers clicked over the keyboard:

I have just received the report that the candidate is moving into stage three. I had considered this impossible. I fear he will move through this stage easily as it has been designed not to test him, but to teach him. I strongly advise you to give me the go-ahead to send in a cyberkiller. Please respond immediately—time is short.

The Committee member hit the send button and hurried from the lobby.

An hour later, during dinner at a restaurant with his family, he briefly excused himself. There was a netphone on the street corner.

The member punched in his access code to check for new messages. There was one. As expected, it was from the president of the World United.

The member shielded the netphone screen from passersby and scanned the words.

Candidate must fail. Proceed with cyberk____.

CHAPTER 32

CYBERSPACE—PIRATE SHIP. The strong smell of wine surprised Mok.

"Wake up, you scoundrel!" a loud voice roared.

Hot breath blasted Mok's face with more of the smell of wine. "Wake up! Wake up! The captain will have us for shark bait!"

Eyes still closed, Mok told himself he was prepared for anything. He had been a royal undertaker for a pharaoh . . . then a count's son in a castle under siege. How could anything surprise him now?

"Wake up! Wake up!" Rough hands shook him.

Mok squinted open one eye and looked into the unshaven face of a man with an eye patch. The wine-stench breath and words came from a mouth of black and broken teeth.

The man jerked Mok into a sitting position. He surveyed Mok and then bellowed with laughter.

"By the depths of Neptune," the man shouted. "Whoever gang-pressed you played a mean, mean joke to shave your head in such a manner!"

"Gang-pressed?" Mok managed weakly. He rubbed his scalp. The stubble was still there from shaving his head at the castle.

"Gang-pressed. You and all the others," the man

shouted in glee. "Fools, the lot of you. It's a simple matter to fill you with wine until we can roll you aboard the ship as crew mates!"

"Crew mates? Ship?" Mok, of course, had not had any wine. He struggled to understand, and became more aware of his surroundings. His bed was a pile of damp blankets in a cramped room of rough wooden beams. It smelled of mold and seawater.

"Ship!" the man shouted. "Of course it's a ship! Weren't you in a harbor town last night? Did you not see the masts and the sails?"

"I did not agree to this," Mok said. He became aware of a rocking motion. The entire room seemed to sway. "Set me free."

More drunken laughter from the man before him.

"But you are free! Free to wander this ship! You can even return to the harbor—if you care to swim among the sharks! Otherwise, welcome to the merriest band of cutthroat pirates to sail the seven seas!"

BACKSTORY III

OLD NEWYORK, A.D. 2076. Benjamin Rufus, a tired old man, walked through the slums of Old Newyork for two hours before reaching the street corner of his memories.

By then, the sweat on his forehead felt as heavy and thick as blood. The morning was hot and muggy, the sunlight filtered through a haze. Concrete and steel reflected the heat. In Old Newyork, no trees or grass provided relief. Because he was ill, the old man half wondered if indeed he had begun to sweat blood. He was afraid to wipe his forehead to find out.

Passersby noticed nothing out of the ordinary about him. He was just another sad-faced old man walking the streets. He was thin and stooped, his hair cropped short and gray. Not even the long coat he wore in the heat was unusual. Many moved through Old Newyork with everything they owned. After all, it was easier to wear a coat than carry it.

A closer observer, however, would have seen a certain peace in the man's face. His wrinkles were not set in anger. His eyes were clear. Not many in the slums at his age showed these small indications of hope.

One thing about this man—impossible to see— would have astounded the passersby. Before step- ping onto a ferry the day before to cross the river to Old Newyork, Benjamin had been among the rich- est men in the world. He had given up everything— name, fortune, freedom—just to reach this street corner in the slums.

The old man did not move for several moments. He paused to draw a breath of courage and looked around with a mixture of sadness and satisfaction. This street corner would suit him now, as it had many years before.

Long ago this area had been a park. A magnifi- cent statue had guarded the entrance to lawn and trees and ponds with fountains. That was before the great Water Wars. When the city was proud and free.

Most of the people now passing by had never seen the park of those earlier times. The heavy, tall statue had long since been pulled down for the value of its bronze. All that remained was the high, wide concrete base, stripped, too, of its bronze plaque.

The park itself was now filled with leaning shacks and honeycombed with twisting, littered paths. The fountains had been drained by people desperate for any kind of water. Skyscrapers behind the park cast shadows on the shacks, like mountains overshadow- ing a village.

Down the street, a waterman sold flasks of water at merciless prices. Bodyguards armed with machine guns protected him. Between the waterman and the old man, vendors of clothes, food, and cigarettes lined the streets, drawing people from their shacks and hiding holes.

Many, many years before, on this same street corner, Benjamin had climbed onto the pedestal of the broken statue before him. He had spoken to the hundreds of people who were scurrying past. Back then his reasons for being here were much different. He had returned today to make up for what had happened because of that first speech.

He drew another deep breath, remembering across the years. He had felt this excitement, hope, and fear then as he had prepared to address the crowd of an earlier generation. It was not easy to speak to a large group of strangers, to gather them together and beg them to listen. Some would laugh. Some would call out insults. And in these slums one could not ask for protection. Not from anyone. Not against anyone.

The excitement, fear, and hope rolled through his belly like kittens tumbling over a ball of yarn. The roof of his mouth, dry from nervousness, tasted of copper. For a long, doubting moment, he considered turning away from the street corner and fading back among the street vendors.

Why was he here? What good would it do? How could he hope to make a difference? Thousands and thousands of slum people were spread over dozens and dozens of square miles of street canyons.

He closed his eyes for a moment of prayer.

Prayer calmed him, gave him strength. Not for the first time, the old man marveled at the joy and love from the Creator of the universe.

Why was he here? In his mind he saw the mother and father and children he had rescued from the work gangs only hours earlier. They and all the other families like them were his reason for coming here.

What good could he do? None, not by himself. He could only trust the power of a message that had given hope to people throughout the centuries. He could only trust the power of the One behind that message.

How could he hope to make a difference? By planting seeds in soil barren of any hope at all.

One final breath to calm my nerves, Benjamin Rufus told himself. One final breath of courage. He took in a lungful of air. And coughed. His lungs rattled with pain. With a wry grin, he told himself he deserved the pain for trying to delay his task.

Benjamin moved to the base of the statue. With great effort, he climbed onto the base. For several moments, he swayed on his feet. He closed his eyes and waited for some energy to return.

A few people stared briefly upward at him then ducked their heads and walked by. What was one more madman among them?

When he felt ready, Benjamin reached inside his coat. Twenty-four hours earlier, he had been one of the most powerful men on Mainside. It had been no problem to buy the small electronic device he now pulled from his pocket. It was shaped much like a flip-phone. He slipped its looped cord around his neck, and the device dangled against his chest.

The old man flicked a small switch. Instantly,

the microphone at the top of the device was ready to broadcast his words loudly and clearly above the din of the people on the street below.

"People of Old Newyork," Benjamin said. He spoke in a normal voice, knowing his lungs would not permit him any more force. "Listen."

The shock of broadcast words cut through the crowds. Through the shacks behind him. People stared with wonder. Many of them had never heard a voice amplified through speakers. How could this man's words ring through the air like thunder?

Instantly, everyone grew silent.

"Gather close," he urged. "Listen."

Slowly, they began to shuffle toward him.

Benjamin noted that one of the waterman's bodyguards sprinted down the street, away from the statue base.

He'd gone to send a message to one of the ganglords. Benjamin knew he had five minutes, maybe ten at the most.

"We all know that there is nothing here of greater value than water," Benjamin said. "Let me tell you about the One who will give you water, so that you will never thirst again."

The crowd muttered excitedly.

"Yes," Benjamin said clearly and slowly. "There is a place waiting for all of you, a place without hunger or fear or thirst. Your greatest hope is because of a man who died on a cross for you. A man from God and of God. A man who rose from the dead."

"No man rises from death!" someone shouted. The crowd hummed with an excited babble of interest and jeers.

"No man born of man," Benjamin Rufus answered calmly. "Let me tell you how this man was different."

As he continued to speak, the old man watched and waited for those who would arrive with spears and crossbows to try to silence him.

CHAPTER 33

MAINSIDE, A.D. 2096. A luxury high-rise building stood near the Hudson River. From its balconies, it was possible to see the distant slums of Old Newyork on the other side of the river.

Inside the building lay one person who had recently been delivered from Old Newyork. But Mok was unaware of his freedom. Plastic tubes connected him to a life-support machine. Other lines were taped to his shaved head and ran to a nitrogen-cooled computer. Two nurses watched his heartbeat and other vital signs with great care. They had instructions to call a team of doctors and comtechs at the slightest sign of trouble.

Down the hall, in a much larger room, the twelve members of the Committee had just gathered around a conference table. A giant vidscreen filled one wall of the room. At the moment no images were on the flat dull-gray screen.

"Cambridge," one of the men said to the Committee leader, "I understand that Mok has moved into stage three."

Cambridge hid a smile of satisfaction. They had all been against his choice of Mok as a candidate. This was the first time one of them had called him

Mok instead of the Welfaro. It was an encouraging sign.

"Stage three," Cambridge confirmed. As usual, he wore jeans and a casual shirt. "Mok has passed through both tests. I expect no problems at all with stage three."

The questioner pointed to the blank vidscreen. "If he is already in stage three, why aren't we able to watch him on the monitor as before?"

Around the room, others nodded and looked at Cambridge expectantly.

Cambridge surveyed them, unbothered by the question.

"You all know the situation," Cambridge said to the whole group. "Mok's body is here, but his brain is wired to a cyberspace sequence. He is in a virtual reality stage where the characters and situations have been set up to respond to his decisions. Just as if the experiences were real."

"Yes, yes," the impatient questioner said, still pointing at the screen. "But why can't we see—"

"He is on a ship on the ocean, not a stationary stage like the Egyptian prison or the castle. Unlike the other cyberspace tests, this one is straining our computer to within gigabytes of crashing."

Cambridge checked his timepiece and made some rapid calculations. "In fact, as we speak, Mok is witnessing a pirate raid. It takes many gigabytes of RAM to coordinate the actions of dozens of men fighting and screaming. Soon, a hurricane will hit. The motion of the ship, the roll of the waves, the creaking masts and pelting rain must all be detail perfect. In short, during this cybersegment, the computer simply can't run the program and still give us a real-time video transmission."

"Later?" another Committee member asked.

"Yes, we can review it later, when there is less memory strain on the computer," Cambridge said. "But remember that our civilized minds will face great shock. Gentlemen, we are talking about an eighteenth-century pirate raid. These men fight with swords, daggers, axes, and short-range pistols. It's savage and cruel beyond our imaginations."

"Savage and cruel!" came the cry from someone near the back. "Followed by a hurricane! What are you putting him through?"

Cambridge allowed a hint of an ironic smile to cross his thin face. "Have some of you actually begun to hope that our final candidate might succeed?"

"Hope is precious," the first speaker said. "Let us at least know that he will have a guide aboard the ship, as he had in previous sequences."

"The presence of a guide would defeat the purpose of this part of the journey," Cambridge said. "And he is on a two-masted schooner, a real pirate ship of that time period."

"Meaning?" someone asked.

"Pace off twenty-four steps," Cambridge said. "That is the entire length of a pirate ship of that era. An open deck twenty-four paces long. And below? Three small cabins forward. One aft. Sleeping hammocks between. With a crew of twenty-five in those cramped quarters, there is no room for a stranger. Not if the cyberspace around Mok is to be believable."

Cambridge regarded the glum faces of the Committee. "All is not lost. I've previously reported of his search for the Galilee Man, as Mok calls Jesus of Nazareth."

They waited.

"We have placed a cross around his neck to remind him of the man of Galilee. And is not Christ, himself, the best guide for any man?"

CHAPTER 34

CYBERSPACE—PIRATE SHIP. In the bright sunshine on the deck of the pirate ship, Mok froze as a large man suddenly stepped in front of him.

"And where might you be going?" It was a snarled demand, the tone backed by the gleaming curve of a cutlass. Had Mok taken another step forward, the tip of the sword would have entered his navel.

"Below," Mok answered, refusing to show his fear.

Mok's hidden fear was well founded. This man, Barbarossa, was the ship's master in charge of all provisions. Mok was carrying some of those provisions—without Barbarossa's permission. This was considered a crime on board a pirate ship.

Mok also knew Barbarossa was a man who enjoyed violence. Mok's dreams, in fact, were haunted by memories of what Barbarossa had done during a raid on a Spanish galleon. That had been before the terrors of the hurricane.

Barbarossa had led the swarming pirates across a rope ladder onto the galleon's deck. Barbarossa had roared with laughter as pistols, cutlasses, and cannonballs cut down the Spanish crew. At the end of the raid, Barbarossa's clothes had been soaked with blood. Others' blood.

Now Mok was face-to-face with this man. All by himself. Unarmed.

"Below?" Barbarossa repeated, blinking with suspicion. "You are going below?"

Barbarossa was a brute. His great sloping shoulders bunched at the base of his skull. His nose, once torn and burned by the explosion of gunpowder, had healed into the waxy shine of a molten candle. This was a man who had once lifted two of his own crew mates by their collars—one in each hand—and banged their heads together with such force that both became simpletons. All they had done was make the mistake of laughing when a barmaid spilled beer on Barbarossa.

"Yes, I am going below," Mok said evenly. He had no choice but to answer this man's questions. Mok knew too well there was no place aboard the ship to run or hide. They had not seen land for five days. All that surrounded them was the blue of water and sky, melted together at the horizon. During his first day aboard, the sight of such vast emptiness had frightened Mok. Now, he welcomed the landless sight as the lesser of far worse evils he had recently witnessed. Vast emptiness was much better than a raid. And much better than the two-day storm that had followed almost immediately, a storm that had darkened the morning sky to night. The ship had pitched to the tops of waves as high as the masts and dropped beside the swells to dizzying depths. All the time the hurricane had lashed the air with rain as hard as the shot used in the pistols.

"You carry water," Barbarossa grunted. "And bolts of cloth. For what purpose?"

Other pirates gathered to listen. They could hear a new storm brewing. Much better that Barbarossa's foul temper be directed at someone else—it kept his attention off them. And, in the long days of idleness between raids, it gave them entertainment.

"The water is for the captured men." Mok saw no point in lying, although he could predict Barbarossa's reaction. "Without water, they will die. They also have wounds that need binding."

"The slaves!" Barbarossa roared, to no one's surprise. "Fresh water for the slaves! You steal from us to give to them?"

The other pirates began to mutter. Of any offense a man could commit aboard ship, stealing provisions was the gravest.

"I have Captain Falconer's full permission," Mok said. In the dank, dark air below deck, chained to the beam of one of the masts, were five men, the only survivors of the now sunken Spanish galleon. Mok could not speak their language, but he did not need words to understand the agony of these men.

"I am the ship's master!" Barbarossa thundered. "I oversee the provisions. You ask me for water. Not the captain."

"Would you have granted my request?" Mok knew the conversation was becoming more dangerous, but he saw no way to leave it.

"No. I would not have. Let the slaves suffer."

Mok decided against the obvious reply. It would be stupid to ask Barbarossa's permission. "The captured men need water. Dead slaves are of no value."

"Neither is a crew member who does not pull his weight." With swiftness unbelievable for such a large man, Barbarossa kicked sideways, hammering Mok at the knees. Mok fell backward. His bowl of water crashed onto the deck beside him. Before Mok could spin or roll, Barbarossa stepped on his chest. He pressed the point of his cutlass into the soft hollow of Mok's throat.

CHAPTER 35

BARBAROSSA GRINNED, showing black teeth.

"A crew mate who does not fight has even less value than a dead slave," he told Mok. "For a dead slave will never turn on you in battle."

Without taking the pressure off Mok's throat, Barbarossa looked to his audience of pirates. "Did any of you witness this mate raising a sword or firing a pistol against the Spaniards?"

Save for the creaking of the ship, the flapping of its sails, and the slap of water against the hull, silence was the reply.

"No," Barbarossa said with triumph. "No one saw you join in our fight."

Barbarossa smiled with angry pleasure. "Only the storm spared you earlier. But now I have the leisure to deal with you as you deserve."

The sword pressed against Mok's flesh. He understood then that Barbarossa had been waiting for any excuse to fight him. Mok dared not try to defend himself.

"Yet, you may redeem yourself and keep your life," Barbarossa's voice shifted to a rumble of amusement, "if you prove yourself as one of us."

The other pirates caught the shift in Barbarossa's mood.

"A sporting event?" one asked. "He fights you?"

A fight meant gambling. While they expected Mok to lose, they could wager on how long he stood, if he lived or died, if he lost any limbs, if he was man enough to not beg for mercy . . .

"Not a fight against me," Barbarossa said. "Against one of the slaves he seeks to help."

Barbarossa stepped away from Mok. "On your feet," he commanded.

Mok stood, resisting the urge to rub his throat.

Barbarossa reversed his cutlass and offered Mok the handle. Mok took it, confused.

"We will bring a slave on deck," Barbarossa said to the other pirates. "He has this sword. The slave will be unarmed."

To Mok, Barbarossa said, "This will be your baptism in blood. Kill, and you survive as one of us. Refuse, and you die in the slave's place."

Mok held the razor-edged cutlass. It would be a simple matter to slash forward and attack Barbarossa. Yet something in the way Barbarossa stood showed he was not only ready but also hoping for Mok to attack him.

Mok dropped the sword.

"No," Mok said. "I will not slaughter any man."

Barbarossa licked his lips. "As I thought. It is the cross around your neck."

Despite the seriousness of the situation, Mok nearly laughed at Barbarossa's words. Yes, Mok wore a cross. But he had no idea how it had gotten there.

The cross around Mok's neck was only the latest of a series of events he could not understand.

"What does the cross have to do with it?" Mok said. He had no understanding of the significance of the silver symbol, let alone any guess as to how or why it had gotten around his neck. He simply knew that he would not kill another man, and that he had dropped the sword without needing to pause to think why.

"There are twenty of us against one of you," Barbarossa taunted. He waved his hands to take in the entire crew. "Will your Jesus save you now?"

CHAPTER 36

JESUS, THE GALILEE MAN. Again, mention of the Galilee Man. Mok's skin tingled at the name of this man who seemed to follow him everywhere.

The pirates began crowding toward him.

"The plank," one said, grinning. "Have him walk the plank."

Mok grabbed the sword from the deck and backed away, aware of how useless the sword was against such a mob.

"Flog him first," another said. "Then have him walk the plank. Let his blood draw sharks."

"Yes! Yes! Bring out the sharks! Drowning is nothing compared to sharks!"

"No, strap him to the mouth of the cannon and shoot!"

Mok felt the backs of his legs bump against the rail of the deck. Behind him were the swells of the depths of the ocean. In front was a mob of men growing more unruly and cruel.

The pirates pressed closer, laughing at Mok's efforts to flail the cutlass and keep them away.

"Stop!" a loud voice commanded.

The laughter and taunts stopped as if sliced by the cutlass in Mok's hand.

"No man dies except by the captain's order."

The pirates parted, giving Mok a clear view of the approaching captain.

Captain Falconer was of medium height and muscular. His reddish-blond beard was neatly trimmed. Normally, he seemed the picture of a country gentleman—an illusion compared to the savage way he attacked and fought enemies. But now his face was haggard, the skin gray as if he were seasick.

"What is happening here?" Captain Falconer asked with quiet authority.

Barbarossa explained. He kept his head raised, staring at the captain with defiance.

"I make those judgments," the captain said. "Not you."

"The same judgment that sent him below with water for the slaves?" Barbarossa asked with a sneer.

"This is my ship, Barbarossa. Speak another word, and you border on mutiny."

Except for the creaking deck and slap of waves against the hull, the ship was silent. The pirates had lost all trace of humor and were straining with tension. If Barbarossa challenged the captain, Falconer would have no choice but to fight a duel. For if he did not take the challenge, Falconer risked losing the ship to Barbarossa.

Barbarossa finally chose to back down. He dropped his eyes and stared at the deck. Mok stored that knowledge and shivered with fear. *Barbarossa, the brute, afraid of Falconer. What kind of man, then, was Falconer?*

The captain turned his attention to Mok. "Barbarossa is right. It is a grave matter that you refused to fight during the raid. Now that the hurricane has ended, it indeed is time I dealt with you. Follow me to my cabin."

CHAPTER 37

MAINSIDE. It was just past midnight. Five hours had passed since the Committee members had left the high-rise to return to their homes and estates.

At one of those homes, one Committee member had gone to sleep on his couch wearing a wrist pager. He wasn't surprised when the vibration woke him. Not that he slept well anyway. Traitors rarely do.

He groaned and sat up, rubbing his eyes. This was why he had chosen the couch instead of his bedroom. He did not want anyone in his family disturbed when he answered the page.

He walked quickly from the living room to an office down the hallway. He shut the door behind him and snapped on the light. Although he had expected this call, the Committee member still checked the number on the pager. It confirmed his guess.

He sat at his desk before the vidphone. He dialed a number. Only four people in the entire world knew this number and who it reached. Three were presidents of the biggest country blocs of the World United government. The Committee member was the fourth. At the moment, he took no pleasure in this distinction.

"That took you two minutes," a voice snapped. An image of the president of the World United filled the screen.

"I am sorry, Your Worldship," the Committee member answered, keeping his expression neutral. It had only taken him thirty seconds, but no one ever disagreed with the man who headed the World United government.

"So tell me some good news," demanded the president. "Tell me that the final candidate is dead."

There was a slight echo to the voice, a delay in transmission. The time gap was the result of scrambling the voice signal between two transmitter satellites. It was impossible for anyone to listen to them with electronic eavesdropping devices.

"As far as I know, Mok is still alive," the Committee member said. He spoke slowly so the scrambling device could keep pace with his voice.

"What!" Rage filled the president's face. He was a bulky man, with white hair and pale skin flushed pinker than usual in his anger. He wore his customary black silk toga.

"As we speak," the Committee member said, dreading his message, "he is asleep."

"We cybered an assassin on board that ship! Why hasn't he killed the candidate?"

"Your Worldship, it isn't that simple. The computer program has been set up to cover thousands of variations, all depending on what decisions the candidate makes in cyberspace."

"Listen," the president snarled. "You told me that when a person dies in cyberspace, his brain circuits are sent into shock, which kills him in real time. What's it going to take for our cyberassassin to step up to the candidate and run him through with a sword?"

"Reality, Your Worldship. Although we were able to cyber in our killer, he must follow the boundaries of the program. He, too, can only do what the situation dictates. The assassin almost had him, but the captain of the ship stepped between them."

"Why?"

"It was part of the program." The Committee member guarded his expression and suppressed his sigh. "When Mok made his decision not to kill the slave in order to save himself, it was programmed for the pirate captain to appear. Over the next several hours of cybertime—which corresponds with our real time—Mok will sleep. The captain wants him to rest."

"Get to the point," His Worldship snapped. "I want simple answers."

"This stage was not really designed as a test for the candidate. After passing through the first two stages, the Committee agreed it was safe to assume he would not kill a slave on the ship. The pirate captain's role in stage three is to prepare Mok for the fourth stage."

This was why the Committee member had advised that the cyberkiller be sent in after Mok.

If he was expecting praise, however, he was disappointed.

"I don't like this," His Worldship said. "Cambridge is a smart man. What exactly do you mean by *prepare?*"

"During the remainder of Mok's time aboard the pirate ship, his only task is to give witness," the Committee member answered. "Cambridge believes that in teaching something, you learn the subject well yourself. It is the same with the act of testifying belief. The teacher gains as much as the student. Cambridge wants Mok's fledgling faith to be strengthened. Not tested."

There was silence from His Worldship. Unhappy silence. When he finally spoke again to the Committee member, his voice was ice.

"We have a candidate here who was the first among many to choose justice in ancient Egypt over the opportunity to escape. During the siege in the Holy Lands, he stood for Christ, even though it meant certain death. And here, aboard the pirate ship, Mok has refused to kill a slave to save his own life. And you are telling me his faith needs strengthening?"

"Your Worldship, I—"

"Enough. I need not remind you of how important it is that Cambridge be stopped. I just want one thing: this final candidate destroyed. When do you expect this to happen?"

"Sometime in the morning, Your Worldship. No one on the Committee knows yet that we have cybered in a killer. He is free to roam the ship and will wait for the first chance to strike."

"Do not fail," His Worldship said.

CHAPTER 38

CYBERSPACE—PIRATE SHIP. Mok rose from a bunk against the wall and stretched. Across from him in the cramped captain's quarters, the pirate Falconer sat on a stool and watched him without expression.

Falconer held open his hand. A small cross dropped from it, then dangled in the air. The chain of the cross was intertwined in the man's fingers.

Mok's hands automatically reached up to his neck.

"Yes," Falconer said. "Your cross. I took it from you while you slept."

Falconer handed him back the cross.

"Although Barbarossa has called for your blood," Falconer said, "I have protected you. I gave you food and drink to sustain you and permitted you a night to rest. Now is time for payment. Answer me these questions: Where are you from? And why do you wear the cross?"

Mok hesitated. Indeed, these were the same questions he had been asking himself. He wondered if even the street canyons of Old Newyork and the Water Wars of his childhood were real. So much had happened to him. First the land of limitless sand. Then the castle. Now he was aboard a pirate ship with a cross in his possession and no knowledge of how he had originally come by it. If only that had been all. But there had also been a troublesome yet helpful dwarf. And a beautiful woman of great mystery.

Falconer mistook Mok's hesitation for reluctance. He lifted his sleeve and pulled out a shining dagger.

"Speak," the pirate captain said. "Or I will remove your tongue so that you may never speak again."

Mok gathered his thoughts. How much could he tell the pirate and still survive?

Falconer sighed and stabbed the dagger into the small table beside him.

"Ignore my threats," Falconer said. "My mind is whirling with confusion. Two days ago, before the great storm, I would have cut your throat and laughed as the ship's cats lapped your blood. Today I am burdened with a promise and a soul that longs to soar."

Falconer stared at the cross dangling from the chain he had returned to Mok. "During the storm, I feared for my life. For the first time ever, I realized I am as mortal as any other man. Me, a man who cannot be bested with a sword. Me, a man who has sent dozens to their graves. I, too, will die."

Falconer sighed again. Mok sensed it was no time to interrupt.

"So in the fury of the storm," Falconer continued, "as the rain lashed at this ship, as the waves tossed us like a cork, I cried out to God. I swore he could have my soul if he kept us safe."

Falconer smiled sadly. "Even for a pirate like me,

an oath made is an oath kept. If I have a soul—and surely I must—if during my greatest fear an instinct told me to call upon the God of the universe, what must I do to give it to him?"

CHAPTER 39

YOU ARE ASKING me all of this?" Mok said. "Am I to answer these questions?"

"You wear the cross of Christ. Aboard a ship of cutthroats, no less. Your conviction must be great. Share it with me."

From the sands to the castle to the pirate ship, legends of the Galilee Man had haunted Mok, teasing him like fragrance upon a wind. For that reason, Mok nearly laughed at Falconer's question. But the earnestness of the pirate was too great, the hunger on the man's face too sorrowful.

"Very well," Mok said, "I will tell you what I know of the Galilee Man."

Mok recalled the audiobook of his childhood. It had spoken of a man who gathered twelve followers and called them fishers of men. It had spoken of a man who described a place called heaven, where the Father waited.

Which part of the audiobook should he pass on to this pirate? Mok closed his eyes, choosing words he had listened to during nights of terror, huddled alone in the slums.

"'I tell you the truth,'" Mok repeated from memory, "'the time is coming and is already here when the dead will hear the voice of the Son of God. And those who hear will have life.'"

Mok opened his eyes. He saw that Falconer was not smirking but listening intently.

"'But he who follows the true way comes into the light,'" Mok whispered. "'Then the light will show that the things he has done were done through God.'"

"But what does this mean?" Falconer asked.

Mok paused, struggling to answer. And as he searched his own heart for words, a strange peace entered him, like a ray of joy itself. *All things were made through him,* Mok heard in his mind, not sure whether the words were memories of the audiobook or a whispering voice in his head. *In him there was life. That life was light for the people of the world.*

A God who created the world. Mok suddenly understood as if a curtain had been lifted to show light beyond. A God who loves all people and sent the Galilee Man to speak directly to them.

The power of this unexplained insight took away Mok's breath. He knew what he would say to the pirate! He knew what the pirate needed to hear!

"'For God loved the world so much,'" Mok said. The peace within him grew as he spoke. Where was the warmth of this peace coming from? "'That he gave his only Son, that whoever believes in him shall, not perish, but have eternal life.'"

"Can it be that simple?" Falconer asked.

"The Son of God himself told us that," Mok replied.

Before he could say another word a loud knocking rattled the door.

"Falconer!" Barbarossa bawled from outside. "Falconer!"

"I will not be disturbed," Falconer shouted, without opening the door.

The door shuddered, then crashed open.

Falconer whirled to his feet and faced the broken door.

Barbarossa stepped inside. Three more men followed him.

"Your command matters nothing," Barbarossa said. He held a pistol pointed at Falconer's chest. "I have declared mutiny."

CHAPTER 40

MAINSIDE. "As I advised earlier," Cambridge told the Committee, "those of you with weak stomachs may wish to take a break. There is food and coffee in the waiting room. You may return after the rest of us have reviewed the battle sequence aboard the pirate ship."

No one moved from the chairs set in front of the giant vidscreen.

"Let me understand," a balding man said, when it was clear everyone planned to stay. He toyed with his pen as he spoke. "We are here to review an episode that has already occurred in Mok's world?"

"Correct," a comtech said, answering for Cambridge. "A replay, so to speak. At this point, while Mok's body is at rest in the lab, he believes he is in the captain's quarters of the ship. As we indicated previously, lack of available computer memory makes it impossible to view Mok in his real time. What we are showing has been pulled from the hard drive and saved. It is the best we can do."

"It is this lag time that makes this meeting urgent," Cambridge said. "I want you to see something. Something I saw early this morning when I reviewed the cybersegment."

Cambridge nodded at the technician, who snapped off a light switch and pointed a remote control at the vidscreen.

For the next ten minutes, the only light in the room came from the swirl of color and confusion on the vidscreen. The committee members watched in horrified fascination. Sword fights, gunpowder blasts, and pirate savagery sent two of the Committee into the waiting room. Neither, of course, tested their weak stomachs by eating anything.

The remainder of the Committee members were so involved in the action that when Cambridge snapped on the lights without warning, the seated men looked startled. They needed a few moments to adjust to the reality of the carpeted room around them.

"What is it?" one asked.

"Take it thirty seconds back," Cambridge said. His voice was hard. "Zoom in on the brute with the deformed face. And freeze there."

In the silence, they heard the slight whir as the storage disk accessed the footage. Then, with clicks on the remote, the comtech brought a closeup onto the screen as requested.

It showed a man in a shirt soaked with the blood of his victims. He had massive sloping shoulders and a sword in each hand. His nose was a stub with the waxy shine of a molten candle. A crazed grin of joy distorted his face.

"This man is our problem," Cambridge said to the Committee. He turned and spoke to the comtech. "You cannot tell me who he is, can you?"

"I . . . I . . . ," the technician stuttered.

"As I thought. Run it back ten more seconds. Then isolate the voices near him. You'll hear someone call him 'Barbarossa.' I do not recall that we cybered anyone of his name or description onto the ship."

The technician replayed the previous ten seconds. The segment confirmed Cambridge's observation.

"Well?" Cambridge said.

"You are right," the comtech said. "Had we created such a character, I would remember the name Barbarossa." The technician shuddered. "And the appearance."

"Then," Cambridge said grimly, "we have a problem. Correction. Two problems."

"Problems?" the balding committee member repeated.

"The first problem is grave. There is a monster of a man aboard the pirate ship. One we did not create or place there." Cambridge began to pace. "Barbarossa is a factor beyond our control. Imagine an actor joining a play without the director's consent. That is our situation. Worse, from his actions, this is an actor on a killing spree. And because we cannot watch the cybersequence as it happens, we have no idea what this man has done in the last few hours."

Muttering began from the Committee members.

The balding man raised his voice. "Who would place this Barbarossa into our cyberspace world? Why? And how could our computer security be broken? Our sequence code was supposed to be impossible to crack."

Cambridge answered slowly. "Those questions, my friends, are our second problem. Graver than the first."

The room burst into the noise of heated discussion. For one of the Committee, however, the indignation, anger, and fear of his words were only for show. For him, the cybersegment was going exactly as planned. Even though they had already discovered the killer.

CHAPTER 41

CYBERSPACE—PIRATE SHIP. "Show no fear," Captain Falconer said quietly to Mok. "If they sense it, they will attack you like sharks on blood."

The pirate captain and Mok stood together on the upper deck of the ship. Below them, and ten paces away, the pirate crew was gathered in an unruly mob. Mutiny was the greatest crime that could be committed at sea. Half the crew called for the immediate death of the captain. The other half—with the gravity of their intended crime now sinking in after the anger of rebellion—wanted no part of the actual murder.

The shouted arguments below took attention away from the captain and Mok. Their hands were bound behind them with rough rope. Only Barbarossa—too far away to hear the captain speak to Mok—paid them any heed. Barbarossa's full-stare concentration on Mok was chilling.

It's as if he hates me, Mok thought. *Yet I have done nothing to harm the man. Is it the cross I wear?*

"Listen to them," the captain said. "Some are calling for us to be marooned."

"Marooned?" Mok asked. His throat was dry with fear. His world had become a whirlwind. It seemed his life was always in danger. Looking down upon swords and angry men was far closer to death than he had yet come.

"Marooned. Set adrift in a rowboat with only a few provisions stored in it. Slight as the chance is, we might drift to land before we die. It is a small mercy, but far better than a rope around the neck."

"Hanging?" With the events of a world so different from Old Newyork tumbling around him, Mok wondered if he had truly gone insane. No, he was not crazy. How could he have created these worlds in his head? The burning pressure of the rope on his wrists was all too real. And his pursuit of the truth behind the man called Christ had started with an audiobook in Old Newyork. The audiobook was not imagined either. How could all of this be? *Hanging?*

"Hanging," Captain Falconer said. "From a rope thrown over the main mast. They are afraid that if I live, the day might come when I return. There is a saying among pirates: 'A dead man gets no revenge.'"

A faint smile showed behind his reddish-blond beard. "They will soon find out that is wrong. Dead wrong."

"What?" Mok asked, snapping his thoughts back to the violent confusion around him. "A dead captain can take revenge?"

The wolflike gleam returned as Falconer nodded. "Yes. Without me, they will die."

"But how can that be?" Mok asked. "Once you die, you are . . ."

"Dead?" The captain smiled, and Mok noticed that the smile reached the pirate's eyes.

"You have heard the Galilee Man tell us there is life beyond, have you not?"

Mok nodded.

"Still," he said, "if they kill me, they, too, will perish."

CHAPTER 42

THEY NEED MY navigation log." Falconer stared straight ahead as he continued to speak. "It is the most valuable thing aboard this ship. Notes and journals about dozens of years and thousands of miles of travel at sea. With me dead and without the journal, they will be lost at sea. And they know it. Until now, that fear has allowed me to control this mob."

"I don't understand," Mok said, forcing himself not to look down at Barbarossa and his executioner's glare.

"Part of my power is my ability with my sword," Falconer explained. "But a captain's real strength is in his navigation experience and skills. Few are those who know how to keep the ship safe at sea, to avoid reefs, to find harbors. The only other person on board with this knowledge is Calico, my second-in-command."

Falconer frowned, pointing with his chin. "Him, the one with an eye patch and the red silk shirt. Barbarossa must have convinced him to mutiny. Otherwise there would be no one to guide the ship."

Mok frowned too. "If Calico can guide the ship, why then, with you dead—"

"Are they lost?" Falconer's smile turned deadly.

"Calico, like any captain, is helpless without the navigation log. And no one knows the precautions I have taken. The chest that holds my navigation log must be opened in a certain way. Otherwise a flint sparks and sets off a charge of gunpowder. Not only will those in the cabin be instantly killed, but the log will also be destroyed, and a fire started. Few things are more frightening than a fire at sea."

Mok knew of the buckets of sand placed all around the ship, of the great care taken with lanterns and cooking fires. He could fully understand the panic that would arise from a blaze below decks in the captain's quarters.

Falconer drew a breath and stared at the mob of pirates. "If I die, so will they. It's not much of a consolation, is it?"

Mok and Falconer shared a grim silence.

Mok's mind, however, was not at rest.

"If they choose to hang us," Mok said suddenly, "tell them the navigation log will be of no use to them."

"Why?" Falconer snorted. "So they will examine the chest before we are killed? So it will explode while we are alive?"

"Exactly," Mok said, hurrying his words. Barbarossa had begun to walk toward them. "Some of the crew will die, which helps our odds in a fight. A fire in your cabin will send others belowdecks. Surely in the confusion we can find a way to escape these bonds, to fight, perhaps to escape in the rowboat. A slight chance is better than no chance at all."

Falconer could not answer, for Barbarossa reached them seconds later. His face, sweating in the noon heat, was hideous.

"Tell me," Falconer began, as if he were merely in conversation over ale with a friend, "how did you convince the crew to mutiny?"

"Your sudden weakness," Barbarossa spat. "Kindness to the prisoners. Saving this wretch from my sword. Only the strong rule, and you are no longer strong."

Falconer's next words to Barbarossa surprised Mok.

"The strong grow old and die," Falconer said. "You, with the strength of five men, will one day be weak and feeble. And what then beyond death? There must be something, Barbarossa. Matters of the soul rule far more than strength. If that is my sudden weakness, it is a strength you cannot comprehend."

Barbarossa laughed. His foul breath hit Mok, even above the other smells of the ship.

"I have the strength of this sword. And the strength of action," Barbarossa said. He lifted his sword. "I will decide your fate while those fools argue. You both die now."

Mok waited. Would Falconer take his advice?

"Then you will die too," Falconer responded with conviction. "I have hidden my navigation log."

Barbarossa's sword wavered. "It is in the chest in your quarters. Calico knows that."

"Can you be certain?" Falconer asked. "If you kill me and do not find the log . . ."

"You lie," said Barbarossa.

"Surely you understand how the ship will then be lost," Falconer continued as if Barbarossa had not spoken. "You can kill us now. But at least our deaths will be swift. Yours will take place much slower. A ship lost at sea is a terrible thing."

Barbarossa put his sword down. He directed his voice away from them.

"Calico!" Barbarossa shouted. The din of the pirates quieted when Barbarossa called out. "Calico! Come here and escort the captain to his quarters. Have him open his chest and show you the navigation log."

No! Mok nearly shouted out that single word. *Not Falconer!*

CHAPTER 43

MAINSIDE. "All of you, gather round," Cambridge snapped. "Witness what we feared most."

The eleven other Committee members left their chairs to stand before the large vidscreen on the far wall of the carpeted room. The screen danced with motion. They saw the deck of a small wooden ship, sails flapping in the wind. Blue ocean and sky beyond. And a mass of shouting men with raised swords.

This world had recently swirled in the mind of a motionless body in another room down the hall. Had they been in that room, they would have heard Mok's heartbeat *blips* rise in volume and speed to match the corresponding stress of the cybersegment.

"There, in the middle of the pirates, it's that brute!" one of the Committee members stammered in panic. "The one named . . ."

"Barbarossa," Cambridge said flatly. "The one cybered into our computer by an outside source. This is the latest we have been able to review."

They stood mesmerized by the giant man. Among all the figures on the screen, his size and savage ugliness drew attention.

"Listen," another Committee member said. "He is calling the crew to murder the captain!"

"Murder!" the first Committee member yelped. "That was not part of the program! Mok was to be allowed rest and a chance to learn more about Christ! We have no control over a mutiny!"

"That is exactly our problem," Cambridge said. "No control. Not with a virtual reality renegade set loose in our cybersite."

With a remote activator, Cambridge lowered the volume on the vidscreen.

He glanced at his watch. "This was taken a few minutes ago. At this point, the comtechs are on standby to upload the action constantly. They are pushing the computer to its limit so we can watch on a two-minute delay pattern."

"You mean Mok could already be dead?"

"No, his body is still alive. But he is in danger," Cambridge said. He paused and looked around the room. "Our options are simple. We leave Mok aboard the ship for the scheduled time. Or flash him to the next cybersite."

Cambridge held up a hand to forestall any questions. "If we leave him aboard the ship, I believe Mok will be killed. Whoever hacked into our cybersite intends the worst. Barbarossa is proof of that. Why else incite mutiny but to create danger for Mok?"

"It is an easy decision then," said one voice. "Flash Mok to the next site ahead of schedule."

"And how long before Barbarossa follows?" Cambridge asked. "Whoever cracked our encryption code to place that savage aboard the pirate ship also has the power to send Barbarossa after Mok into the next cybersite. You know what Mok faces next. With Barbarossa there, Mok's odds go from grim to impossible."

"The solution then?" someone countered.

"Modify our encrypted security code. Our hacker won't be able to follow. That's the good news."

He surveyed them all. "The bad news? Our com-techs tell me the code is so complex it will take half an hour to change. Real time here is real time in cyberspace. That means Mok must face another half-hour aboard the pirate ship before we can safely send him ahead. A half-hour with Barbarossa."

"What if Mok jumps overboard? Even with his hands tied, surely he can tread water for half an hour. The ship will sail on without him and—"

Cambridge shook his head. "Remember? His cyberworld is like a stage. Our computer memory is not large enough to make the oceans beyond the ship real. If he steps off the stage—the pirate ship—he will enter a cybervoid. The sensory shock will scramble his brain circuits. If it doesn't kill him, it will turn him into a vegetable."

"Leave him on board for a half-hour!" In direct contrast to Cambridge, the first Committee member was an excitable man. He was pointing at the muted vidscreen and the waving swords. "A half-hour in a full mutiny? But if he dies there, he'll die here!"

Cambridge nodded. "Yes. The slash of a sword, a

rope around his neck, musket balls through his ribs. Any of it will kill Mok in either world. Somehow, he must survive the next half-hour."

CHAPTER 44

CYBERSPACE—PIRATE SHIP. As Calico walked toward them, Mok nearly buckled with the horror of it. To save his own life, Falconer would have to disable the trap and hand over the navigation log. Then they would surely be killed.

Barbarossa pushed Falconer toward the approaching Calico. Falconer stumbled and turned his head to speak to Mok.

"You spoke of the Son of God," he said quietly. "And I believe. No longer do I fear death as I did during the storm."

Did that mean Falconer would sacrifice his own life to give me a chance to escape? Mok wondered.

Mok couldn't ask the question aloud. Calico spun Falconer around, and they marched away. That left Mok alone with Barbarossa.

"Now," the giant snarled, pulling his sword loose, "you wretched Welfaro orphan, I will finish with you what I began."

"No!" Mok said, with such force that Barbarossa paused. *Wretched Welfaro orphan?* Mok thought. Here on a pirate ship, how could this brute know of Old Newyork? How could he know Mok was an orphan?

"No? You are bound. I have the sword." Barbarossa unsheathed the sword completely. Its hilt was dull brown with dried blood.

"You called me a Welfaro. I must know why." Again, Mok spoke with such intensity that Barbarossa paused.

"Don't play games with me," the giant snarled. "Surely you know by now I have been sent for you."

"Sent? Who sent you? Why?" *This brute must know what's been happening to me,* Mok realized.

"What does it matter to you?" Barbarossa said. "As soon as your head leaves your body, you will no longer exist. Here or there."

Here? Or there? Mok wanted to beg for answers. It seemed he wanted that knowledge more than he wanted life. Yet the sword was raised. The fire in Barbarossa's eyes would not be quenched with mere words. Mok would now receive neither life nor answers.

He refused to beg.

Barbarossa laughed again. A look of insanity filled his eyes.

Then, incredibly, an explosion rocked the ship. Falconer! He had made the sacrifice. Knowing of the trap, he had decided to open the chest in such a way that the gunpowder exploded.

Barbarossa grunted in puzzlement and looked behind him.

Now! Mok told himself. Later, he could mourn for Falconer.

Sword still raised, Barbarossa stared back at the

black smoke that bloomed from the lower decks. Mok dived past him and sprinted down the steps.

There were shouts and confusion.

Mok's first thoughts were to hide below. All he needed was five minutes alone to loosen the ropes around his wrists. Then he could fight, or perhaps get to the rowboat and drop it into the water. Better the open sea than Barbarossa's sword.

Mok reached the lower quarters seconds later. He did not know if Barbarossa pursued him.

Screams filled his ears.

The prisoners! They were trapped.

For a moment, Mok hesitated. If he helped them, he might not escape.

The screams grew louder.

Hadn't Falconer given his life to save others?

Mok turned toward the screams. He could not let them burn without trying to save them.

CHAPTER 45

MOK DODGED pirates running in all directions. Although he knew time was passing quickly, his next moves were blurs of concentration in the confusion of smoke and flames and running bodies.

Mok found the armory. He secured the handle of a sword between his feet to hold it upright and sawed loose his bounds. Then he grabbed the sword and rushed to the prisoners. One by one, he freed them, explaining his plan in loud shouts, hoping they could understand him.

Mok led the freed men to the armory. They grabbed swords and dashed to the open decks. There, a few pirates fought, but as time passed the fight faded. The pirates had a more urgent problem. The fire.

Finally, Mok and the prisoners reached the rowboat. As Falconer had promised, it held provisions, stored in small casks.

From the side of the ship, Mok looked at the open water below. Freedom. All he had to do was get off the ship, and he would be free.

The prisoners began to loosen the rowboat. Time seemed to crawl by with the pace of a snail. When the boat was ready to be lowered into the water, the prisoners jumped in and called for Mok.

He set one foot in the rowboat. They were waiting for him to push off toward the water below.

Freedom, Mok thought. Whatever problems faced them on the open sea, at least they had escaped death by fire, rope, or sword.

Then a hand grabbed Mok from behind. The other prisoners fell back in fear.

"Thought you could escape?" It was Barbarossa!

The brute held a dagger to Mok's throat. None of the escaped prisoners could make a move to help Mok as he had helped them.

"Now," Barbarossa said, spinning Mok around to face him. "With no ceremony, you die."

In his mind, Mok called upon the Galilee Man of his childhood audiobook. Mok called, telling himself the Galilee Man was not legend, but truth. He prayed that belief in the Galilee Man led to eternal life as the audiobook had promised.

Barbarossa lifted the dagger and began to slash down at Mok's chest.

And Mok's world dissolved in black beyond any shimmer of light.

CHAPTER 46

MAINSIDE. When he was young, the Committee member had nightmares of drowning in mud. In his dreams, he would run and run and run, but the deep mud slowed him down until it dragged him below the surface.

Now, as he stepped off the elevator and into the lobby of the high-rise building, he felt the same fear. Other Committee members were engaged in cheerful conversation. But it seemed as if he were sinking in the mud.

Twice before, he had stepped off the very same elevator to reach the very same netphone across the lobby. Twice before, he had promised the most powerful person in the world that Mok would not survive the next cybertest. Twice before, he had been wrong.

And for a third time, he had to report failure.

It was like straining and straining to run through the mud. But it sucked him deeper and deeper.

The Committee member barely cared this time if anyone was watching him. They could assume he was checking for e-mail after the long meeting.

He began to type in the number for the president. A president who would be totally outraged to hear that Mok had moved on to the fourth cybertest.

Seconds later, the system prompted him for his e-mail message. The Committee member slowly typed his message:

> **The candidate is now at stage four. It may be days before I can find the new sequence code to send the cyberassassin after him. What are your orders until then?**

The Committee member hit the send button and walked out of the lobby with shoulders slumped.

When he reached his home a half-hour later, he ignored his family and went straight to his office. He powered his computer, plugged in his access code, and checked his electronic mailbox. The president of the World United had already replied:

> **Fool. We have already discussed what to do. And you know where and how to do it. Ask yourself. Him? Or you?**

CHAPTER 47

CYBERSPACE—THE AMERICAN WILD WEST. Night thunder woke Mok. Not thunder from lightning, but thunder accompanied by dust. He couldn't see the dust, but he could taste it. The thunder rumbled and rumbled.

He did not understand.

When his eyes adjusted to the darkness, he saw he was halfway up a hill. The far edge of the valley was a line of black against the lighter sky. He also saw the source of the thunder.

Giant animals. Hundreds and hundreds of them passed below, massed in a great long herd.

Mok shook his head wearily. He was too tired and too weak to care anymore. He curled up and went to sleep, lulled by the steady rumbling of the moving beasts.

He slept until the sun was warm upon his face. Without sitting, he opened his eyes and scanned the wide, empty grasslands of the valley. The giant animals were gone.

Mok turned over and dozed. He did not wake until a persistent fly brushed against his face. He waved it away without opening his eyes. It returned.

Finally Mok muttered in anger and sat upright.

He froze as he opened his eyes and began to yawn.

It had not been a fly that tickled his face but a feather—attached to the end of a spear. And the owner of the spear, a bronze-skinned warrior wearing only a loincloth, sat on a horse and stared down at Mok without a smile.

BACKSTORY IV

OLD NEWYORK, A.D. 2076. From a half block away, the ganglord saw the crowd gathered at the street corner ahead. He was a giant of a man, a fighter of many years. Beneath his protective leather pants and vest, his tough hide was covered with old scars. As was his shaved head. During his many years of fighting, each scar along the way had taught him something new. He had learned those lessons well. It had been years since anyone had dared to challenge him, years since he had been forced to fight.

And now someone dared to speak in public against the laws he, Zubluk, had set.

Squinting against the glare of the sun, Zubluk smiled grimly and touched the sword hanging at his side. Even though four of his men walked behind him—armed with spears and swords and crossbows—this appeared to be an occasion when the ganglord himself would enjoy doling out the punishment.

As the ganglord and his bodyguards moved closer, they heard the old man's words.

"There is a truth," the old man was saying to the crowd. "It is a truth that will set you free from any earthly burden of pain or poverty or ganglord slavery."

Zubluk's grim smile became a frown. Dangerous as the old man's words were, there was also the matter of how loudly and clearly he spoke. Only electronic technology gave a voice that kind of power. Mainside technology. The man was not a Welfaro, for one of the slum dwellers would have immediately sold such technology for water.

What is a Mainsider doing in the slums? Zubluk wondered. The World United government did not permit anyone to cross the rivers back to Mainside. Ever.

Zubluk was not stupid. No man reached his level of brutal power without brains. He knew Mainsiders also had other technology and weapons far more effective than swords or crossbows. And Zubluk had heard rumors of a man in the Scorpions' territory who had used an electric arc to defend a family from slavers.

Zubluk and his four men reached the edge of the crowd. The people's attention was directed forward to the old man and his words. The ganglord spun an old woman around, and she shrieked at the sight of his shaved head and scarred face. She put up her hands to block a blow.

"Bah," he said, and pushed her aside. He did not have time to waste on crushing insects when much bigger prey stood before him.

Her cry had drawn the attention of others, and the slum dwellers reacted in instant panic. Murmurs traveled ahead, like ripples of water from a dropped stone.

"Zubluk has arrived! Zubluk has arrived!"

The ganglord strode ahead, unafraid of the people massed around him and his men. No Welfaro had ever dared to fight a ganglord, let alone one with Zubluk's terrifying reputation.

Zubluk reached the front of the crowd. He got his first clear look at the old man.

Benjamin Rufus looked just like any other tired old man fighting the heat in the Welfaro slums of Old Newyork. He was thin and stooped, his gray hair cropped short. Yet there was something in the old man's eyes—something rare in the slums. A joy. A peace. And no fear.

From where he stood on top of the statue base, the old man immediately saw the giant ganglord and his four bodyguards. Yet the old man's words did not falter.

"Look no farther than your own love, fear, joy, and hatred," he said to the crowd in calm, slow words. "Look no farther than the empty longing of your hearts. Surely these longings tell you that your body is more than just flesh. These longings let you know that you carry a soul. Let this knowledge then point you toward the God who breathed your soul into you. Let me tell you about his Son, who came into this world to save you."

"Silence!" roared Zubluk.

"You cannot silence truth," the old man answered.

"You can silence a man," Zubluk said. "You can rip his tongue from his head."

For a moment, Zubluk considered unsheathing his sword. But there was the matter of the dangerous Mainside technology. Zubluk's shrewdness outweighed his need to show bravery.

Zubluk waved his four massive bodyguards forward.

On the statue base, the old man smiled with a trace of weariness.

When the bodyguards were less than ten paces away from the old man, he pressed his elbow against his side. This released his 'tric shooter from a strap attached to his forearm, hidden beneath his coat. Without pausing, he lifted his arm and aimed at them, chest high. He pulled the trigger. In as little time as it took to move his arm from left to right, an arc of bright blue light swept across the four men. They crumpled with screams of agony.

Rufus brought the gun back to center and aimed it directly at Zubluk. But by then it was too late.

The giant warlord had stepped back into the crowd and grabbed a woman. He wrapped one massive arm around her shoulders and held her in front of him as a shield. With his other arm, he pressed the blade of a knife against her throat.

The old man's gun arm wavered.

"You'll never make a head shot from that distance," Zubluk snarled. "Drop it, or she dies."

The woman did not cry out in fear. She remained still, watchful.

"If she dies," Rufus said. "You lose your shield. I only stunned your bodyguards. But if you kill her,

I won't stop at stunning you. I'll stream the juice until you die too."

For several moments, there was silence. The great crowd had frozen.

"I know you," Zubluk said to Rufus, almost as if there were no woman, no knife, no 'tric shooter. "I have seen you before."

"Perhaps," Rufus said, "but it matters little. I have a message to bring to the people of Old Newyork."

"Not while I rule," Zubluk said. "I will hunt you down and—"

Zubluk broke off with a curse of pain as the woman snapped her head down and clamped her teeth on his wrist. She bit so hard that his blood streamed from her mouth. Then she twisted and pushed away from him.

Rufus took advantage of the confusion and streamed Zubluk. The crackling arc of bright blue light hit him squarely in the chest. With a single grunt, he fell first to his knees then face forward onto the ground.

The woman did not flee. She walked directly toward Benjamin Rufus. She was of medium height, dressed in rags, and smudged with dirt. A shawl covered most of her face, and it was difficult to see her age.

At the base of the statue, she reached up.

"Take my hand," she said to the old man. "Let me help you down. Then come with me. You will need someone to keep you safe here in the slums."

CHAPTER 48

MAINSIDE, A.D. 2096. The members of the Committee had just gathered around a conference table.

Cambridge stood at the front of the room near a gray vidscreen. He waited for the others to quiet. The intensity in his eyes and his reputation set him apart from the other members of the Committee.

Cambridge turned his head slightly. It gave him a view through the tenth-floor window, a view of the distant slums of Old Newyork across the Hudson River.

The sight reminded him that those slums were the reason for their meeting.

The view also put another picture into his mind. A picture of the candidate Mok, now motionless on a padded cot in a smaller room just down the hallway, his body connected to a life-support machine. Two nurses tended to the still body. Both watched the heart rate and other vital signs with great care.

Cambridge turned his mind back to the meeting. He gazed up and down the conference table and waited for individual discussions to end. Cambridge felt a great sadness. He knew one of the Committee had betrayed their cause.

The room slowly grew quiet. Finally all eyes were on the tall man at the front.

"I would like to begin with prayer," Cambridge said. "Our candidate nears the end of his cyberquest. And not one day too soon. All of you know how important the Senate vote is at the end of this month. The lines have been clearly drawn. We need Mok to swing one or two crucial votes in our direction."

"What is the candidate's chance of success?" asked one of the members.

"All I can tell you is what you already know," Cambridge said. "He has passed three stages. In Egypt, he showed that he believes in justice. The siege tested his beliefs. He learned to testify with his growing faith on the pirate ship. His experience in the Wild West will help him prepare for the task beyond."

There was a long pause. Everyone knew what was planned for Mok. But he had to survive these final stages. Otherwise, Old Newyork and its thousands of weary and helpless poor would lose all hope.

"Let us take this to our Lord in prayer," Cambridge said.

All twelve men bowed their heads. One, however, did not turn his mind and heart to prayer. His thoughts were turned to betrayal—and how to stop Mok. For he had been given his instructions by the president of the World United, the most powerful man alive. The words of prayer continued around him.

When Cambridge finished and opened his eyes, he felt more at peace. How important, he told himself, to look past trouble to the Father who waited beyond.

"You've seen the vidmonitor," Cambridge said as a way to break the silence. "You all know we have safely cybered Mok from the pirate ship to the western plains."

"Will the cyberassassin be able to follow him to the new site?" one of the Committee asked.

"No," Cambridge said, hiding his irritation. "The new code is too complex to crack. Whoever managed to hack into our computer is now helpless to follow Mok."

"Excellent," another Committee member said. "The testing of our candidate can continue."

"It's good and bad," Cambridge answered. "Mok is safe, at least from the cyberassassin. But we still don't know who sent the assassin in, or how."

"Is that a problem? After all, the most important thing is the test," the same person said.

Cambridge shook his head to indicate a negative. "There is still the ultimate goal of the Committee. If we don't find out who was behind this betrayal, everything is at risk."

Cambridge cleared his throat. "And that means a change of plans."

All of the Committee members leaned forward.

"My full attention must be here," Cambridge said. "I won't be able to supervise Mok. We're sending the girl back in."

Excited babble broke out.

Cambridge raised his hand for quiet.

"Yes," he said, "I understand the difficulties. It means last-minute adjustments in the program. And she'll have to do the best she can in a dangerous situation. But we have no other choice."

Cambridge looked around and waited for any disagreement. None came. Cambridge ended the meeting. One by one, the members filed out of the room.

An hour later, Cambridge met with the senior Committee member and, as a safeguard against one person dying with the security access code to Mok's cybersite, gave the member the new security code. A half-hour later, Cambridge called another Committee member and gave him another security code. By midnight, each Committee member knew a different code.

Only then was Cambridge satisfied enough to prepare himself for sleep. Whoever had betrayed the Committee was a desperate man. Cambridge prayed he had done everything he could to protect Mok.

CHAPTER 49

CYBERSPACE—THE WILD WEST. The land around Mok brought back memories of his time in the desert of ancient Egypt. There the horizons had also stretched far in all directions, and the sun had been high in an endless sky.

Here, however, tall grass, not drifting sand, rippled before the wind. Here, the sun's heat was warm, not blazing. And here, the bronze-skinned man with a spear did not wear a tunic as the Egyptian palace guards had, but merely a cloth around his waist.

"Your brain is the size of a pea," Mok said in conversational tones to the man. "And your ugliness is only exceeded by your smelliness."

The man did not reply. He was on horseback. Mok followed on foot behind the horse. Twice Mok had tried to escape. The man had patiently ridden Mok down and jabbed him with the spear. Mok had quickly learned to follow.

Mok had also quickly learned the man did not speak. By Mok's estimation, they had traveled for two hours since the man had woken Mok by tickling his face with the feather attached to a spear. Not once in all those miles across empty land had this man answered any of Mok's questions. *Where were they? Who was he? Where were they going?*

After repeating his futile questions for the entire first hour, Mok had become convinced the man could not speak English. Either that, or he was deaf.

"Not only that," Mok said, looking for ways to amuse himself as they crossed the monotony of land, "but you dress like an idiot and people laugh at your bellybutton."

No reply, of course. Mok spent another five minutes insulting this man, then tired of the little game and fell into silence. It was broken only by the wailing of prairie wind, the sharp alarm whistles of small animals that scurried into holes in the ground, and the occasional piercing screams of hawks that circled the sky above.

Mok turned his mind to his final moments on the ship. There had been a giant savage of a man— Barbarossa. The giant had called Mok a Welfaro. How was it that Barbarossa had known anything of Mok's life in Old Newyork? And by the giant's admission, he had been sent after Mok. *From where? By whom? And why?* Last, and most confusing of all, the giant had said something about Mok dying in two places. Had Mok somehow still been in Old Newyork at the same time he was on the pirate ship?

Barbarossa's dagger had plunged down at Mok's chest, yet Mok had not died. He had somehow been transported to starlit hills that overlooked a herd of huge, thundering beasts. By dawn, the beasts had gone, but Mok remained, asleep until this man on the horse had woken him.

Mok could not forget Barbarossa's words. *Two places?* Was that somehow the truth? Mok was here but not here? Then remained more questions. How? And most important, why?

How could Mok be here yet also in Old Newyork? Here, he felt the thud of his feet against land, the wind against his face. The bright sun made Mok's eyes water. He could reach down and touch the rough fabric of his shirt and pants. His legs were tired from constant walking, and his throat was dry. Here was as real as life had been in Old Newyork.

Here . . .

Mok wrinkled his nose.

The breeze brought a disgusting smell, a stench far worse than anything he had discovered in Old Newyork. And Old Newyork's rotting mounds of garbage had provided many unpleasant smells.

Mok looked past the silent man on horseback in front of him. Dozens and dozens of birds filled the sky beyond the next hill.

Five minutes later, Mok discovered why. He and the man on horseback crested the hill. Mok saw hundreds of huge animals—dead. The ground was stained brown from their blood. Mok remembered then that a thundering herd of animals had passed him in the night. Were these like those animals?

As they neared the animals, Mok could hardly breathe. Flies rose in clusters at Mok's shadow. He felt staggered by the waste of it all. Who had slaughtered these animals?

The bronze-skinned man half turned in the saddle and looked down on Mok. "It is your people who kill our buffalo in this manner," the man said. "They take only the hide and tongue and leave the rest. My anger is kindled against all with pale skin."

Buffalo. These animals were called—

Mok felt the flush of embarrassment fill his face. The man *did* speak English. He'd understood everything Mok had said.

"My name is Yellowbird Sings," the warrior said. "I am Pawnee. You are now a prisoner of my tribe. The elders will cast judgment upon you for these things your people do."

CHAPTER 50

A HALF-HOUR LATER, Yellowbird Sings led Mok down a narrow trail into a valley folded between the hills. Halfway down, Mok saw large upside-down cones. As they got closer, he realized the cones were made of animal skins supported by poles tied together at the top. Smoke rose from the tops of these cones. From cooking fires inside?

Mok followed the man on horseback into the center of camp. The grass in the camp was well matted. Bones and pieces of hide littered the paths between the cone shelters, and the firepits overflowed with ashes. These people had camped here for some time.

As Mok walked, he watched the women and children as carefully as they watched him. Some of the mothers scraped at hides. Old women squatted near fires, stirring pots with sticks. Children clutched the women and peeked around their legs at Mok.

Despite the people that Mok could see, there was an eerie quiet to the camp. Then they came upon five dead men, all bronze-skinned like the man on horseback. All wore similar waist-cloths. All sprawled on the ground, clutching bottles.

Mok gasped at the sight. Then he understood they had not died, but passed out.

The man on horseback muttered something and climbed down. He shouted in a language that Mok could not understand. A woman hurried toward them. She wore a buckskin dress with fringes.

He spoke quickly to her.

She listened without interrupting. When the man finished his rapid-fire questions, she answered him.

Mok made little sense of her words, for she, too, spoke a language he could not understand. He heard one word clearly: whiskey.

She swept her arm and pointed beyond Mok and the bronze-skinned man.

Mok saw a large wagon, heaped with bloody hides.

Buffalo, he told himself.

Two men dozed in the shade beneath the wagon. These were not bronze-skinned men barely clothed but grizzled, bearded men in long, filthy coats.

The bronze-skinned man walked closer and jabbed at the men with his spear.

The two men roused themselves and rolled out from under the wagon.

Mok saw them closer. They were both short and pudgy. Both wore battered felt hats with holes in the brim. Their beards were crusty with the grease and caked dirt that also covered their filth-stiffened clothes.

"Hey, buck," one of the men said without any fear. "You haven't been in this camp for a few days, have you? I'll give you the rules. You want whiskey, go skin some of the buffalo we shot." He pantomimed to make his point as he spoke.

"Understand?" the other said. "No hides, no whiskey."

"I know what this firewater does to my people," the bronze-skinned man said. "You are not welcome at this camp. You will leave now."

"Is that so?" the one on the right said. He pulled a pistol out from under his coat. "How you going to make us leave? All I see on you is a spear."

The man on the left stepped forward and, without warning, punched the bronze-skinned man in the stomach. The one on the right hit him across the head with the butt of the pistol.

The bronze-skinned man fell. Both white men started kicking at his head and ribs.

Mok reacted without wondering why. He dived into both men, flailing with his arms.

Seconds later, Mok, too, was on the ground, blinking at the men above him. Mok stared directly into the dark holes of two pistols pointed at his forehead.

CHAPTER 51

SHOOT HIM, JACK. Put some daylight into his skull."

"Let's throw him on a fire instead. Fool deserves it for taking the Pawnee's side against ours."

Mok flung himself away and banged squarely against the wagon wheel. The men grabbed him by the ankles and began dragging him. Mok tried kicking, but he was helpless.

Just as they reached the fire, Mok heard the thunder of rifle fire. Both his attackers froze.

From the ground, Mok saw the silhouette of another man on a horse.

"Get to your feet, son," the man said. "This is one man of the Lord who ain't afraid to use a Winchester to help preach the Good Word."

Mok got to his feet and dusted himself off.

"Now," the man with the rifle continued. "You two varmints drop your pistols and clear out. Otherwise there'll be plenty of daylight showing between your eyes. This Winchester don't miss."

The two whiskey traders dropped their guns and backed away.

The man surveyed the camp from his horse. He wore a black shirt, black pants, and a black hat. He was a big man with a neatly trimmed goatee and dark, slicked-back hair.

"The name's Preacher John," he said. "What do folks call you?"

"Mok."

"Never laugh at a man's name, I say," Preacher John said. "Still, I got to wonder what was going through your folks' heads when they came up with that one."

Preacher John shook his head.

"Anyway, son," he said to Mok, "good thing I rode in when I did. Now let me ask you a question. Are you saved? And do you want to help me bring the Word to these Pawnees?"

"But . . ." Mok pointed at Yellowbird Sings just getting to his knees. "He said I was a prisoner of this tribe."

"*You* are," the preacher in black said. "As for me, I ride this land freely with the Word of God protecting me as I move among the tribes."

He smiled. "So let me ask you again. Will you help me bring the Word? Because if you won't, I'll hand you right back to those two varmints."

"I'll help," Mok said. After all, how could this possibly bring any harm?

CHAPTER 52

MAINSIDE. The man stood for a moment in front of a sink. Water ran from the tap over his hands. He felt no fear. At this late hour, the only other people who might walk into this washroom were security guards. The guards would recognize him instantly and leave him alone. They would not know his plan.

And, had any guard pushed the door open, it would have seemed, of course, as if the man were simply washing his hands. Instead, he was hardly aware of the water as he examined his face carefully.

He thought it was a wonderful face to have. By the time morning arrived, he would be on a private jet headed for Mexico, where he would have nothing for the rest of his life but sun, time, and money.

The mirror showed blond hair carefully brushed back in the latest Technocrat style. His teeth were shiny white and perfect—all capped of course. His nose was straight, his cheekbones high as current fashion dictated. Most Technocrats had plastic surgery at least once every ten years, and the reflection in the mirror showed the results of such care and attention.

These are the eyes of a man about to become very rich, he told himself. From the mirror, blue eyes gazed back at him in triumph. He winked at himself, laughed softly, and stepped away from the sink to dry his hands.

Moments later, he stepped into the quiet of the carpeted hallways. It did not take long to reach his destination. He stopped in front of the door. On the other side was the body of the candidate, held in suspended animation while his mind and senses traveled in the virtual reality of cyberspace.

He knew there were others inside the room with the candidate. Others who must be forced into sleep.

The man knelt in front of the door. He took a small plastic tube from his pocket. Squeezing it hard, his fingers broke the smaller tube inside. Immediately, chemicals began to mix in the tube.

He slipped the tube beneath the door. It was highly unlikely that either of the nurses inside would notice. At this late hour, they were probably fighting sleep anyway.

Thirty seconds was all it would take. The chemicals would burn through the plastic and release an invisible gas, consisting mainly of a chloral-hydrate base.

He would have preferred something with cyanide. It would kill everyone in the room without risk to himself. But his instructions had been precise: the male nurses were not to be killed. Once Mok was dead, he was to plug the machines in again. It would look like a natural death, and the nurses would take the blame for falling asleep on duty.

So it would be the chloral-hydrate mixture. A single breath of it was enough to knock any person unconscious. In another five minutes, the gas would clear from the room through the ventilation ducts. But he would give himself extra time to be sure. He did not want to fall into the same trap he had just set for the nurses.

The man moved to the end of the hallway. He leaned against the wall as he watched the seconds tick by on his watch.

Exactly ten minutes later, he returned to the door. He had a key to enter. All of the Committee members did.

Quietly, quickly, he stepped inside.

He grinned in triumph at what he saw. Both nurses—big, solid men—were asleep on their chairs, heads dropped onto their chests.

And in the middle of the room was the candidate, lying still. A blanket covered him. Tubes ran from various parts of his body. The steady *beep-beep* of the heart monitor was the only sound in the room.

The man grinned wider. This was reason for more triumph. How difficult would it be to kill someone who lived only because of a life-support machine?

With a quick twist of his fingers, the man locked the door behind him. No sense in taking the slight chance that a security guard might stop by and check the room.

Satisfied that nothing would stop him now, the man stepped toward the body.

Blip! Blip! Blip! Blip!

As the killer with blond hair and a perfect face

took his last few steps toward Mok's motionless body, the heart-rate monitor suddenly pulsed faster.

The killer stopped and cocked his head. His own heart began to race faster too. Could Mok actually know of his approaching death? Was his heart rate speeding up in sudden fear?

No matter, he told himself. It wasn't as if Mok could rise from the cot and fight back. He was in suspended animation and lying beneath a blanket.

Blip! Blip! Blip! Blip!

The killer then realized that the heart-rate monitor showed Mok's excitement in cyberspace. He must have entered a new danger level. His heart—behind in this world—was reacting as if Mok's body were indeed where his mind believed it was.

Blip! Blip! Blip! Blip!

With a snort of laughter at his jumpiness, the killer squatted beside the life-support machines. He closed his hands around the first electrical cord plugged into the wall.

How simple. Just a yank of this cord and the one below, and Mok was dead.

Blip! Blip! Blip! Blip!

The killer wiggled the first cord loose. With a final snap, it pulled from the wall.

Instantly, the heart-rate monitor shut down.

All that remained was the final electrical cord. With Mok dead, the blond-haired man's dreams would come to life—while the dreams of the Committee died.

CHAPTER 53

CYBERSPACE—THE AMERICAN WILD WEST. Mok stood beside the large wooden-spoked wheels of a wagon. Except for the strong odor of the mule harnessed just upwind of him, Mok had no complaints about his surroundings. A prairie breeze hardly more than riffled the waist-high grass beyond the wagon and Indian camp. Blue sky and horizon stretched as far as Mok could see in all directions with not a single cloud against the deep blue.

Mok smiled briefly, lifting his face to the sun and closing his eyes as he relaxed.

He had long given up on trying to believe his new life was some sort of dream. Like the hot sun on his face and the sounds of the Pawnee camp on the other side of the wagon, the details around him were too vivid to be merely his imagination.

But Mok had not given up on trying to explain these events. Determined as he was to make sense of it, though, he had decided the only way to keep his sanity was to accept and survive each new world.

As Mok stood with the sun warming his face and chest, he realized with surprise he felt a degree of happiness. For the first time since he had been shot with the blue arc of light, he was not facing danger. No execution loomed at a pharaoh's command in this world. No castle siege or pirate assassin threatened his life. This world, at least now that the buffalo hunters had gone, was calm. Enjoyable. And the wide sky and far horizon gave him a feeling of freedom.

"Son, how long do you intend to stand there and collect flies? We got ourselves a wagon to unload."

Mok opened his eyes. The man in the black shirt was standing in the wagon above, holding a sack of flour.

"Yes, sir," Mok said.

"Call me Preacher John. Or just John. But I've already told you that."

Preacher John threw down the sack of flour. Mok caught it with both arms and staggered under its weight.

It had only been a half-hour since the preacher had saved Mok. In that short time, Mok had learned the man's full name was John Richards. He called himself a missionary and was known among all the tribes as the Great Helper.

As he had explained to Mok, he was just as interested in bringing earthly hope as he was in delivering the Word of God. Much of that earthly hope consisted of the contents of the wagon: blankets, used clothing, sacks of flour and sugar, and various medicines. Mok's job was to help unload this wagon. After Preacher John gave the Pawnee Indians the Word, Mok would help distribute the supplies among them.

Mok set the sack of flour down and straightened, just in time to catch another sack.

Men and women had begun to gather around them and the wagon, talking excitedly and smiling broad smiles. Supplies!

As Preacher John had explained, these Pawnee were supposed to receive monthly food and blankets from the government. But the agents were notorious thieves and passed on little of these necessary and often-promised supplies. Without the preacher and his efforts, the upcoming winter would be difficult.

Mok worked steadily. The pile of supplies on the ground grew higher as the wagon emptied. The Pawnee stood and waited as they watched Preacher John and Mok.

Mok was so intent on the steady rhythm of unloading that he didn't notice all talk around him had stopped.

"Son," Preacher John called down from the wagon, "I believe now is as good a time as any to see how much good you'll do me."

Mok wiped the sweat off his face and looked up at the preacher. All Mok saw was the outline of the big man, black against the sun. Preacher John tossed a small object at Mok, and he caught it more from reaction than thought.

"You'll be needing that," Preacher John said.

Mok studied the strange object in his hand. It was made of dark, gleaming metal. Heavy. Tube on one end. A handle on the other. It was like the objects the buffalo hunters had pointed at Mok's head.

Mok looked upward again, a question obvious on his face.

"Six bullets in that Colt .44," Preacher John said. He pointed. "And six braves waiting to see what you might do with it."

Mok turned his head to look. The crowd of Pawnee around them numbered at least fifty. All had frozen to silence. The crowd parted widely in the middle. Six tall, muscular braves walked through the crowd toward Mok and the wagon. All were armed with war spears, shields, and knives. All were painted with fierce expressions of anger.

"I expected this," Preacher John said. "Every group has its share of young troublemakers. I come to preach and give freely. Yet, they would rather take without first listening to the Good Word."

Preacher John shook his head sadly. "Yes, sir. On occasion, some even have it in mind to scalp me and leave me for the buzzards."

CHAPTER 54

PREACHER JOHN hopped down from the wagon and stood beside Mok.

"No one gets anything from Preacher John unless they listen to him preach," the big man in black said. "I've always found a way to stop the troublemakers myself. But I'm curious to see what you'll do. Being as you agreed to help and all."

The braves moved closer. They stopped twenty paces from Mok and Preacher John and the unloaded supplies. They stared at Mok and Preacher John in silence.

"You've got the Colt .44," Preacher John said. "Still, I don't advise you to shoot them. Makes it real tough to get the rest of them to believe it when you tell them the part about how Jesus is love."

The warriors continued to stare. Ready for battle, they wore only flaps of cloth hanging from their waists. The lack of clothing showed that all six were heavily muscled. Their silence—and the unspoken threat of muscle—was more unnerving than any shouts of anger.

Mok stared back. He had no idea what to do.

Preacher John dug a small cigar from his shirt pocket. He put it in his mouth, lit a match by snapping the end against his thumbnail, and drew his first puff from the cigar.

"On the other hand," Preacher John said in an unworried drawl, "it don't do no good to let them just up and walk away with any of the supplies. Gives the others no reason to stick around and listen to the Word."

"Oh," Mok said.

The warriors began to advance slowly.

"By the way you're holding that .44," Preacher John said, "a person might think you'd never shot a pistol before. That ought to make things real interesting."

"You won't help?" Mok said.

"Want to see if you're worth keeping around," Preacher John said. He took another puff from his cigar.

Mok looked down at the Colt .44. He was gripping it by the barrel with his left hand. He put it into his right hand. His fingers fell naturally around the handle of the pistol.

The braves were only ten steps away.

The lead brave grunted something in a language Mok couldn't understand.

"He's saying he wants all the supplies," Preacher John translated. "He says step aside."

The warrior lifted his spear. He cocked it back as if he was going to hurl it at Mok's chest.

"This here is known as a showdown," Preacher John said. "I advise you to do something. These Pawnee will lose a lot of respect for you if I have to draw my other Colt and defend you."

Mok's mouth had turned dry. He couldn't even

find enough moisture to swallow. The blade of the spear looked crusted with blood. It didn't take much imagination to see how easily it could impale him.

It crossed his mind to call himself an idiot for believing this new adventure might be peaceful and filled with freedom. Any second now, the warrior was going to throw that spear. And it would hurt.

Mok's fingers tightened with nervousness. His index finger caught on the trigger. An explosion rocked the air as the pistol seemed to jerk itself in his hand.

Mok looked down with disbelief. He'd never seen anything like this in the slums of Old Newyork.

Gunsmoke drifted up to his face.

Murmuring filled the air.

Mok looked back at the warrior with the spear. He was still standing, but he was staring down. There was a neat little hole in the lower section of the cloth that hung from his waist. The bullet had passed clean between his legs.

All the others in the crowd were pointing at that little hole and the daylight that shone through.

The warrior looked up at Mok. His face was puckered with a combination of disbelief and relief. He dropped his spear and put his hands up, as if begging Mok not to shoot again. The warrior stumbled as he began to back away.

The other Pawnee began to rock with laughter as the young warriors fled.

Preacher John patted Mok on the shoulders.

"Well," he said to Mok. "I suppose that's one way to run them off. Now let's get down to business."

CHAPTER 55

JOHN RICHARDS CLIMBED back onto the wagon and began to preach to the people gathered below him. He spoke Pawnee, which Mok could not follow.

Mok, at the side of the wagon, let his mind wander as he watched the men and women and children listen to Preacher John.

The Word. Preacher John had called it the Word. Preacher John was speaking the Word about the man named Jesus. Mok's thoughts spun again to the audiobook of his childhood.

From it, Mok had learned about a man from Galilee who promised a home for any who believed in him. The Galilee Man had given his life on a cross to save others. And, in the streets of Old Newyork, Mok had wondered again and again if the Galilee Man was legend or truth.

Until his adventure on the pirate ship, Mok had thought it nearly impossible that a man would give his life to save others. In Old Newyork, it was the opposite—too many often took lives to save their own. Yet on the pirate ship, Captain Falconer had been willing to die simply to save Mok and the prisoners on board.

Now, Mok was beginning to understand what a gift

that sacrifice had been. It made him hungry to know even more about this Galilee Man. Mok looked forward to time alone with Preacher John to ask his questions.

It was late in the day and the sun cast long shadows when Preacher John stepped down from the wagon. Yet the Pawnee had waited patiently. Some of them had shown great interest in the preacher's words.

Preacher John waved the Pawnee forward. Then he and Mok handed out the supplies to families.

Occasionally, Preacher John would point at one of the young teenagers. There would follow a rapid discussion in Pawnee with the teenager's mother and father, accompanied by many hand gestures on the part of both Preacher John and the parents.

After this happened a fourth time, Mok stopped his efforts with the sacks of flour and turned to Preacher John.

"What are you discussing?" Mok asked. "And why with some families but not others?"

"Simple," Preacher John said. "I am inviting them to send their older children to the white man's school. I spent much of my preaching time trying to convince them that the only way they can survive in the white man's world is to have some of their children educated in the white man's way. The Pawnee need their own doctors and lawyers and teachers."

Preacher John wiped his brow. "See, son. Words just aren't enough. We have a call to feed the hungry and mend the sick. Once these Pawnee can help themselves, they'll be much better off."

Mok shook his head in admiration. He decided right there he would do his best to help this great man in his efforts.

It gave Mok new energy as he lifted and handed out supplies. He was nearing the bottom of the pile when he looked past the last few families in front of him.

He saw something that made him forget his sore back.

A few hundred paces away, a young Pawnee woman guided an older woman by the elbow as they walked slowly through camp.

It cannot be, Mok told himself. Yet it was. Although her hair was braided, and she wore leather buckskins, there could be no mistake. This was Raha, the pharaoh's daughter. She had also been Rachel, the servant girl in the castle. She seemed to be haunting him through time. All of Mok's doubts and uncertainties overwhelmed him again. What madness surrounded him? How could it be real that he was among a tribe of Pawnee, helping a great preacher?

At that moment, Mok knew only one thing. He must speak to her.

CHAPTER 56

HE FOUND HER at nightfall. She was brushing the long hair of the older Pawnee woman. Both were singing quietly near a fire.

"Who are you?" Mok asked without a wave of greeting.

He held his breath. The long shadows of dusk made it difficult to see any expression on her beautiful face. What if she replied in Pawnee? What if she pretended not to know him again? What if it wasn't the young woman who had dogged his footsteps from one world to another?

She did not reply.

"Who are you?" Mok asked again, this time with an edge to his voice.

Both women stopped singing. The older woman turned her head and spoke to the younger one in Pawnee.

"I am Voice-in-the-Wind," the young woman finally said in English. "And my adopted grandmother says you have a rude manner of speaking if indeed you have approached me for courtship."

The older woman spoke again. The younger woman listened, then translated. A smile showed as she spoke.

"My adopted grandmother says, however, it may be worth my while to listen to a man of such handsomeness, if only he can be trained to speak more gently."

"You speak Pawnee to her and English to me," Mok said, trying to ignore the flush of embarrassment he could feel hot on his face. "How is it you know my language?"

"I have been sent," she said simply. "For you."

If she had slapped him across the face, it would have had only half the effect of her words.

"Sent?" he sputtered. "Who sent you? Why? From where?"

She continued to smile, but said nothing else.

"Please," Mok said. "You must help me. Were you with me in Egypt? At the castle?"

"Yes," she replied. "But I can tell you little more."

Again, questions flooded Mok. All the questions that had tormented him. She *was* the key. She had the answers. He fought the urge to shake her shoulders to force the truth from her.

"You know, then, what has happened to me? That I was born into the slums of Old Newyork?"

"Yes. But that world is more than two hundred years in the future."

Each of her answers only spun more questions for him. He was almost dizzy with the confusion of what to ask next.

"Another has followed me too," he said, his words tumbling out. "Barbarossa, aboard the pirate ship. He tried to kill me. Tell me, please. Why has all of this happened to me?"

Voice-in-the-Wind smiled mysteriously. "All I can tell you is that I have been sent for you."

"Sent from where?" Mok tried again. He stepped closer. "Who sent you?"

She had the answers. All he needed to do was force them from her.

"I have been sent to warn you. John Richards is not what he appears to be. Tonight, watch him."

"Preacher John? He not only speaks of love, but he also shows it."

"Beware of false prophets," she replied, "who come to you in sheep's clothing. Inwardly they are ravenous wolves."

Each time she spoke, it was like another blow. These very words had come from the Galilee Man.

"I had an audiobook as a child!" Mok said. "I listened to those very words."

"The audiobook is known as the New Testament," she explained. "It was no accident that you found it. For our plan was already in place before you were born."

"Plan?" He almost fell to his knees to beg. "A plan in place for me before I was born? Please, tell me what you can."

"Watch the preacher tonight," she said. "And remember this: What will it profit a man if he gains the whole world and loses his soul?"

Again, words from the audiobook.

"Tell me," he pleaded. "How have I been sent from Old Newyork?"

"How?" she said. "Too often men ask how, when the important question is why."

"Why, then? Tell me, why?"

He reached across the short space between them and shook her shoulders.

The old woman barked out words in Pawnee. Mok ignored her.

"Why?" he repeated. "How can I make sense of this?"

"Whatever world you find yourself in," she said, "that is always the question. For isn't every life a quest?"

Mok's bewilderment began to turn to anger. Before he could speak, however, three warriors stepped into sight. They pointed their war spears at Mok.

He stepped away from Voice-in-the-Wind.

"You will not see me here again," she said. "But remember my words. Watch the preacher. And take heart. The messenger is not the message."

Voice-in-the-Wind took the old woman's hand. With great dignity, they both walked away.

Mok glared at the warriors, so confused and frustrated that he would have welcomed a fight. They, however, seemed to remember the lesson that Mok had taught earlier with his Colt .44. They followed the two women and left Mok standing alone—with only haunting questions as company.

CHAPTER 57

MAINSIDE. Silence had replaced the steady *blip-blip-blip* of the heart-rate monitor. Mok's heart was still beating, of course. But the monitor was dead. Just as Mok would be in minutes.

The killer was crouched beside the wall. His ears adjusted to the new silence. He heard the snoring of the male nurses in their chairs. He heard the *plop-plop* of liquids in the tubes attached to Mok's arms. He heard a gentle *whoosh-whoosh* of the life-support machine as it pumped air through Mok's lungs.

The *whoosh-whoosh* wouldn't last long. Once the killer pulled the final cord from the wall, the life-support machine would also shut down.

He reached for the cord. Wiggle, wiggle. The killer grunted with the effort it took to pull the big plug.

It popped loose.

The killer expected new silence. Instead, the life-support machine continued its gentle *whoosh-whoosh*.

What was wrong? The killer thought it through. He decided the life-support machine had a backup battery system. The Committee wouldn't risk letting a candidate die in cyberspace by not being prepared for a power outage.

The killer moved to the back of the machine. He studied the wires. It took him a short while to figure it out. Then, with no hesitation, he pulled two other cords.

The machine stopped. As did Mok's lungs.

The killer clenched his right fist in triumph.

Dead, dead, dead. Mok was as good as dead.

Rich, rich, rich. The killer was now rich.

He backed away from the machine.

All he needed to do was wait a few minutes. Without the life-support machine, the body would starve for oxygen. No person could live without air for long.

The killer glanced at the door. The only thing that could go wrong now was an unexpected visit from the security guards.

One minute passed.

The snoring of the nurses continued as Mok's life slipped away.

Two minutes. Three.

Surely Mok was dead now, the killer told himself.

He forced himself to wait another few minutes. That time passed. All life on the table was gone. Without doubt. Absolutely. Positively.

The man slapped his hands together at a job well done. He replugged the cords into the back of the life-support machine. He plugged the other cords in place.

The life-support machine began moving Mok's lungs again. But the killer knew it was like pushing air into rubber balloons. Those lungs would never use oxygen again.

The heart-rate machine proved the killer right. It picked up no heartbeat at all. Mok had flat-lined.

Dead. Dead. Dead. Which meant he was rich, rich, rich.

The killer spun on his heels and walked with confidence toward the door. Once he was in the hallway, nobody could prove he had killed Mok. It looked as he had been instructed to make it look. It looked as if Mok had accidentally died as the nurses slept, not watching the monitors.

The killer pictured his walk down the hallway. His ride down the elevator. His walk through the quiet empty lobby to freedom. To the money he had been paid to kill Mok. To Mexico and a long retirement.

As he opened the door, he froze.

Four men stood in the hallway, two of them security guards. Before the killer could step back, one of the security guards pointed a 'tric shooter at his chest.

"This is set on kill," the guard said, "not stun. If you move, I pull the trigger."

The killer reacted with anger. "What kind of outrage is this! As one of the Committee, I have every right to be here."

"But not every right to unplug those machines." This speaker was white haired, the one named Cambridge. "The connections in there were set up to send instant alarms if the electrical current was ever broken."

The killer had stopped listening. He was staring beyond Cambridge at another Committee member.

One identical to him. Same hair. Same nose and cheekbones. Same perfect teeth.

That Committee member was staring back at the killer with horrid fascination.

"Cambridge!" the Committee member said. "This man is my double!"

"So it seems," Cambridge said calmly. "But should we be surprised? With a three-D computer scan of a photograph to work from and enough time, even the poorest plastic surgeon can remake a face."

Cambridge continued to speak as if the killer didn't exist. As if Mok had not been murdered.

"This shows that whoever sent him has been planning against us for some time," Cambridge said. "And planning well. If we hadn't caught him, the video monitors would have shown it was you in the room."

"Me?" The Committee member visibly sagged. "You would have thought I was the betrayer?"

"Stimpson, my friend," Cambridge said. "Even had I seen it on camera, I would have had difficulty believing it."

Cambridge half turned his head and spoke to the security guards. "Take this man away. We will question him later. I doubt we will learn anything about who sent him, but the effort must be made."

Cambridge fixed his eyes on the killer. A hired man who had let his face be shaped to match a photograph.

"I do not know what decisions you have made in life to bring you to this desperate place of greed,"

Cambridge said. "But there is still hope for your conscience."

"I don't understand," the killer said.

"In there," Cambridge answered, pointing, "you did not take a human life. Much as those who sent you had planned, so had we. Once the security code was breached, we took steps to counteract what might be tried next. We set a trap of our own."

Cambridge smiled without humor. "Under the blanket lies a plastic dummy. Mok lives elsewhere."

CHAPTER 58

CYBERSPACE—THE AMERICAN WILD WEST. Mok sat with his knees up and his arms wrapped around them. He shivered as he watched Preacher John's tent. Hot as it had been during the day, it seemed impossible the night could be as cold as the pinpricks of light from the stars above.

Mok would have much preferred to be wrapped in blankets. He could be sleeping, warm, under the wagon where Preacher John had sent him after the campfire had died.

Instead, he sat among low bushes. Preacher John's tent was only ten paces away. It glowed from a lantern inside. Mok guessed that the preacher was reading from the Word, as he called his Bible.

Outside in the cold, Mok was forced to endure the bites of mosquitoes, afraid to slap at them in case Preacher John heard him. Mok could only find consolation in thinking that between the cold and the mosquitoes, he would certainly not fall asleep.

More irritating than the cold and the mosquito bites, however, was the feeling that he was acting like a fool. After all, he was watching the tent only because of what Voice-in-the-Wind had told him. If indeed that was her name. In the land of sand, she had been Raha. During the siege, she had been Rachel.

From a distant hill, a coyote began to wail. A coyote on another hill answered in the same high-pitched yipping. Mok shivered more, this time not from cold. The sound was eerie, but in this new prairie life, he had no idea if it was a sound of danger.

Mok heard rustling in the grass as mice and other small animals scurried through their night activities. Already he had heard a *whoosh* and seen the shadow of an owl against the moon as it swooped down and took its prey from those rustling creatures.

Again, he wondered about the many questions that had been with him since speaking to Voice-in-the-Wind only hours earlier.

She had been sent to warn him. She knew he came from Old Newyork—more than two hundred years in the future. She had not been surprised to hear that Barbarossa, who had tried to kill him on the pirate ship, had also known of Old Newyork. It was as if both had been sent through time to follow him.

Mok blinked. He heard his last thought echo through his head.

It is as if both have been sent through time to follow me.

Could that be it? Could that somehow be the answer to all the mysteries that surrounded him?

Think hard, Mok told himself. *Think.*

Growing up in the slums, he'd heard story after story about Mainsiders. They had little boxes to speak into that could send their voices into other boxes across the world. There were the flashes of silver that crossed overhead with a roaring thunder that followed far behind. These giant tubes, if you wanted to believe the stories, carried Mainsiders through the air. There was the audiobook that Mok had had in childhood, a small box that spoke to him about the Galilee Man. The blue light he had been shot with, and how it had sent him into blackness, was surely from Mainside.

New thoughts tumbled over old thoughts so quickly that Mok had trouble staying with them. If it had been a Mainsider who had shot the blue light, then perhaps there were other Mainside things he could not understand. After all, if they could send their voices across the world and send their bodies through air, perhaps there was a device that also sent Mainsiders through time.

Mok left that thought in the back of his mind. He brought up other memories. What had the girl's last words been in the castle? *I'm sorry, but this was done to save you.* As if, perhaps, someone at the controls of a time device had reason to move him elsewhere. Like to the pirate ship, where he'd found himself immediately afterward.

And what had Barbarossa said on the pirate ship? *As soon as your head leaves your body, you will no longer exist. Here or there.*

Here, as in wherever Mok had been sent. Or *there*, as in back at the device that moved a person through time.

Yes, he told himself with growing excitement. A device that sent him through time! This explained it! It wasn't all a dream. In dreams, a person did not bleed when hit or feel cold and bruises and hunger. In dreams, a person could not make up all the things and wonders that Mok had seen. But if he were actually traveling through time into different lands, it all made sense.

Yes! The dwarf named Blake, who had given him advice in Egypt and at the castle, had appeared and disappeared at will. Voice-in-the-Wind had done the same. And Barbarossa. They must all be Mainsiders, all able to travel through time.

Mok grinned in the darkness. This new answer, of course, led to other questions. Like why had Mok been taken to the Mainsider time device? And why was he being moved from place to place? After all, he'd rescued the pharaoh's daughter. It would have been nice to stay and accept her reward in any manner she decided to give it to him. It would have been wonderful, too, to have remained with Count Reynald and his family as the son of an important man. Even among the pirates, if his new friend Captain Falconer had not died, Mok could have made a life much better than any he'd had in the slums.

Still, Mok felt a definite triumph. He'd found a way to explain the insanity. All he had to do now was live through whatever—

Mok instantly shifted his attention to a dark figure moving toward Preacher John's tent. The figure called out words in a low voice Mok could not hear.

The tent flap lifted as Preacher John invited the visitor inside. In the brief moment before the tent flap fell again, a flood of light outlined Yellowbird Sings, the Pawnee warrior who had found Mok alone in the vast prairies.

Was this why Voice-in-the-Wind had told Mok to watch the preacher? Was he going somewhere with Yellowbird Sings?

Mok waited, holding his breath to hear better. A murmur of voices reached him. But neither man stepped out of the tent again.

Mok quietly got to his feet. He pushed branches of the bush aside as he moved toward the tent. Moments later, he was crouched beside the tent, listening.

CHAPTER 59

ALTHOUGH HE WAS close enough to hear their words distinctly, Mok could not make sense of their conversation. They spoke Pawnee. He had just decided it would be wise to move away from the tent when they switched to English.

"Enough talk in your tongue," Preacher John said. "For this discussion, we speak English. It's safer. You're the only Pawnee in this camp who speaks English. We can be overheard, and it will not cost us our lives."

"What about the one named Mok? He speaks English."

"Strange name, but I like him," Preacher John said. "He is strong. He is brave. He is smart. I have decided to keep him as a helper."

"What?" Yellowbird Sings said angrily. "You promised me gold for his capture."

Mok cocked his head. Gold for his capture?

"There is something about him," Preacher John said. "No fear. A sense of awareness. I believe it would be a shame to make him a slave."

Mok blinked. Had he heard right? A slave?

"But we made a deal. I deserve my money for him."

"No," Preacher John said. "He stays with me. It

won't take him long to learn Pawnee. He looks innocent. And from the sounds of it, he actually believes the Word. Someone like him will help us greatly as we go from camp to camp."

Mok's heart began to pound wildly. Something was wrong. Terribly wrong.

"But I should get something. You didn't have to put up with him on that long ride. Some of the things he said. That people laughed at my—"

"Enough," Preacher John barked. "This afternoon, the elders let me choose eight of their strongest young boys and girls. We leave tomorrow. In a few days, we'll have them at the mine. Then you'll get your fair share of gold."

Mok had heard enough to understand. Preacher John wasn't taking the Pawnee children to schools to educate them. He was selling them.

But how could Mok explain this to the Pawnee elders? The only people in camp who could translate Mok's English into Pawnee were Preacher John and Yellowbird Sings. He couldn't ask them to help him tell the elders.

There was Voice-in-the-Wind. She spoke English and Pawnee . . .

Mok straightened to move away from the tent. He would find her tepee in the darkness and tell her she had been right about Preacher John. She could warn the elders.

Mok took a step away from the tent. And tripped over a rope tied to a tent peg.

It might have been his grunt of pain. Or it might

have been the way the tent shook from the vibrating rope. Either way, it was enough to alert the two men inside.

As Mok scrambled to his feet, the men stepped out of the tent.

Preacher John leveled his pistol at Mok's stomach.

"It don't take much more brains than a fence post has to figure out you heard too much," Preacher John said. "Get inside the tent."

CHAPTER 60

THE TENT WAS big enough to easily stand in. Lantern light showed a folding cot, draped with blankets. A small luggage chest served as a table, holding a box of bullets, a small oilcan with a dirty cloth across the top, and a long-handled wire brush. Preacher John had taken off his black shirt. It was hanging from a rope stretched across the tent.

He stared at Mok, chest hairs curling from the neck of his dirty undershirt, his pants held by suspenders. Yellowbird Sings stood behind Preacher John, guarding the tent flap entrance.

"You impress me, boy," Preacher John told Mok, holding his pistol steady at Mok's belly. "It seems you had enough sense to know I wasn't a real preacher. And I've spent a long time fooling people."

Mok kept his chin steady. *The messenger is not the message,* Mok thought. *That's what Voice-in-the-Wind said. But what did she mean?*

"Thing is," Preacher John continued, "folks with less than admirable intentions often gravitate to thumping the Bible. People expect preachers to be good, God-fearing folks. Those few of us who aren't find it easy to take advantage of that. Pretending to be a preacher is the best sheep's clothing a wolf can find."

Mok suddenly understood Voice-in-the-Wind's warning. Preacher John's heart was false, but the words he spoke were true. Mok decided to remember to pay attention to people's actions as well as listen to their words in the future.

He watched as Preacher John reached with his free hand to where his shirt hung. He took a cigar from its pocket. Without taking his eyes or pistol off Mok, he found his matches and lit the cigar.

"Look at you," Preacher John said. "I might put lead in your belly any second. Yet you ain't showed a scrap of fear."

Preacher John squinted at the cigar smoke drifting into his eyes. He reversed the pistol, and handed it butt first to Mok.

Mok's eyes widened with surprise. He was no pistol-shooting expert, but he had certainly learned already the power of pulling the trigger.

"That's right," Preacher John said. "Now you've got the draw on me. Do me a favor, and hear me out before you decide whether to plug me with holes."

Another long puff on the cigar. "I want you to join me," Preacher John said. "We'll be partners. I can make you a wealthy man."

"That's why you gave me the pistol?" Mok asked.

"The man holding the gun has no need to lie," he answered. "And I'm interested in what you truly have to say about my offer."

Preacher John grinned a handsome smile. "So what do you say? There's gold mines in the mountains where work bosses don't ask no questions about the workers I deliver. These Pawnee are easy pickings. I've been moving through this territory about a year now, and outlaw or not I already have enough gold to buy me a dozen mansions back East. And this ain't nothing the law gets too excited about. In other words, this is easy money and no chance of jail time. Throw your hand in with me, and you'll never have to worry about money the rest of your life."

Mok didn't even need to consider it. He'd spent his life in Old Newyork dodging the work gangs. They often spread through the city looking for children to capture as factory slaves. And what he'd learned in his search for the Galilee Man was enough to tell him there were more important things than money. He had to remember no farther than the audiobook of his childhood.

"'Do not lay for yourself a treasure on earth where moths and rust consume,'" Mok said with a trace of a smile. "'But lay up a treasure in heaven.' Surely Preacher, you know that."

Preacher John smiled back through his cigar smoke. "You really believe that Bible verse, son?"

Mok nodded.

"Enough to die for it?"

Mok shrugged and held up the pistol.

"That ain't much of an answer, son. You think I was dumb enough to give you a loaded gun?"

Preacher John used his cigar to point at the chest with the oilcan, dirty cloth, and wire brush. "I was cleaning my pistol as I spoke with Yellowbird Sings here. When we heard you outside, I didn't stop to put the bullets back in. After all, more often than not, just the sight of a gun is enough to win a fight."

Preacher John's grin widened. "But putting the gun in your hand got you to speak honest like I wanted you to. Sad thing is, your answer just cost you a lifetime in the mines. My Pawnee friend will get his outlaw gold for capturing you after all."

Yellowbird Sings spoke from the tent flap. "We have trouble."

"What?" Preacher John said sharply.

"Warriors, maybe two dozen. Headed this way."

"Too many to fight," Preacher John said. "We'll hear them out. This boy won't be able to tell them a thing. He don't speak Pawnee."

"This is not good," Yellowbird Sings said softly, fear in his words. "They have two children with them. Pawnee children."

"What's wrong with that?"

"They are wearing clothing from the mine. John, they must be escaped slaves. Those elders have our game figured out. They will stake us to an ant pile in the morning sun."

Mok would have enjoyed spending more time watching the sheer terror that crossed Preacher John's face. But time was something he didn't have.

The tent began to spin with a blackness that was now becoming familiar. And Mok was gone.

CHAPTER 61

MAINSIDE. Fear clutched at the Committee member so tightly that he could hardly press his fingers against the numbers on his private vidphone. It gave the Committee member no satisfaction to look around his private home office and see the expensive art on the walls. Money had far less value when a man feared for his life.

After two tries, he managed to punch in the number correctly. Within seconds, a closeup of the face of the president of the World United appeared on the screen.

"Yes," the president snapped.

"Stage five, Your Worldship," the Committee member whispered. "He has moved to stage five."

"What! You told me the candidate would be killed here in real time, that the life-support machine would be unplugged."

"It . . . it did not happen. Cambridge guessed that we . . . I would be desperate enough to try something. He took precautions."

"Do not, I repeat, do not tell me that Cambridge captured our man. It took a year for surgeons to get his face duplicated perfectly."

The Committee member remained miserably

silent. It was answer enough for the president.

"You are a dead man," the president told the Committee member. "If this were an open line and half the world were listening, I would still make that threat. You . . . are . . . a . . . dead . . . man."

"Your Worldship, I can promise you that our candidate will fail. On my life, I make that promise."

The president glared into the vidscreen. "I've heard your promises before. Why should I believe you now?"

"I have the new security code," the Committee member said, almost stammering. "Our cyberassassin can follow him to the next cybersite."

"Don't call me until the candidate is dead," the president snarled. He hit a button on his end of the vidphone connection.

The Committee member sat staring at a blank screen.

CHAPTER 62

CYBERSPACE—PARIS, A.D. 1943. Cold.

That was Mok's first impression. The cold and gray of a winter twilight.

He stood on a sidewalk staring at old buildings built close together along the street. He wore black. Black pants. Black overcoat. Black mittens.

None of this surprised him. He had learned to expect the unexpected. Given time, he would learn where he was.

But he didn't know how much time he'd get.

Cresting the hill where the cobblestone street disappeared between the buildings, the first wave of soldiers swept toward him.

BACKSTORY V

OLD NEWYORK, A.D. 2076. With imagination, it was possible to see that a large tunnel had once curved through the ruins where Benjamin Rufus and the woman stood.

Shafts of sunlight shining through cracks in the street above gave an almost eerie view of the remains. Dozens of broken slabs of concrete—some three times the height of a man, some worn and crumbled to less than a foot tall—had fallen against each other, leaving large and small jumbled openings in all directions.

"Subway," Benjamin Rufus whispered. "This was once the subway."

His overcoat hung on him. He coughed deeply after he spoke, so she had to wait to ask her question.

"Subway?"

"Before the Water Wars," he said, "trains . . ."

He paused, seeing in her eyes that she did not understand *train*.

". . . were large steel boxes on wheels that moved people through here. The bombs of the war collapsed the tunnels."

Her smile was timid. "You know much."

He returned her smile, looking past the dirt

smudged like shoe polish on her face. She was only shoulder high to him, dressed in rags, with a shawl covering most of her head.

"You were born here," he said. "I was not."

She looked at the ground, pausing to gather the courage to speak, then lifted her head again.

"Zubluk," she whispered, "the most feared ganglord of all. He said he knew you. How can that be if you were not born here?"

The old man closed his eyes, recalling his past. "It is a long story," he answered. "*If* we have time, I will tell you."

"We have time," she said. "I know Zubluk will not rest until he finds you. But here you will be safe. Not once have the work gangs found me here."

She shuddered at the memories of the giant brutish ganglord and his bodyguards. "But if you go above ground . . ."

Benjamin Rufus nodded and began coughing again. This longer, harder fit shook his body.

She left him quickly, disappearing behind a giant slab. She returned with a blanket, which she wrapped around his shoulders.

"Thank you," he said. "You have offered me safety and warmth, but I do not even know your name."

"Terza," she replied simply.

"My name is Benjamin Rufus," he said. Nothing about him gave her a clue that until the night before, he had been one of the most powerful men on Mainside.

"You took a risk to save me," he said. "Yet you know nothing about me. Why put your life in danger?"

"I listened to your words to the crowd," replied Terza. "That was enough. You spoke to my heart. It is as empty as you said. To hear that my body was more than flesh, that I had something more . . . a soul . . . it was like clear, cold water to a dry throat. I want to know more about God. About his Son. It seemed worth the risk to find the hope you described."

"God builds an emptiness into each one of us," he said. "It remains empty until we find him. Nothing else will fill it. Not money, not fame, not excitement. Believing that God came to earth as Christ, and seeking God through the Son will fill that emptiness. It brings life beyond death."

"How do you know this?" Terza asked. "I have never heard of such things . . ."

Benjamin Rufus sat down, using one of the concrete slabs as a bench. "Are there no Christians in Old Newyork?"

She frowned. "I don't think so. Unless you mean Churchians. But what little I know of them sounds nothing like the message you bring."

The frown he returned was question enough.

"They hold secret meetings," she answered. "They have rules. Many rules. Those who don't follow the rules are condemned. They remain friends with only each other and do not accept those who do not share their beliefs."

Rufus shook his head in sadness. "Like the Pharisees of Christ's time."

He saw the question in her eyes.

"I'm sorry to say I have an advantage." Benjamin Rufus sighed. "You can't be blamed for what you do not know. Just as I cannot take pride in what my background has given me."

"I know you come from Mainside," she said, "even though you have not told me so. You could not be here because the government sent you as a prisoner, otherwise your forehead would be marked. Why are you here?"

"The answer is simple," he said after a moment's reflection. "There have been two or three generations here without an understanding of the message of Christ. They live without hope. The next generation must not live that way."

"You will pay with your life to deliver your message of hope."

"Yes," he said. "Of that I have no doubt. I only pray it is later rather than sooner; where the ground is rocky and dry, many seeds must be sown in many places for the fruit to grow."

The woman sat beside him. "Begin with me. Perhaps I can help put seeds in places you cannot go."

CHAPTER 63

MAINSIDE, A.D. 2096. Cambridge sat alone in his office. If he raised his head from the computer screen before him, he would see sky and river and the far shoreline that marked the island of Old Newyork. The only thing luxurious about the office, however, was the vastness of its view. Despite the money and resources available to him, he had not treated himself to expensive carpet or walnut paneling or a large desk or rare art.

In fact, his office simply held the desk at which he sat and the computer, which held his total attention. The screen showed a three-dimensional image of a young man dressed in black walking a cobblestone street on a winter afternoon.

This young man actually lay still in a smaller room just down the hallway. Despite the short physical distance between them, Cambridge and Mok shared the same space. Cyberspace. Mok lived it as Cambridge watched.

Cambridge rested his chin on his hand.

Please God, do not let Mok fail, Cambridge prayed. *He's come this far. Don't let him fail.* Mok's success was crucial to keep heat bombs from destroying Old Newyork.

Yet, watching the computer screen, Cambridge could not hide from the knowledge of how thin the line was between success and failure. The cyberprogram linked Mok's mind to a virtual reality so close to life that if Mok died in cyberspace, it would scramble the nerve circuits in his brain, killing him in real time as well.

Worse, this would be Mok's most difficult cybertest. And he had come so close to the end . . .

Cambridge thought with pride of the other stages of Mok's cyberadventure. Egypt, the test of justice. The Holy Land castle siege that tested his beliefs. A pirate voyage that helped him learn to share those beliefs. The Wild West, where he was tempted with riches over truth. And now . . .

And now—Cambridge slammed his hand down on his desk in anger—Mok must face betrayal. Not betrayal built into the events of virtual reality, where every choice Mok made could shift the program in almost infinite directions.

No. This betrayal came from one of the twelve Committee members. Betrayal after nearly two decades of working together in secrecy to follow the plans laid by Benjamin Rufus.

So, instead of observing Mok with the growing hope of success, Cambridge was forced to watch the computer screen for a cyberassassin.

Even now, Cambridge could hardly believe it.

One of the Committee had sent a killer into cyberspace. That killer's only goal was to stop Mok at any cost.

CHAPTER 64

CYBERSPACE—PARIS. Gray sky. Clouds hung low over drab, dirty buildings. Traces of snow drifted onto the cobblestone streets. Several parked vehicles half blocked the sidewalk. Men and women, with heads bowed, walked the sidewalks in heavy, dark overcoats, their breath becoming small clouds of vapor in the late afternoon winter chill.

Mok noticed all of this, but only briefly.

His attention focused on what was far ahead of him, where the cobblestone street disappeared between the cramped buildings that lined both sides. At the top of the hill, he saw five men marching toward him. They wore uniforms and each carried a rifle slung over his left shoulder. As the men marched down the slope of the hill, Mok saw the helmets of another row of soldiers begin to top the hill from the other side. The helmets rose higher, followed by shoulders, then waists, until those soldiers, too, crested the hill and began to march down toward Mok.

Followed by another five.

And another five.

Row after row of soldiers filled the street. And behind all of this, Mok heard a rumble, growing louder each passing second.

Yet the men and women on the sidewalks continued their business as if nothing were strange about waves of soldiers filling the street.

As for Mok, the rumbling noise gave him an eerie dread. It was a sound so unnatural, so ominous, that without realizing his feet were moving, he found himself in an alley.

It cut his view of the street to the small gap just ahead of him, but it seemed the safest move, considering he had no idea where he was or what was happening.

Seconds later, the first row of soldiers passed by the alley, marching precisely in step.

An old man staggered into the alley, bent almost double by the weight of a sack on his back. The man lurched toward Mok, intent on passing through the alley.

Mok saw the old man's face only briefly. Deep wrinkles sketched a picture of sorrow, pain, and weariness. It pierced Mok's heart to instinctive compassion.

The rumbling was so loud that Mok did not try to speak. Instead, he touched the old man's shoulder as the man passed by.

The old man dropped the sack and half lifted his arms, as if trying to ward off a blow. Mok saw his clothes were ragged and that the man had a large six-pointed yellow star sewn on one sleeve.

"No!" Mok shouted over the rumbling noise. He pointed at the fallen sack. Potatoes had spilled onto the cobblestones. "Let me help carry!"

Before the old man could reply, two things happened.

The first was something Mok did not understand until it was explained to him later. Nothing in Old Newyork had taught him about the machines of war. Following the soldiers, German panzer tanks passed the alley. Their loud engines drove steel treads that crunched and roared over the rough cobblestones. From the corner of his eye, Mok saw the long barrels and the turrets, the dull green plating of the tank shell, and the series of wheels that turned the caterpillar treads.

The second thing, however, Mok did understand; he had seen the gangs in Old Newyork.

A dozen kids swarmed the alley.

They began to pelt the old man with sticks and stones and garbage.

CHAPTER 65

INSTANT ANGER SWEPT through Mok. He dashed forward.

Although Mok was outnumbered, the boys were younger and smaller. And the boys were not filled with rage. Mok snatched a stick from one of them and began to swing.

They backed off in surprise. Something in Mok's face turned their surprise to fear. Wordlessly, like a pack of wolves working together, the boys spun on their heels and dashed back toward the street.

Mok stood with his fists clenched around the stick, his chest heaving. He watched until the last of the boys disappeared. Only then, as he calmed his breathing, did he turn back to the old man.

Mok gasped.

Blood ran down the man's face from a gash on his forehead.

In his pockets, Mok found a handkerchief and bits of colorful paper.

Mok let the paper fall to the cobblestones and stepped forward with the handkerchief to press it against the old man's forehead.

"Money," the man said, his eyes wide. "Don't let the wind take it!"

Mok kept his hand gentle against the man's forehead.

He half turned to see where the man was pointing. All Mok saw were the bits of colored paper.

"Money?" Mok repeated. In Old Newyork, tokens of titanium were called money.

"Enough to feed my wife and me for a year!" The man struggled to get away from Mok, to reach the money.

"Paper is money?" Mok said.

"And money is food!" The man took the handkerchief from Mok. "Pick it up before those children return."

Mok did so, putting it back in his pocket. When he straightened, the man was staring oddly at him.

"I am called Mok," he said. "I hope you are not hurt badly."

"Thaddeus," the old man said. He pulled the handkerchief away and grimaced at the sight of the blood. "How have you lived your whole life without knowing money? And how do you have so much?"

Mok gave a grim smile. "I wish you could answer those questions for me. I wish you could answer many more as well."

"You do not make sense," Thaddeus said.

Mok stooped and began to pick up the man's scattered potatoes.

"Think of me as someone newly dropped onto the street," Mok said. "And please tell me. Where are we and what year is this?"

"Paris," Thaddeus answered, more puzzled. "Nineteen hundred and forty-three."

"And that?" Mok asked, pointing at the strange thing on four wheels just beyond the alley. He'd never seen one in Old Newyork.

"An automobile. How can you not know that?"

"Automobile," Mok said, more to himself than the old man. "I *have* heard of those. From before the Water Wars."

"Water Wars?" Thaddeus echoed. "This is the Second World War. The Germans now occupy Paris. What are the Water Wars?"

Mok had gathered the remaining potatoes. Then he lifted the sack.

"I'll carry these," Mok said, "if you will lead."

A strange expression remained on the old man's face. "Surely you see the Star of David on my sleeve."

"Yes," Mok said, unsure of what the man meant.

"I'm a Jew," Thaddeus explained. "That's why the boys followed and tried to rob me. No one helps Jews in these times."

"I do," Mok said.

Thaddeus smiled for the first time.

"May God bless you," Thaddeus said.

Mok smiled and followed the man's slow pace. The alley twisted and turned several times. Above them were the windows of apartments, black and bleak in the dying sunshine. Garbage lined both sides of the alley.

Mok remained behind Thaddeus until the alley finally emptied onto another street.

Thaddeus stopped and moaned with horror.

At first Mok saw only the street, the drab buildings,

and some gathered soldiers. On the ground, in front of one of the buildings, sat an old woman, surrounded by piles of clothing.

"Run away," she cried when she saw Thaddeus. "Run!"

He hurried toward her instead, his arms wide. "Miriam! Are you all right?"

The old lady tottered to her feet. Her face was crooked with grief.

"You should have saved yourself," she said. "You should have disappeared back into the alley."

"I could never leave you," Thaddeus said. "What happened?"

"Our home, Thaddeus," she said. "Tonight of all nights, they have taken our home."

CHAPTER 66

THADDEUS SEEMED TO GROW stronger and taller as he comforted his wife. She buried her face in his chest. He held her close with his right arm and soothed her by stroking her gray hair with his left hand.

"We have each other," Mok heard Thaddeus say to her quietly. "We have each other. We will always have our love. No one can ever take that away."

The old woman hugged him tighter. The sleeve of her overcoat had a yellow star sewn onto it.

Jews, thought Mok. *A yellow star to mark them. What are Jews? Why are they marked?*

Miriam stepped back from Thaddeus. She bit her lower lip to hold back her tears as they gazed on each other.

Sadness hit Mok. Not at their grief. But because their love was so strong. It made him aware of how alone he was.

"Why have they done this?" Thaddeus asked her.

"They said an army captain wants our home," Miriam said. Her voice trembled. "All our cherished keepsakes and furniture. Everything we've put together in our lifetime. His!"

Thaddeus whispered something else. Mok was close enough to hear, but not sure if he heard correctly.

"The radio," Thaddeus said. "Did they find the radio?"

Miriam whispered her reply. "Not yet. Nor the little book . . ."

Thaddeus shook his head in warning as he looked past her at the soldiers.

Two of them, large men armed with machine guns, walked toward the couple.

"Enough," one of the soldiers grunted. "Pick up your belongings and come with us."

"Come where?" Thaddeus asked. Not in desperation, but in anger. "Isn't it enough that you take our home? You take our freedom now too?"

"We have orders to put you on a train to a work camp outside of France," the soldier said. "Move now or I will break your teeth."

The soldier lifted his machine gun and threatened the old man with the butt. He jabbed it toward Thaddeus's face for emphasis.

Until then, Mok had not moved. The scene had taken his attention so fully, he had forgotten the weight of the sack of potatoes on his shoulder.

Yet as the soldier forced Thaddeus to cower, Mok stepped toward the couple, not sure what he could do to protect them against an armed soldier, but unable to stop his impulse.

"Is this your grandson?" the soldier asked as he noticed Mok. "If so, where is his star? You know Jews who don't wear the star may be executed."

"He is not a Jew," Thaddeus said quickly. "I paid him to carry my load."

The soldier grinned at Mok, showing stained teeth. "I'll take the money then. You should know better than to help a Jew. Perhaps we'll put you on the train too."

Suddenly, the soldier's grin froze. He backed away from Mok and the couple.

He barked a few words in German at the other soldiers. They all stiffened and stood at attention.

Thaddeus looked behind him. His face showed instant concern.

"The Gestapo!" he hissed to Mok. "The worst of the Nazis. Walk away now as if you don't know us, and you might be safe."

"But you . . ."

"Forget about us!" Thaddeus said. "We'll pray the car is just passing by. If not, there is no need for you to suffer with us! Go! Now!"

Mok peeked over his shoulder.

A long, gleaming black automobile glided down the street toward them. Its windows were dark. Small flags waved from the hood of the car.

Mok was paralyzed by indecision. How could he leave these people? But if he stayed, how could he help them against soldiers and the Gestapo, whatever the Gestapo was?

Mok hesitated too long.

The car stopped. Mok could not see through the darkened windows.

A tall man in a highly decorated uniform stepped out of the vehicle. All the soldiers instantly saluted. Thaddeus and Miriam huddled against each other.

"Jews?" the Gestapo officer asked, pointing at the building behind the soldiers. "From that apartment?"

"Yes," a soldier said. "These are the ones. To be shipped to a work camp. We were only following orders."

"Idiots! With all these possessions?"

"Standard procedure," the soldier stammered, "for all Jews. Let them take what they can carry."

"Not these," the Gestapo officer snapped. He pulled a pistol from a fine leather holster. He pointed it at Miriam's head. "Get into the car. Both of you."

"But we have our orders," the soldier said. "If we do not return with them, our commanding officer—"

"These Jews are helping others escape the country," the Gestapo officer snarled. "No punishment will be too harsh for them."

He waved his pistol at Thaddeus and Miriam. The soldiers fell back, and the old couple shuffled, frightened, toward the car.

The Gestapo officer swung the pistol and turned it on Mok.

"And you? What is your involvement with these Jews? Are you with them?"

To his shame, Mok wanted to lie. He wanted to deny he knew them, or had sympathy for them.

Yet the lie took too long to get to his lips. For a long moment, he stared back at the officer, while flakes of snow drifted down between them from the cold gray sky.

"Your silence is answer enough," the man barked. "Get into the car!"

CHAPTER 67

AS THE DRIVER gunned the car forward, the Gestapo officer on the passenger side half turned to look at Mok, Miriam, and Thaddeus in the backseat. The officer lifted his hat from his head and smoothed his thick, dark hair with his hand. He had a movie star face, with black eyes and a thin mustache.

"So, my friends," he said to them, "where would you like me to take you?"

He dropped his hat in his lap and smiled at the surprise on the faces of his prisoners.

"You heard me correctly," he said, still smiling. "I am offering you freedom. Where would you like me to take you?"

"Freedom?" Thaddeus asked.

"Let me explain," the Gestapo officer said. "My name is Wolfgang and . . ."

He unbuttoned the top of his uniform, reached inside, and pulled out a silver chain. He dangled it so that on the end of the necklace they could see a six-pointed star within a circle.

"The Star of David," Miriam gasped. "A symbol of hope for the Jews. But you are a—"

"A Nazi? Sworn to dispose of the Jews?" he said. She nodded.

"Indeed, I am a high-ranking Gestapo officer. But also a secret sympathizer to the Jews. It is a crime how they are treated. My driver and I have taken to cruising the streets, looking to rescue those Jews we can. It is but little in the face of what has been happening. Yet at least I am doing what I can."

Except for the hum of tires over the cobblestones, there was silence as Miriam and Thaddeus looked at each other.

"Can we believe him?" Miriam whispered. "Do we dare hope?"

Thaddeus spoke to her in a low voice. "No, my love. This is a trap."

He repeated his words to Wolfgang, louder, almost defiant: "This is a trap."

Wolfgang arched his eyebrows. "A trap?"

"You told the soldier you were taking us because we were helping others to escape. You could not know that if you were simply driving by as you say."

The officer stared at them for at least a half minute. Then he laughed loud and long. "What priceless humor!" he finally said. "I thought I was telling the soldier a lie. So, you *have* helped other Jews escape?"

Thaddeus did not answer.

Wolfgang shook his head in admiration. "What a fortunate day. Of any who might deserve help from me, then, it would be the two of you. I give freedom to the freedom givers."

The driver made a turn. Although the streets were

crowded with people, they parted quickly for the car that so obviously carried the Nazi elite.

Wolfgang reached into a pocket of his uniform. He pulled out a thick wad of folded money.

"For you," he said, reaching over the seat. "It will help you. Now tell me, where do you want to go?"

Neither Miriam nor Thaddeus accepted the money.

Wolfgang sighed. With his other hand, he offered them his pistol.

"Here," he said. "Would I hand you this if I meant you harm?"

Mok spoke for the first time since entering the car. "Check it for bullets."

Thaddeus took the pistol. He clicked a button and the clip fell from the pistol's handle. It was full of bullets.

"Good," Mok said. "I'd hate to get tricked twice."

"Twice?" Thaddeus asked. "This has happened to you before?"

"Another time and place," Mok answered. "It's too long a story to bother telling."

"Are you satisfied?" Wolfgang interrupted. "We must hurry. If I don't return soon, I will have too many questions to answer."

"Satisfied," Thaddeus said. He handed Wolfgang back the pistol and, with a motion very smooth for a man so old, took the thick wad of money. "Turn the car around and take us to a small café near the river. Le Café Bordeaux."

"Le Café Bordeaux!" Miriam said. "Surely you can't mean to go there. After all, the—"

Thaddeus squeezed Miriam's knee to keep her silent.

"Le Café Bordeaux," Thaddeus said firmly.

"You must leave Paris," Wolfgang protested. "More and more they are rounding up the Jews. If you get caught again, I cannot guarantee I will be able to save you."

"Wolfgang," Thaddeus answered, "leaving the city is exactly what we intend to do."

"I don't understand," Wolfgang said. "A café? Where people meet for food and drink?"

"If you want us to escape, please take us there," Thaddeus answered. "I can say no more."

CHAPTER 68

MAINSIDE. In another office, miles away from Cambridge, another Committee member also faced a computer. He, like Cambridge, watched the 3D image of Mok's cyberjourney. Unlike Cambridge, however, this man's face seemed joyful.

He sat back in his chair with his feet propped on his desk. He was home alone and did not expect any interruptions.

His right hand rested on the vidphone. The number he had keyed in would connect him to the president, the most powerful man among the global union of civilized nations.

Any second now, the Committee member told himself, any second now he could hit "send" and connect the call.

He grinned at the computer screen. Any second now a brute of a man would appear among the people passing by the small café in wartime Paris.

The Committee member could clearly see the sign in the background: Le Café Bordeaux.

When this brute of a man appeared, he would bring Cambridge's plan to an end. This man had been sent to prison for murdering three people at their dinner table, then sitting down to finish their meal before robbing their house.

The president of the World United had freed him on one condition—that he allow himself to be hooked up to a virtual reality computer and sent into cyberspace. His task was simple. Kill Mok.

The mechanics had been easy to arrange. The killer was attached to a computer hundreds of miles from the Committee site. The Committee member had supplied the encryption code to allow him access to the Committee's private cybersite. Then the killer had traveled into cyberspace to search for Mok.

The cyberassassin had failed once. But Mok had expected that attack.

Here, on the streets of Paris, the killer would simply step out of the crowd and knife Mok in the chest. End of Mok. End of program. End of Old Newyork.

The Committee member smiled to think of the wealth waiting for him. He smiled wider as he saw the image of a large man with a fierce scowl move into the doorway of Le Café Bordeaux.

Moments later, the image of a dark limousine rolled to a stop in front of the café. The door opened. Mok stepped out, only a few feet away from death. The cyberassassin would kill Mok in cyberspace— Paris, 1943. And in real time—Mainside, 2096.

As he watched the killer knife Mok, the Committee member hit the send button on the vidphone.

The president of the World United had given him an order to call the moment that Mok died.

CHAPTER 69

CYBERSPACE—PARIS. The Gestapo car pulled up in front of Le Café Bordeaux. Mok opened his door and stepped into the street, almost into the path of another car. The driver honked as the car nearly brushed him. Mok caught a glimpse of the driver's face, pale behind the windshield. But the car passed too quickly for him to apologize.

Mok walked around the car to the sidewalk. He gave support first to Miriam, then to Thaddeus, as they, too, stepped out of the car.

The moment they closed the door, the Gestapo car eased away and disappeared down the street. Wolfgang had no reason to stay; he had wished them well and said his good-byes as they neared the café.

Mok shivered as he looked around. The car's warmth had been much nicer than the cold twilight.

The café was a small building sandwiched between larger buildings. The windows glowed from candlelight inside. Diners sat at tables near the windows. It looked like a warm, cheerful place.

Mok waited for Miriam and Thaddeus to move toward the café, eager to be warm again.

Instead, Thaddeus took Miriam by the arm and headed away from the building.

"Hurry," he said. "And you, too, young man. Come with us."

"But the café . . . ," Mok said, confused.

"No," Thaddeus said sharply. "I don't trust Wolfgang. He may be simply letting us go to find out how we smuggle other Jews to England."

"Smuggle?" Mok asked. A lot had happened in a short time, and he couldn't make sense of it all.

"The Nazis have done terrible things to us Jews," Thaddeus said. "Whole families have disappeared, sent to work camps. Miriam and I have worked with resistance fighters to help some Jews get out of the country. But we must do it secretly. The Jews must be smuggled out."

"I don't understand," Mok said.

"If we don't, Jews will die. Jews will—"

"I mean, I don't understand why it is so important for the Nazis to harm the Jews. What have you done to deserve such hatred?"

"It is simply that we are different. For some people, that is enough. The color of our skin perhaps. Or our different beliefs. It's a sad thing to judge people without first knowing their hearts . . ."

"And Wolfgang is enough of a man to stand against this?" Mok asked.

"If Wolfgang is truly for us, it won't matter where he thinks we went," Thaddeus said. He pointed at the warm glow of the café. "But if he wanted me to give him a clue as to where the smuggling begins, he is welcome to believe it is Le Café Bordeaux. The owner is a Jew hater and has made money turning

243

Jews over to the Nazis. It wouldn't surprise me, in fact, if *he* told the Nazis about Miriam and me."

"In other words," Mok said, now understanding why Miriam had at first protested in the car, "if Wolfgang suspects the owner, he'll harass him."

Thaddeus grinned. "Exactly, my friend. Perhaps soldiers will even raid the café tonight. And in the meantime, twenty Jews depend on Miriam and me this evening."

"Twenty . . ." Mok didn't have time to finish his question. Thaddeus and Miriam had begun to walk away.

Mok hurried to catch up.

Without slowing down, Thaddeus said to Mok, "I have wondered whether you, too, are a spy for the Nazis. Yet my heart and mind tell me no. I take a different way home every day, so you could not have known I would be in the alley where we met. Nor could you have known a gang would attack me."

"A gang?" Miriam asked. She stopped her husband to put her hands on his face to search his eyes. Then she noticed the gash on his forehead. "Are you hurt?"

"No," he said with a chuckle. "This young man fought them all. It could not have been a fight arranged to earn my confidence. So now, unlike I do for Wolfgang, I give him my trust."

He pulled her close and hugged her. "And, as the God we love knows, we desperately need to be able to trust someone."

"Yes," Miriam said simply. "Yes, we do."

Thaddeus turned to face Mok. Nearly all the day's light had disappeared. Shadows covered the old man's face. Snow lightly dusted the shoulders of his overcoat.

"Over the past week," Thaddeus said, "many Jews have come to us for help. We have found a place for them. Tonight all of us are to escape. To lose our home tonight is the worst timing possible . . ."

"You want me to help you reach the others?" Mok asked.

"No," Thaddeus said. "They are not far away. Miriam and I can get to them ourselves. We have until midnight to meet with them and the resistance fighters who have been helping us. However, I beg you to use that time to go to our home. I doubt the army captain has begun to move in yet, and there is something you must get for us."

"What is it?" Mok asked.

Thaddeus drew a deep breath. "For months, I have used a crystal radio to listen to Nazi broadcasts. When I can, I send news across the Channel to England to whoever might be listening."

Mok hung his head. "I'm sorry," he said. "I don't understand what *crystal radio* is. Or *channel*. Or *England*. Where I come from . . ."

"There's nothing to be ashamed of," Thaddeus said quickly. "No one has complete knowledge. You, I'm sure, know things I do not."

Mok accepted this encouragement with a smile.

Thaddeus smiled back and said, "So let me explain some of what I know."

Thaddeus took a few hurried minutes to tell Mok about the crystal radio, and about the fifty miles of water between the countries of England and France. Thaddeus explained that it was so dangerous to be caught with the radio, that he would take it apart and hide the pieces when he wasn't using it.

When he finished, Mok nodded. "This radio is valuable. You want me to return to your home and retrieve it from the hiding places?"

"There is more," Thaddeus said. "Not just the radio. Something else. Something you must find and bring to us. We will be waiting in a barge—"

He noticed Mok's confused look and added, "a flat-bottomed boat—at the river's edge."

Mok waited.

"You see," Thaddeus said, "certain things come easy to some people. I was born with a head for numbers."

Miriam patted his shoulder. "What this wonderful old man is trying to tell you is that he is a genius. Truly a mathematical genius. Before the war, he lectured at the university. He has many books published on the subject of encryption."

Again, Mok asked for an explanation.

"Codes," Thaddeus answered. "No one can understand the messages sent without the key to the code. During war, it is how top-secret information is passed."

Thaddeus noticed that passersby were forced to walk around them. He waited until no one was near. Finally he spoke again.

"Young man," Thaddeus said, "I have cracked the code the Germans have used over the last few months. That information will be extremely valuable to those who fight the Germans and wish to end the war."

Mok asked, "What exactly am I looking for?"

"A small black book," Thaddeus said. "I would not ask you to put yourself in danger, but I cannot return to my home. Neither can Miriam."

"I will do my best," Mok said.

"You must do more," Thaddeus said. "Not only does the book contain the code I've cracked, but it also has hundreds of details on Germany's plans for a surprise invasion against England. If we can get this plan to the right people, the Germans can be stopped."

Thaddeus gripped Mok's shoulders and stared him in the eyes.

"Do you understand, my friend?" Thaddeus said, almost pleading. "This book can not only save thousands upon thousands of lives, but it can also change the course of history. And now it seems you are our only hope."

CHAPTER 70

GETTING INTO THE APARTMENT had been simple. The streets were dark and the soldiers stationed near the building ignored Mok. Thaddeus had given Mok a key to the back downstairs entrance and to the apartment on the third floor.

Inside the apartment, Mok had no trouble finding the radio pieces. He had used a small candle in his search, and the radio components were exactly where Thaddeus had told him to look. He held them now in a small sack. Thaddeus had been clear with his instructions: take all the pieces of the radio and discard them far away from the apartment. The Nazis must not realize that a former mathematics professor and encryption expert had been using a radio.

Simple as it had been so far, Mok's nerves were like thin copper strands being pulled tighter and tighter. The darkness beyond the tiny light of the candle unnerved him. The shadows of furniture seemed to become Nazis ready to pounce. And there was the silence, broken only by Mok's shallow breathing. At any second, he expected soldiers to burst through the door. And he would be trapped.

Mok forced himself to take a couple of deep

breaths before lack of oxygen and fear could make him dizzy. He reminded himself that all he had left to retrieve was the book . . .

A book that could change the history of the war.

Mok tried not to think of the book's importance. He looked for the painting of a sailboat along the far wall.

In a cabinet to the left of the painting, Thaddeus had said, *you will find a false bottom. Empty the bottom shelf. Then trigger the hinge by feeling for a button beneath the cabinet.*

He tiptoed across the hardwood floor, careful not to bump into anything.

The flicker of the candle finally showed him the painting. It led him to the cabinet.

Mok set his sack down on the floor.

He quietly opened the cabinet door. It held shelves of china plates and bowls, arranged neatly in rows. He got on his knees and set the candle down, then began pulling the china, piece by piece, from the bottom. When all the pieces were on the floor, Mok dropped even lower and groped beneath the cabinet. His fingers brushed the cabinet legs and finally touched a button near the back, exactly as Thaddeus had promised.

With a satisfying *click*, the button responded to the pressure of his finger.

Mok looked inside the cabinet and saw that the bottom of it had released upward on a spring hinge. He lifted the panel higher, and saw the small notebook in the space beneath.

Mok briefly closed his eyes in relief. He let out a breath, unaware that he had been holding it.

Mok reached for the notebook. And froze as a boot slapped the hardwood floor only inches behind him.

Before he could turn, the candle went out.

"Does it frighten you," a voice whispered in the darkness, "to think of the power this little book has given you?"

CHAPTER 71

FOR LONG, LONG MOMENTS, Mok waited for the blow against his head. He waited for the knife in his back. He waited for the kick to his kidneys.

Nothing happened.

His fear built until it rose to the point of cold anger. Mok decided to face the presence behind him, not take a blow crouched like a dog. Slowly, he stood. Slowly, he turned.

He strained his eyes in the dark. Finally, he saw the outline of someone before him. Someone chest high.

"Let me repeat my question," the voice whispered. "Does it frighten you to think of the book's power? The lives of thousands upon thousands are in your hands."

Now, Mok's mind shrieked. *Now!*

He dived forward, hoping surprise might overpower whatever weapon the intruder had.

He hit the intruder hard and low. They banged to the floor in a tumbling heap. Mok found the man's neck and grabbed and twisted. There had been times in Mok's life when he'd had to fight to save his life. He knew the feeling of desperation and how to turn it into a weapon.

The other fought back, gasping and choking.

Mok squeezed tighter.

Without warning, the intruder went limp.

Mok let go and backed away. He stood poised, ready to fight again at the slightest movement.

Seconds passed.

"Have you finished your obnoxious soldier games?" the man finally croaked. "Or must I play dead a little longer?"

Mok knew the voice.

"Stinko?" Mok asked. "I mean, Blake, is that you?"

"Yes," Blake answered. "Much against my will, I am here.

"I've pegged you as nothing but trouble from the beginning," Blake continued, "and this only proves it. Don't think I'm happy because you actually re-membered to use my real name."

Mok took a moment to relight the candle. The flame showed that the dwarf's face still held all the grumpiness it had before.

"Well, don't think *I'm* happy at the way you chose to say hello after all this time," Mok snapped. "I ought to choke you again."

Blake groaned as he struggled to his feet.

"Go ahead," Blake said. "My pain can't get worse anyway. And it will give me an excuse not to de-liver my message."

Mok's mood instantly shifted away from irritation. *Blake knew something about the strange worlds Mok had entered.*

"Message?" Mok demanded. "From whom? About what?"

"No, no, no, no, no," Blake said quickly, smugly—delighted at Mok's response. "You don't get those answers tonight."

"When?" Mok said, back to irritation. He set the candle on one of the cabinet's shelves. "You owe me. Or someone owes me. I didn't ask to be put into this."

"We don't ask to be born, either. But no one hands us all the answers. All we can do is search for them."

"That's what this is?" Mok demanded. He inched closer to the dwarf. "A search for answers? What kind of stupid—"

"A search, like life," Blake interrupted. "This is no different for you than any life. You have a training ground to learn and make decisions for what comes after. An opportunity to seek the answers about where you are going and why. After all, life is a quest, sometimes glorious, sometimes brutal, sometimes sad and painful, sometimes . . . hey!"

"I've figured some of this out, you know," Mok said in conversational tones, as if his hands were not again firmly around Blake's neck. "Someone is sending me through time. The same person who sends you after me and pulls you out again. How else could you and the girl follow me? And that cretin who tried to kill me. You don't even have to tell me how. I just want to know why. And if you don't tell me, I'll start squeezing and won't stop until my fingers meet in the middle."

"Nice try," Blake said, tapping his toes with impatience. "But I know you won't. And so do you."

"How do you know?" Mok asked, trying to force a sneer into his voice.

"Because you've come this far. Another type of person would never have made it out of Egypt, let alone go through the other worlds as you did."

Mok sighed and gave up. He dropped his hands to his sides. "I hope you're enjoying yourself."

"There are moments," Blake said. "Like when I blew out your candle and whispered from behind. I'll bet you almost wet y—"

"Just give me the message," Mok said, weary now. "Isn't this part of it? You deliver a message and then go away, so I can suffer through something I don't understand."

It was Blake's turn to sigh. "If you insist on taking the fun out of it."

"I do."

"Then here it is," Blake said. "Power for the sake of power is close to evil. Yet all of us have power to some degree. And to do right with the power we have often demands lonely, difficult choices."

Mok understood the seriousness in Blake's voice.

"The book?" Mok asked quietly. "Is this the power you mean?"

"There is more than one way to get the code book to England," Blake said. "You will arrive at the boat along the river in less than half an hour. I can promise you that. When you get there, think about what the book could mean to the world."

Without warning, without a shimmer, the dwarf disappeared.

CHAPTER 72

MAINSIDE. Cambridge faced the entire Committee in a conference room down the hall from Mok and his life-support machine.

Behind him, the vidscreen was gray. Unactivated.

Cambridge waited until the Committee members were seated.

"You may be wondering why I called an emergency meeting this early in the morning," Cambridge said. "Especially since the hourly updates e-mailed to most of your home Netsites show the candidate surviving well as he learns to deal with racial hatred and the difficulties of leadership."

Cambridge looked them over, one at a time. Some wore fitness suits. None bothered to dress in the togas that signified Technocrats. Few of them felt the need.

"But one of you," Cambridge continued, "believes something different. In fact, one of you is under the impression that Mok died last night."

Instant babble greeted Cambridge's statement.

He held up his hand for silence.

Instead of speaking again, however, Cambridge clicked a remote control at the vidscreen. It showed

Mok nearing the barge on the river, city lights twinkling in the background.

"But as you can see, Mok is alive," Cambridge said. "Very alive."

Beneath the conference table, one of the Committee members clutched his hands to his knees in a reaction of panic.

Impossible, this Committee member thought. *I watched Mok die last night. I reported it to the president of the World United. Millions of dollars are about to be wired into my offshore banking account.*

The Committee member listened to Cambridge as if his life depended on Cambridge's next words. Which it did.

"Why, then, have I called you here if Mok still lives?" Cambridge asked. "Because I know who among you tried to kill him."

CHAPTER 73

CYBERSPACE—PARIS. In the apartment, Mok stood in the dim light of the candle, staring at the spot where the dwarf had disappeared.

It was true, then, that someone was sending him through time. It was true, then, that there was a reason. A direction. And Mok knew now that he was watched, for the dwarf had known of Mok's actions in the other times and places.

But he still had so many questions. What was the reason? What direction? Why was he watched? When would it end?

He knew that there was only one way to find out: by going ahead and continuing through life . . . by moving forward, doing his best with the knowledge he had . . . and by continuing to learn.

Mok grabbed the sack that held the pieces of the radio. Although not as important as the code book, it was still crucial to remove them from the apartment.

Mok blew out the candle and carefully left the building. Just as carefully—despite Blake's promise of safety—he crept through the alleys of wartime Paris. Within the half-hour, he had reached the Seine River.

Paris was well over a thousand years old, and the river had long since been tamed into a wide, slow channel of water. Both banks were walls built of concrete blocks. The water smelled faintly like damp, moldy cloth. Occasional slaps of water hit the hulls of the boats tied to those walls, and city lights bounced off faint ripples.

It took Mok only a few minutes to find the barge Thaddeus had described. It sat low in the river. There were other flat-bottomed boats as well, designed to move cargo slowly down the sluggish river. Each had living quarters on top of the cargo hulls.

Mok knew from what Thaddeus had said that twenty Jews, as well as Thaddeus and Miriam, would later be hidden in the cargo hull, near the bow, behind a false wall. At midnight, French resistance fighters—those secret fighters of the Nazis who occupied Paris—would bring the other Jews.

To this point, everything had gone as Thaddeus had promised. Everything had gone, too, as Blake had promised. Except for one thing.

The lights in the windows of the barge.

Mok checked to make sure he'd found the right boat. The dim numbers on the hull were the ones Thaddeus had made him memorize. But there was something wrong.

Thaddeus had made one thing very clear to Mok. The window at the front and the window at the rear would both be lit. Only those two windows. That was the signal that everything was all right. If light shone from any other window, or if either of those two windows was dark, something had gone wrong.

And the rear window was dark.

CHAPTER 74

NOTHING ELSE about the barge seemed unusual. Mok saw no soldiers, no movement. The deck was empty except for coils of rope.

Had Thaddeus forgotten to light the rear window?

Mok wanted to go forward. He wanted to run away. The dwarf's words came back to him. *Does it frighten you to think of the book's power? The lives of thousands upon thousands are in your hands.*

Mok held the small flat notebook tightly against his chest, a reminder of its power. If he went forward and something was wrong, what would happen to the book? If he ran away, could he get the book to those who fought the Nazis?

To do right with the power we have often demands lonely, difficult choices.

Mok decided to go as far as possible—until it appeared danger should turn him back.

He crouched low, moving slowly from shadow to shadow, grateful that his dark clothing helped him to stay hidden. Ten slow minutes later, he was on the deck of the boat, creeping lightly.

Mok reached the front window. He listened. No sounds.

He drew a deep breath and inched his head

upward to peek inside. And nearly fell backward.

The light inside clearly showed a small, neat cabin with bare walls and a small dining table. Seated at the table were three people. Miriam, Thaddeus, and Wolfgang—the Gestapo officer.

This was not a social event.

Thaddeus and Miriam had their hands tied to the arms of their chairs. Wolfgang, his back to the window, held a pistol in his right hand.

Mok crouched down.

What should he do?

Think, he told himself. *Find a safe place to think.*

Mok crept backward, retracing his steps. He scanned the street, saw no one, and slinked off the barge into deeper shadows.

Hidden, he was deeply conscious of the small notebook. The code book could save thousands upon thousands of lives.

Again, in his mind he heard the dwarf's message.

There is more than one way to get the code book to England.

Indeed, there was. Mok had money. He had survived the street slums of Old Newyork; Paris would be far simpler. Given time, Mok could somehow find a way to get the code book into the right hands.

Yet . . .

He would have to leave Thaddeus and Miriam in the hands of Wolfgang, a Gestapo officer who obviously knew too much about the couple. If Mok ran now, he would condemn his friends to certain punishment, torture, and maybe death.

And probably the same fate awaited the twenty Jews who were to arrive at midnight.

Still, the dwarf's words haunted him. *Think of what the book could mean to the world.*

Mok realized the choice was simple. Twenty-two lives against thousands and thousands of lives. Sacrifice only twenty-two and save all those thousands.

But his heart told him differently. Mok could not bring the faces of those thousands into his mind. But all he had to do was close his eyes to see the love that Thaddeus and Miriam had for each other, to see them as they had first embraced on the street, to see Thaddeus comforting Miriam, to see Miriam's fear that a gang might have hurt Thaddeus.

How could Mok let them die?

He now understood what Blake had meant. *To do right with the power we have often demands lonely, difficult choices.* He might be able to ask advice, he might know the rules and laws, he might even face direct commands. But in the end, whatever he chose to do would be a decision he made alone. And how much harder when the choice is not clear . . .

The code book seemed to press heavier and heavier against his chest. Against his heart.

Church bells rang, rolling through the night. Ten bells. Thaddeus had explained to Mok that he could measure time by the bells. Two hours left until midnight when the twenty other Jews would arrive. If Mok did nothing, they would be captured.

As Mok waited and agonized in the deep shadows, he realized something else. He had a third choice: to not make a decision between two choices.

Save thousands and thousands? Or save Thaddeus and Miriam and the others on the barge?

Over and over again, the questions went through his mind.

Mok gritted his teeth.

And finally he decided.

He moved out of the shadows. Without looking back, Mok walked away from the river into the darkness of Paris at night.

CHAPTER 75

MIDNIGHT BELLS rang from a distant church. While the drifting snow had long since stopped falling, bitter cold remained. The sound of the bells seemed as brittle as the air that carried it.

Midnight. When the twenty would gather to be smuggled to safety.

Mok had returned to the river again. This time, however, he did not crouch and move with stealth from shadow to shadow. Instead, he marched boldly onto the barge. He crossed the deck without hesitation, went to the front cabin, and knocked softly.

"Come in," Thaddeus called.

Mok stepped in. He saw only Thaddeus and Miriam. Until Wolfgang, hidden behind the open door, calmly shut it.

"Finally," Wolfgang said, pistol at Mok's face. "Our little pigeon arrives."

Mok let his mouth drop.

"Come, come," Wolfgang said. "Must you be so surprised? We Gestapo are far ahead of the pitiful resistance movement."

"Thaddeus?" Mok said.

"I am terribly sorry," Thaddeus said. "We were—"

"Fools," Wolfgang broke in. "Thinking I had

actually let them go. You see, informers told us of their plan to escape with twenty other Jews. I arranged for them to be thrown out of their apartment. I arranged to be there to offer them help. But, of course, it was a trap."

"A second car was following behind," Thaddeus said, miserable. "It was the one that nearly hit you. When Wolfgang drove away, spies in the other car jumped out down the street and came back to follow us. When they realized Le Café Bordeaux was not our meeting place, they simply captured us again."

"I put a gun to his head," Wolfgang said. "But this stubborn old man was willing to die before telling me where he intended to meet the others. So I told him he could watch his wife die slowly instead." Wolfgang smiled with evil. "Then he told me everything."

The Gestapo officer glanced at his watch. "I expect the other Jews to arrive within minutes. There are soldiers below in the cargo hold waiting to capture them and send them to work camps. Since you have helped these Jews, you must suffer with them."

Mok showed fear. "No!" he cried. "I have something you want. Let me trade that for my life!"

"What could you have that I might want?" Wolfgang asked with a sneer.

Mok pulled a piece of paper from his pocket. He unfolded it and handed it to the officer.

"What is this?" Wolfgang asked, glancing at the scribbled notes.

"One page from a notebook that belongs to Thaddeus."

"No!" Thaddeus shouted. "You cannot tell him about the code book!"

"For my life I can," Mok said. Mok turned to Wolfgang and continued to speak. "You'll see that Thaddeus has unlocked a radio code. The top half shows the radio message. The bottom half shows what the code means."

Wolfgang stared hard at Mok.

"Sit against the wall," Wolfgang finally ordered. "I want to read this without wondering when you will jump at me."

Mok sat.

A half minute later, Wolfgang spoke again. "This is indeed important. Tell me more."

Mok did. Mok told Wolfgang about the crystal radio. About Thaddeus and his background. And about how Thaddeus had sent Mok back to the apartment for the code book.

When Mok finished, Wolfgang stroked his mustache. "Why shouldn't I just kill you now and search your body for the code book?"

Mok reached inside his jacket and pulled out a small black notebook. He tossed it to Wolfgang. "Because the one I carry is a fake. The other one is hidden. I intended to go to England with the Jews and, once safely there, sell the location of the real one for a fortune."

"Which you will now give to me instead?" Wolfgang asked, smirking.

"All I want is my life," Mok said.

"You cannot make that trade!" Thaddeus shouted. "It is worth our own lives to stop the invasion of England!"

"Shut up, old man," Mok said. "You are much nearer the grave than I. Life is still precious to me."

Thaddeus gaped at Mok. "You vile traitor. At least the Nazis make no disguise of their hatred. You pose as a friend and turn on us. May your soul rot forever. May—"

To stop Thaddeus's rising rage, Wolfgang lifted his hand to strike Miriam.

"Enough," Wolfgang said. "I want the code book. Where is it?"

Mok smiled. "Hidden on the barge, so I would have it near once we made it to England. Yes, I know you could easily kill me once you find it. But I believe this proves I can be of service to you in the future."

Wolfgang smiled back. "That is more than a possibility. You do appear to be a capable young man. Tell me where it is."

"No farther than the inside of a life jacket on the far side of the deck." Mok made motions as if to rise. "Shall I get it for you?"

"Am I stupid enough to let you go alone?" Wolfgang said. "Hardly. We'll go together. And quickly, before the other Jews arrive to be captured."

Mok stood.

"Hands on your head," Wolfgang said. "I will follow you."

Mok opened the door slowly and then obediently placed his hands on top of his head. The cold night air hit him hard. He took a deep breath and stepped forward, knowing the outcome of the war depended on the next few seconds.

CHAPTER 76

MOK MOVED SLOWLY. He did not want Wolfgang walking quickly.

One step. Two. Mok waited . . .

Then it happened. The loud thump. A muffled yell. The two resistance fighters on the roof had tackled Wolfgang!

Mok began to turn in triumph. But a loud roar and a bright burst knocked him to the deck.

Mok fell, twisted, one leg bent beneath the other.

For several shocked seconds, he didn't move. He stared up at the glow of lights from the city bouncing off low clouds.

He struggled to figure out what had made the noise and the bright burst. He tried to sit up.

He could do neither.

Pain hit. A surge of white heat flamed from his chest and spread through his body.

Still, Mok did not understand.

"He's been shot!" Mok heard a voice say. But the voice seemed distant, as if coming from the far end of a tunnel. "Get a cloth to stop the bleeding."

Shot?

A face bent over him.

"Can you hear me?" the man asked. It was one

of the resistance fighters. A small, compact man. Mok knew his name. Pierre. They'd spoken less than a half-hour earlier. "Can you hear me?"

What a dumb question, Mok thought. He said so to Pierre. In Mok's mind, he was talking clearly. But for some reason, Pierre didn't seem to understand.

Another man crouched down beside Pierre. Thaddeus.

"He's in shock," Pierre said to the old man. "I don't know what we can do to bring him back."

What did Pierre mean, bring him back? Where was he going? Mok tried to disagree, but he couldn't make his lips speak.

Darkness began to close in. Not the sudden whirling darkness that had sent him to the Holy Land from ancient Egypt.

This was a different darkness. A cold darkness where silence seemed to echo.

Sadness filled Mok. How could he now explain everything to Thaddeus? How he'd gone to retrieve the radio pieces because he knew Thaddeus would need it to find another way to escape. How he'd waited near the barge for the resistance fighters to appear with the Jews. How he'd told them of his plan to fool Wolfgang into stepping outside. How he'd actually thrown Wolfgang the real code book, hoping he could bluff Wolfgang. How . . .

Dimly, Mok saw that Miriam was on her knees, holding his hand, and Thaddeus was bent in prayer.

And dimly . . .

The blackness and silence became complete.

CHAPTER 77

MAINSIDE. Cambridge paced before the Committee. "Each of you, I'm sure, remembers the day we discovered a killer had been cybered onto the pirate ship."

Nods came from around the table.

"You will remember how our comtechs took so long to cyber Mok to the next site."

More nods.

Cambridge continued. "That night, I called each of you privately. I asked you to be the secondary backup of the password code that allowed access to the cybersite."

Again, more nods, this time with puzzled faces. Behind Cambridge, the three-dimensional images of Mok in cyberspace flickered silently across the vidscreen. But all eyes were on Cambridge.

Especially the eyes of one man. A man whose throat was dry with fear.

"Well," Cambridge said, "I gave a different password code to each Committee member. Ones that would put you each into a different ghost-site."

"Ghost-site?" one of the Committee asked.

"Ghost-site," Cambridge said. "A site that mirrored Mok's actual cybersite. But was not hooked to

Mok's virtual reality. We had twelve ghost-sites. That's what took the comtechs so long—getting those sites ready."

"I don't understand," another member said. "Why go to all the trouble?"

"Then all we needed to do was monitor the ghost-sites," Cambridge answered. "Since each of you was given a password to a different site, when the cyber-assassin appeared on a specific ghost-site, we would have our traitor. And last night, we discovered who it was."

Cambridge closed his eyes briefly, as if dreading the announcement.

Before he could speak, someone pointed at the screen and shouted.

"Mok! He's been shot!"

BACKSTORY VI

OLD NEWYORK, A.D. 2078. "Rufus, you have no place left to run!"

From far down the long, cool tunnel, the gang-lord's shout of anger echoed among the broken slabs of concrete. One wide section, the height of two men, leaned at an impossible angle, supported by the smaller pieces it had fallen upon. A shaft of sunlight streamed through a sewer grate in the street above, casting deep shadows. It was here that the man, the woman, and the baby crouched, hidden.

"Die! Die! Die!" This demented shouting came from the opposite direction in the tunnel, repeated again and again by the ganglord's warriors. The sound bounced off the jagged edges of the jumbled concrete and seemed to surround the three fugitives.

"I love you," the woman, Terza, whispered to the man.

"As I love you, my wife," Benjamin Rufus replied. He smiled sadly in the darkness of their hiding spot and tightened his arm around her shoulders.

"Can't we have more time together?" she asked. "Not even another day?"

"Shhh," he cautioned. He heard the braveness in her voice as she fought her tears. In his own sorrow, he hardly trusted himself to speak without choking on his words. He whispered, "That my illness has not taken me during my two years in the slums is a miracle. I, too, want to ask for more time. It takes effort to remember that I should instead give thanks for every extra hour God has allowed me to live with you."

The baby in Terza's arms gurgled with happiness, unaware of their danger. Benjamin held them both close, and his wife leaned her head on his shoulder. As the shouting grew closer from both sides, the man and the woman prayed in silence.

Benjamin murmured, "Remember our greatest hope, my love. For those without faith, death in this world means the end. But we have the joy given to us by Christ. Time here is short. But beyond waits an eternity of love."

"Can you be sure?" she asked as her tears began to fall.

"I have had my doubts," he said. "It is part of being human. But as death approaches, God strengthens my certainty. He *is* the Creator of this universe. I do not fear Zubluk because I do not fear death."

"Just another day together," she pleaded. "Another week. We can escape now and keep running. I cannot bear to say good-bye."

"No," Benjamin said quickly. If he allowed himself to consider it, he might take whatever time his body had left, even though he was weakened by illness. "You must leave now. Before they see you."

"I love you," she said one final time.

In answer, he found her hand and lifted it so she could feel the tears on his face.

Then Benjamin Rufus rose. He helped Terza climb the slab of concrete. She and the baby escaped through the sewer grate above.

When they were gone, he replaced the sewer grate and settled beneath the concrete slab again. And waited for the ganglord to arrive.

"I know you are here," Zubluk said into the grays and blacks of the tunnel shadows. "You were betrayed by one of your own. For only a few bottles of pure water, he told us how to find you."

"I am here," Benjamin replied from his hiding spot. He was confident that the echoes would make it difficult for them to locate him exactly.

"And your wife and child?"

"Do they matter? It is only me you want."

"I want you to pay," Zubluk said. "You have caused me too much trouble. If they are not with you, I will track them down."

Benjamin Rufus did not have to see Zubluk to know how the angry man looked. The giant always wore black leather. A fighter of many years, his battered face bore many old scars. As did his shaved head. Behind him would be his warriors. Equally fierce. Equally merciless.

"Tell me," Zubluk said. "Why? You've lived two years in the slums. Why?"

"Do you mean to distract me while your men circle around?" Rufus asked.

Zubluk laughed. "No. You're already a dead man. With you trapped like this, I don't need to play games. It is truly a question that has bothered me since you returned to the slums."

"Returned?" Rufus said. He had his own reason to keep the conversation going as long as possible. It would give his wife and baby time to get farther away. "Returned to the slums? So you know."

"Yes," Zubluk said. "I know who you are. So why did you come here from Mainside? From freedom and wealth and power and comfort? You were one of the few who ever escaped this island."

"Because where I once was blind, now I see," Rufus answered.

"Don't speak riddles with me," Zubluk snarled.

"Had you listened to the message I brought," Rufus said calmly, "you would know it is not a riddle."

"Bah!" If Zubluk thought it strange to converse with a voice coming from the darkness, nothing about his snort showed it. "A man died on a cross thousands of years ago. What does that matter to us today?"

"It is not his death that is important. But that he rose again and lives to this day. Believe, Zubluk.

Fall on your knees and believe. Even after all the terror you have inflicted on the poor people here, you will be forgiven and welcomed home."

Zubluk roared with laughter. "You speak as if I were about to die. Not you."

"I know I will die," Rufus said. "My body has been failing. Even without you and your sword, very soon my spirit will leave its frail prison. I am ready. But I fear you are not."

Silence. Benjamin Rufus had spoken with such certainty that it rattled the scarred ganglord.

Rufus listened for the scuffle of leather that would tell him the warriors were closing in. He heard only the quiet drips as water condensed on and fell from the cool walls of the tunnel.

"Zubluk," he called out. "Did you not wonder why it was so easy to find me? So easy to trap me?"

More silence. Rufus touched a small plastic box attached to his belt. Had enough time passed? Were Terza and the baby safe? Had she been able to clear others from the street above?

Rufus closed his eyes in brief prayer. He opened them again, straining for the first signs of Zubluk's warriors.

Finally, he heard it. Someone kicked a pebble. Zubluk's men had found him. It was time to act.

"Zubluk," Rufus said. "Do you now understand? I came from Mainside with a message. It is a message the people of the slums must be freed to hear. I have weapons you do not. And I am already dying."

"Get him!" Zubluk roared.

Shadows dived toward the space beneath the large slab of concrete.

Benjamin Rufus pressed the button on the small plastic box. A button that sent a tiny electronic signal to plastic explosives wedged into crevices of the tunnel wall.

There was a flash and the horrible thunder of thousands of tons of falling concrete. A great plume of dust rose into the slums from the sewer grate.

Then, half a minute later, there was silence again. Complete silence.

CHAPTER 78

MAINSIDE, A.D. 2096. "Oxygen! Now!" The doctor snapped the order without looking over his shoulder. It was a small room, and the doctor fully expected the medtech behind him to bring the portable tank and mask within seconds.

Head still down as he examined the body on the cot, the doctor spoke in calmer tones to the man standing beside him.

"Cambridge," he said. "I don't know how long we can keep Mok alive. The monitors all show signs of major trauma. Blood pressure down. Shallow breathing. Feeble heart rate. It's as if a bullet has actually hit Mok."

The doctor shook his head and finally looked up from the patient. "I almost wish he were bleeding."

"Because . . . ?" Cambridge prompted. His face, thin and hawklike, looked tight with worry.

The medtech handed over the oxygen tank. The room contained little beyond medical equipment and Mok's body. Aside from the medtech, the doctor, Cambridge, and of course Mok, no one else had been allowed into the room.

The doctor placed the oxygen mask on Mok's face.

As he turned dials on the tank, he said, "If he were actually bleeding, emergency surgery would stop the blood loss and stabilize him. As it is now, his body is reacting to what his mind believes, and we have no way of convincing his mind that the bullet and the wound don't exist."

Cambridge sighed. Mok was linked to a computer program designed to make virtual reality so believable it was impossible to tell it wasn't live. Once Mok believed death had struck him in cyberspace, it would scramble the nerve circuits in his brain, killing him in real time.

The doctor, short and red-headed, took another blood pressure reading. His lips tightened with concern.

"We must save him," Cambridge said in hardly more than a whisper. "Mok has just passed the final test. Without him to sway the World Senate vote, the heat bombs . . ."

Cambridge cut himself short. The doctor already knew the urgency. He didn't need the extra pressure of Cambridge telling him how thousands and thousands of slum dwellers might be fused into a molten puddle of glass and concrete and steel.

"At this point," the doctor said a few moments later, "oxygen doesn't seem to be helping. We'll need to risk emergency interference. Let's go to the back-up plan and send a doctor into cyberspace after him. Maybe virtual surgery will keep Mok from dying."

"I wish we could." Cambridge closed his eyes and pressed his hands against his face. "But we've lost Mok on the vidscreen. The comtechs are hoping we can land him at a new cybersite any second. Maybe then . . ."

It had been so close. So very close. Mok had been five minutes from returning as a hero. Cambridge agonized over what had gone wrong. How had cybersecurity been breached? Mok was not supposed to have been shot. Yet Mok believed the bullet wound so real it was draining his life.

Mok's breathing grew more shallow beneath the oxygen mask. Cambridge didn't need a medical background to know it was a bad sign.

"I have no choice but to inject him with adrenaline," the doctor said. "If that doesn't work, I don't know what else to do. Or how long he'll live to let me try something else."

Cambridge put his hand on the doctor's shoulder. "I'll tell the Committee you're doing everything possible. As for us . . ."

"Yes?" the doctor asked, reaching for a hypodermic needle.

"We'll be praying," Cambridge said as he headed out of the room. "For a miracle."

CHAPTER 79

CYBERSPACE—JERUSALEM. Shouts. Wailing. Babble.

Dust. Heat. Sun. Shadows.

Slowly, one by one, Mok made sense of each new impression. It seemed an icy blackness was melting away from him, bringing him into growing light.

He became aware of hard stone pressing against his body, of rough walls around him. He smelled rotting vegetables and fruit.

With the returning sensations came another: pain.

Mok lay on his side, and as he pushed himself up, pain lanced him. Pain from his back and shoulder.

He groaned. The sensation was white heat as he forced himself to his feet. He almost fell and leaned against the wall. He felt warmth on his ribs. With shock, he realized it was blood. His blood.

Memories returned.

He'd been on a river barge. At night. In Paris. Leading a Gestapo officer holding a pistol into a trap. He'd heard a bang of exploding air. He had twisted and fallen, staring up at the city lights bouncing off the low clouds. Faces had come into view. Faces that had then faded.

And now? Where was he?

Waking up in a new time and place was no longer strange to Mok. It had happened too many times already.

Indeed, Mok had learned that he could do little to control each new situation. If he waited and watched, he would discover his role. In all the previous times, though, he had never woken with his own blood soaking the clothing he wore.

Dizziness began to take Mok. Not the dizziness that signaled he would soon find himself in another time and place. But a frightening dizziness that instinct told him meant death.

He needed help.

Ahead, where the alley emptied into a street, he heard wailing and shouting. People. People who might help.

Mok staggered forward, leaving blood smears where he lurched against the stone of the wall.

A part of his mind took in the shapes of the archways and the tiled roofs. It reminded him somewhat of the streets he'd seen in Egypt, except this seemed more crowded.

The noise and babble grew louder as he neared the street. Mok found himself panting to get breath. He wanted to lie down and close his eyes, hoping for darkness to return and let him drift away.

A few more steps. People backed into the

entrance of the alley, as if the crowd on the street had forced them to retreat.

Mok fell. His grunt of agony drew the attention of a large man looking over the shoulders of people in front of him.

The man turned to Mok. He bent over Mok and lifted him to his feet. If the man felt any disgust at the blood on his hands from Mok's wound, he did not show it.

"My friend," the man said, "you are in a bad way."

The man was black haired and bearded, with a square face and dark eyes. Despite his bulk, he did not appear intimidating.

"Where . . ." Mok gasped at the effort it took to speak. "Where are we?"

The man frowned. "Jerusalem. During Passover. Did thieves beat you so badly that you cannot remember?"

"It hurts," Mok said. He could not remember ever in his lifetime in the slums asking for help. Weakness meant death in Old Newyork. But Mok had little more strength than a newborn baby. And there was something gentle about this large man. "Please . . ."

Mok couldn't croak out any more words.

"I will do what I can," the man said. "Yet we cannot move until the procession passes by."

Mok leaned against the man, on his feet only because of the man's arm around his waist. The man pushed through the small knot of people.

They grumbled but quieted at the sight of Mok's wound.

Only half conscious, Mok turned his head to look at the commotion headed toward them.

It took him long moments to sort out what he saw. There were soldiers, armed with short swords. They led a man, torn and bloody. Behind the man followed a large procession. The women in the crowd wailed and cried out.

It was not the loud public grief of the women that held Mok's attention, but the bloody man guarded by soldiers. The man was bent almost in half as he dragged two large beams of wood, tied together in the shape of a cross.

CHAPTER 80

THE MARKET STREET began down a hill, so Mok clearly saw the activity below him. The soldiers whipped and prodded the man carrying the cross. It was a great load, and the man fell. One soldier kicked the man. Others spit on him.

Wailing rose from the women behind the soldiers.

Somehow, with agonizing slowness, the man got to his feet again, bowed beneath the heavy cross. He pushed up the hill. It was obvious the man was near the point of exhaustion.

Still, the soldiers jeered.

The man's slow progress finally brought him near Mok. Mok saw that the man's face streamed with blood from puncture wounds caused by the crown of thorns he wore. The man fell again. Once again, soldiers kicked him.

This time, however, the man could not get up.

The tallest soldier surveyed the crowd. Looking up the street, his eyes turned on the man supporting Mok.

"You," the soldier commanded. "What is your name?"

"I am Simon," the man said, moving slightly to

shield Mok from the soldier's sight. "Of Cyrene."

"As I thought. From the country. You have a big, strong back. You carry the cross."

"And if I don't?" Simon asked.

"No one disobeys Roman commands," came the answer. "You'll die by the sword where you stand."

Simon looked around him. The crowd was silent, awaiting his answer.

"Someone take him," Simon said, setting Mok down gently. No one moved forward.

"This young man is hurt," Simon appealed to the people around him. "He needs help."

No one moved forward except the Roman soldier. He waved a menacing sword toward the farmer. "Take the cross now or die."

"I am sorry, my friend," Simon said to Mok. His voice held no hurry. No panic or fear. "I have no choice but to leave you. If he kills me, I cannot help you later."

Simon dug into his pocket and brought out a coin. He pressed it into Mok's hand. "Take this. Perhaps someone will accept payment to bind your wounds. I will return and look for you."

Mok nodded, too tired to thank the man from Cyrene.

Simon stepped into the narrow street. He walked with his shoulders square, keeping his gaze level to those of the crowd who stared at him. He bent his back to accept the weight of the cross. His strong legs pushed upward. The wooden beams rested solidly without wavering.

The soldiers kicked the other man to his feet.

"No!" a woman wailed. She had dark hair, and tears glimmered on her face. "This man is innocent! Let him live!"

Other women cried the same cry.

The man of the cross turned to them. "Women of Jerusalem," the man said, "don't cry for me. Cry for yourselves and for your children."

Whatever else the man said was lost to Mok, for the people around him began to press forward.

Mok tried to rise but was too weak. He fell back.

Through the legs of the people in front of him, Mok saw the procession begin to move up the hill again. Soldiers in front. The man among the soldiers. Simon behind. And the multitude of people following.

A few steps later, when the whipped and beaten man came opposite Mok, he stopped.

As if directed by an invisible hand, the people in front of Mok parted.

Mok, bleeding and exhausted from his own pain, raised his head. His eyes met the eyes of the man of the cross. A man with no significant features. A face neither ugly nor handsome. Hair neither long nor short. A build not powerful, not weak. Someone easy to overlook in a crowd. Except for his eyes.

The man's face was white from utter weariness. His beard was matted with blood and spittle. Yet the eyes . . .

The depth of the man's eyes lifted Mok's heart, thrilled Mok with an unspeakable peace.

The man reached out with a trembling hand.

A soldier knocked the man's hand away. Yet the man reached again toward Mok.

Mok was drawn to his feet. He somehow found the strength to reach out to the man of the cross.

"You are loved," the man said to Mok, his soft voice clear in the crowd's surging noise. "I know of your burdens, your pains. Follow me to my Father, and you shall find a home. Never again will you be lonely and afraid."

One of the soldiers stepped between them. The man stood strong, just for a moment, and his fingertips brushed against Mok's. It was the lightest touch, like the graze of a dove's wing.

The crowd's noise filled the space between them. The soldiers jeered. And the man was gone, shoved before Simon and the cross, up the narrow street.

Mok stared at his fingertips, as if there might be a mark there. How could that slight touch have filled him with such utter serenity, such clear understanding of the love of the God of the universe?

It was such an incredible mixture of joy and peace that it took several minutes for Mok to comprehend something equally strange and unexpected and beautiful.

He no longer felt weak. The white heat of pain had disappeared. He no longer bled.

Mok had been healed.

With disbelief, he stared up the hill at the crowd that had left him behind.

But Mok did not want to be left behind. He began to run toward the man of the cross.

CHAPTER 81

MOK COULD NOT FIGHT his way to the front of the procession. The crowd was too big, the street too narrow. He followed, all the while trying to make sense of his new surroundings.

He was in a city, of that he had no doubt. Every few paces, other streets led away from the one he walked. Crooked and twisting, they seemed to form a maze. Except for arched openings, the buildings of plastered white formed continuous lines so that the streets were almost like tunnels leading away in different directions. The people wore robes of all colors, many of the women with head coverings.

Jerusalem, Simon had said. *Jerusalem during Passover.*

It had been years since Mok had last held the audiobook of his childhood. Only fragments remained of what he could remember from that audiobook. Yet those fragments had sustained him during his years alone, struggling for survival in the desperate street slums of Old Newyork.

Jerusalem during Passover.

Mok's strongest impression of the audiobook had not been details, but hope. The legend of a man from Galilee, a man who had done wonderful things and helped many poor and lonely people, had given him hope. Mok wished he could be more certain of his memories, but hadn't the audiobook spoken of a place called Jerusalem?

As he wondered, the crowd spilled through a giant stone archway out of the city. With the buildings no longer surrounding him, Mok was able to see that they were among hills, which explained the angle of the streets. The land dropped steeply into a valley and rose just as steeply on the other side. He noticed the dusty green of stocky trees rising in small groves from the brown of arid land. Beyond, Mok saw the tops of other hills lined against the pale blue of the sky.

He did not spend much time surveying the view, for the crowd had spread, and he was able to push forward. It took him only minutes to reach the front.

What he saw shocked him. He briefly stepped back in horror.

The cross that Simon had carried lay on the rocky ground. Simon was gone. The man of the cross, the man who had healed Mok, stood with his head bowed beside that cross. The Roman soldiers continued to guard him.

But this was not what horrified Mok. No, it was the sight of two more crosses, both of those also lying flat on the ground.

Nor was it simply those two crosses. Rather, it was the activity at each cross that shocked him.

For a man had been laid on each of those crosses. Those two men had been beaten, and soldiers held their arms along the beams of the crosses.

Mok had arrived at the very moment when a soldier had lifted a massive hammer and begun to pound an iron spike into the wood of the cross—through the hand of one of the men.

Thud. The hammer came down. *Thud. Thud.*

The man shrieked in agony. Half of the crowd roared approval while the other half wailed in protest. Unfazed by the reactions of the spectators, the soldier moved to the man's other hand and began the process again.

The second man, held by soldiers to the second cross on the ground, began to cry in fear. The third man, with the eyes of eternity, simply continued to stand quietly with his head bowed.

When the solider began to pound spikes into the ankles of the first man, Mok turned his head, unable to bear the sight of the blood. But the sounds still reached him.

Not once among all the cruelties that Mok had seen in the slums of Old Newyork had he ever seen anything close to this. He felt his stomach flipping, and Mok had to struggle to keep from vomiting.

It wasn't over.

The soldier with the hammer moved to the second man. Others lifted the first cross into place. On top of the hill, it stood outlined against the sky.

And other soldiers took the third man, the one who had healed Mok, and placed him on the third cross still on the ground. He did not protest. He did not cry out in fear. He quietly allowed the soldiers to stretch his arms into place.

"No!" The loud cry ripped itself from Mok, almost before he was aware he had joined the wailing of women nearby. "No!"

Mok knew nothing about why the men were being nailed to the beams of wood. He knew nothing about the men. Nothing except the depth of the third man's eyes and his gentleness and his promise to Mok just before their fingertips had brushed.

Even with what little he knew, Mok was as certain as he breathed that the third man did not deserve to be hung on a cross.

"No!" Mok cried. He rushed forward.

A soldier saw him and slammed his head with a sideways swing of his spear. Mok tumbled backward and lost all sight and sound to an overwhelming darkness. Not the familiar whirling darkness of cyberspace, but the painful darkness of losing consciousness.

CHAPTER 82

MOK WOKE to perfume. His head was cradled in a woman's lap. She gently wiped his face with a cool cloth.

"Who are you?" Mok asked.

"Mary Magdalene," she answered. "I have promised myself to care for you when I am able. But please forgive me. I cannot take you away from here yet."

Mok blinked. He saw he was still on the hillside. Surrounded by a crowd. All three crosses now stood against the sun.

The woman mistook his silence and hurried to explain more. "You tried to save our Teacher," she said. "You deserve help. But we cannot leave him."

She began to weep.

Mok ran his tongue over his teeth. None were broken. He eased up to a sitting position. His head throbbed, but aside from a tender spot where the spear had hit his skull, he felt no other damage.

The woman continued to weep. Another woman sat beside her and tried to comfort her.

"Mary, Mary," the other woman said, "remember his teachings. Remember his love."

"Who is that man?" Mok asked them both.

295

"And why have they done this to him?"

Mary drew a deep breath. She straightened her posture. "He is Jesus of Nazareth. And the Romans have crucified him because—"

"Jesus of Nazareth!" Mok forgot his pain. "The Galilee Man!"

Mary nodded, puzzled at Mok's excitement. "Yes," she said with some hesitation. "He is from Galilee."

Mok stared at the cross in awe. Jesus was not a legend, but truth! Mok had found the Galilee Man of his childhood audiobook!

In the same instant, Mok's joy turned to bitter sorrow. This Jesus was beaten and hanging from a cross—about to die. Where was the hope in that?

Unless the rest of the audiobook had also spoken the truth. Unless this Jesus would rise again from the dead as the audiobook had promised.

Mok marveled in silence. If the man named Jesus rose from the dead, he truly was the Son of the God of the universe. And if the Son of God had come to earth, how could any person knowing of it not choose to follow Jesus?

Yet . . .

Mok shook his head. Beaten and hanging from a cross. Could Mok really believe what seemed impossible, that this man would come to life again after death had taken him?

Mok wanted to believe. Mok also doubted.

He turned to Mary to ask her more questions.

But she was no longer there. Nor was the crowd. Nor anything else but the familiar darkness that told Mok he was about to be spun into a new time and place.

CHAPTER 83

MAINSIDE. "Unbelievable!" the red-headed doctor said. "Cambridge. Look at this!"

Cambridge crossed the medical room in three quick, long steps. He stood beside the doctor at the cot where Mok lay motionless.

The doctor pointed at the various monitors of Mok's life-support system. "Everything is back to normal," the doctor said. "Pulse. Blood pressure. Even brain waves."

"Back to normal?" Cambridge asked.

"He was only moments away from death," the doctor said. "I can tell you, in all my years as a doctor, I have never seen such a dramatic and complete recovery."

Cambridge bowed his head briefly. The doctor respected the silence. When Cambridge looked up again, the doctor continued.

"You and your prayers deserve full credit for whatever happened in cyberspace," the doctor said. "Nothing I did seemed to help."

Cambridge was about to reply, but he froze. And pointed.

On the cot, Mok opened his eyes.

A few moments later, Cambridge pushed Mok's wheelchair to the window to let him stare out at the view. Cambridge moved to the corner of his desk and sat casually, half facing Mok, half facing the window.

Cambridge composed his thoughts. So much was happening so fast. Less than an hour earlier, Cambridge had confronted the Committee, about to reveal the traitor among them. Then the medical crisis with Mok had taken him away.

The Committee members were still under guard in the conference room, divided by the knowledge of a traitor among them, yet strangely united by their prayers for Mok. Cambridge had to deal with Mok before he returned to the Committee.

"You came from there," Cambridge finally said, pointing at the hazy, distant street canyons.

From his wheelchair, Mok squinted against the sunlight. It had taken half an hour to completely revive him. He had been motionless on the cot for so long that his muscles were still too weak to allow him to walk.

"Why should I believe you?" Mok asked after a long, thoughtful pause. "From what you said about this cyberspace . . ."

Cambridge hid a smile. In the time since Mok had returned, Cambridge had not been able to tell him much. An illiterate Welfaro would be expected to spend days trying to comprehend computers and cyberspace and virtual reality. Yet Mok had grasped the concept immediately.

"What I said about cyberspace was that the computer supplied your brain with the sights, smells, sounds, tastes, and feel of an artificial world. The program would adjust to the decisions you made, as you were making them. To your mind then—"

"I know, I know. To my mind then, the new worlds were completely real," Mok said. "Which is why I wonder if this, too, is part of cyberspace. You, too, could be part of the program. All of this could still be happening in my mind. It could simply be another cybersegment."

"It could," Cambridge finally allowed, impressed at Mok's logic. "Given the effectiveness of virtual reality, I'm not sure how I can convince you otherwise. Perhaps I can only ask you to listen as if you truly had returned."

Mok watched the distant skyline for several minutes.

Cambridge, acutely aware of the Committee crisis in the conference room, showed no signs of impatience. It was infinitely more important to convince Mok to join their cause.

"All right," Mok said, turning back to Cambridge. "It matters little to me how I was sent into those other worlds. I do, however, want to know why. If you promise to answer that, I will listen."

YOU WERE BORN into a world without hope," Cambridge began. "It is a giant prison where water is more precious than a person's blood."

Cambridge paused soberly. "Not that I need tell you this in great detail."

"No," Mok said quietly. A lifetime of memories of the harshness were enough reminder.

"Hopeless as it might seem," Cambridge continued, "I doubt those who live there would choose death over life."

"No," Mok said again, more quietly. He had seen how hard people fought to stay alive.

"Here on Mainside," Cambridge said, "the wealthy and powerful have determined that your life and those of others in Old Newyork are not worth sustaining. The World United government wishes to destroy Old Newyork. Most of the steel has been scavenged. They see no reason to continue supplying water. At the end of the month, they intend to . . ."

Cambridge stared away from Mok, at the slums, lost in contemplation of the horror.

"Yes?" Mok prompted.

"Heat bombs. Far, far more effective than the atomic bombs of another age. The concrete and glass of the entire island will fuse. No man, woman, or child will survive."

"What?!" Mok half stood, then grunted in pain and fell back in his wheelchair.

Cambridge got up from his desk and began pacing the office as he spoke. "You asked me why you were sent into cyberspace. Let me answer by telling you about a man named Benjamin Rufus. Decades ago, he founded Benjamin Rufus Holdings, a giant Internet company, and became one of the wealthiest men on the planet. Twenty years ago, he gave up wealth, power, everything— to go from Mainside into Old Newyork. Why? He wanted to begin change there."

"He could have sent someone else," Mok said.

"Perhaps. But he had reasons to go himself. On Mainside he left behind his corporation, its money, and a committee of men directed to use the profits to accomplish what Rufus planned to begin himself in Old Newyork before he died. He wanted to estab- lish a better life for the people in Old Newyork. Especially for its children.

"There are hundreds of thousands in the slums," Cambridge said. "It seemed an impossible task, with the ganglords and the slave factories and the total chaos of a giant prison without laws. But Rufus began an underground church in Old Newyork, bringing the message of eternal hope to a place where the gospel of Jesus Christ had been lost over the generations."

"The Galilee Man!" Mok said.

Cambridge smiled. "Yes, Jesus of Nazareth. Yet mere words of hope were not enough. In the slums, we continued Rufus's mission by developing hidden pockets of Christians who helped others. Not Churchians, who simply preached and judged those who would not follow their rules, but followers of Jesus, who acted, mostly in secret, to help others."

Mok smiled. "Now I understand the stories. Time and again in the slums, I heard about women and children who were rescued or given food but didn't know who to thank for the help."

"Yes," Cambridge said. "It was not yet time for them to move openly. Even then, these small groups who led by example were able to bring others to follow the Galilee Man. Hundreds of groups formed over the years, but no group included more than a dozen people.

"Because of the thousands and thousands in the slums and the threat of ganglords, we needed to maintain secrecy until we were ready. Our final goal was to send a single leader into the slums, a leader who could use the full wealth and power of Benjamin Rufus Holdings to unite these underground Christians in an open struggle against the evil in the slums."

Cambridge stopped pacing. He stood beside Mok's wheelchair.

"We had set up the cybertests to find a leader to send into Old Newyork to unite the underground movement," Cambridge said. "This leader has to be strong, trustworthy. For this leader, once free in the slums with the money and help from us on Mainside, would literally have the unchecked power of a king."

Cambridge put his hand on Mok's shoulder. "Remember Egypt? We need someone who has a sense of justice so strong that he would face death rather than let another die for him. The castle? We need someone willing to stand firm in his faith, no matter how great the pressure to do otherwise. And so on. Each stage was a way to test our candidate. A dozen of the best-educated Mainsiders failed. We had no leader. Until you."

"Me?"

"Only you passed, Mok. Only you made it through all the cybertests. My great regret is that you were sent into the test without your permission. You were the only candidate who didn't realize he *was* a candidate. Almost the way a baby is born and must live through the quest of life."

"I would have accepted the challenge had you asked," Mok said.

"That pleases me," Cambridge said. "Yet with all the choices you made in all those times and places, there remains another. Will you accept the leadership? Because now, even that slight hope for Old Newyork is in danger."

Cambridge shook his head sadly. "I told you of

the government proposal to simply erase Old Newyork. Certain real estate developers can't wait to get their hands on the land. The bill has been drafted. Tomorrow, it goes to a final vote. Our sources tell us that of the fifteen hundred senators, seven hundred will vote in favor of dropping the heat bombs, seven hundred will vote against, and one hundred are undecided."

"What can I do?" Mok asked.

"Stand up before the World Senate. Help us convince fifty-one out of those final one hundred not to vote for the total destruction of Old Newyork."

Mok frowned. "They have no reason to listen to me."

Cambridge allowed himself a mysterious smile. "I believe they do. Please remember two things about what I'm going to tell you next. First, it must remain a sworn secret between us until the time is right."

"And second?" Mok asked.

"What I have to tell you will make your decision to help us much more difficult than you can imagine."

CHAPTER 85

ONE HOUR LATER, Cambridge and Mok stood at the head of a long table in the conference room.

The Committee members waited for Cambridge to speak. Cambridge gestured at the coffee cups and plates of half-eaten food scattered around the table.

"You have waited with great patience," Cambridge said. "I believe you will have found it worth your while."

Cambridge smiled. "Let me introduce Mok. You've shared his cyberadventures. You've been grateful for his decisions. And now, by a miracle, he is with us after the World War II shooting. I'm pleased to say he has accepted our request to return to Old Newyork."

When the applause died down, Cambridge looked at his watch.

"Some of you may find it hard to believe that only half the morning has passed since you gathered for our emergency meeting," Cambridge said. "I regret the guards in the hallway, but as you know, one of us has betrayed the cause. Were it not for Mok's medical crisis . . ."

Many of the Committee nodded. All of them understood.

"Anyway," Cambridge said, "it is time to finish the difficult task that began this morning."

Cambridge turned to Mok. "You should know what has happened. While you were in cyberspace, a killer was sent after you."

"Barbarossa," Mok whispered. "On the pirate ship."

Cambridge nodded. "And in real time, another killer made an attempt—here in this building. That assassin was caught. Plastic surgery had made him identical in appearance to Committee member Stimpson."

All eyes turned to Stimpson. He sat at the far end of the table, a blue-eyed man with blond hair carefully brushed back.

"It was a stroke of genius on the part of whoever paid the assassin," Cambridge said. "Our surveillance cameras clearly showed the killer's face. Had he escaped, we would all have believed he was Stimpson, not an impersonator."

Murmurs of sympathy spread around the table for Stimpson.

"Yet," Cambridge said to Mok, "we did find a way to trap the Committee member who betrayed us. He was responsible for using the sequence code to allow the killer Barbarossa into cyberspace after you. This occurred during your time in the cybersegment set in France."

Cambridge then turned to the others. "I won't drag this out further. This morning, all of you heard the details of how we set up ghost-sites in cyberspace to monitor your activities. When one of you made a move against Mok, we learned exactly which one of you is the betrayer."

Cambridge pointed at a man sitting on the left-hand side of the table. He was a dark-haired man of medium height and medium build.

"It is you, Phillips," Cambridge said. "This Committee has been dedicated to its cause for twenty years. All this time you have worked with us, eaten with us, shared with us. There should be no punishment too great for one who betrays friends. However, that is not for us to decide. Harming you will harm your family, and they do not deserve to share in your punishment. Instead, we will send you away, trusting that God's judgment will be rendered when he sees fit."

Phillips bowed his head as shouts of anger echoed through the room. Several men leaned across the table, as if to grab him.

"No!" Cambridge ordered. "We will not add a crime of revenge to his crime of betrayal."

In the following stunned silence, Cambridge turned to Phillips. "Have you anything to say?"

Phillips shook his head.

"Then go," Cambridge said. "We have greater concerns than your miserable existence."

Phillips pushed his chair away from the table. Silently, he left the room. Not one Committee member turned to watch his departure.

CHAPTER 86

IN THE MORNING SUNSHINE, Cambridge and Mok stood at the bottom of the wide marble steps of the Great Congress Hall of the World United government. Hundreds of men and women of all nations filled the steps, talking to each other in groups of twos and threes and fours.

Mok looked younger than he had the day before. A blue silk toga had transformed him from a slum dweller to a handsome young Technocrat.

Mok scanned the scene, intent on observing as much as he could. This site and these politicians, Cambridge had explained, ruled the destiny of the world's billions of people.

The building before him reflected that importance. It seemed to reach as high as a mountain, with huge columns of polished stone supporting the arched marble of the entrances.

A bell began to ring, chiming three times and pausing before ringing three more times. Again and again. People began to flow up toward the main entrance.

"It is time," Cambridge said. "Everything depends on the next few hours."

The ceiling of the hall was a large, graceful curve at least three stories above the assembled senators. It reflected sound so clearly that the speaker at the front of the giant hall did not need a microphone to address the fifteen hundred people assembled.

He raised his hands and received instant silence, the traditional respect given to the president of the World United. Mok and Cambridge, sitting in guest seats near the back, heard clearly, for the interior was built for the slightest sounds to travel without echoing.

"As you all know by your agenda," the president said, "we will begin by reviewing the status of the slum area known as Old Newyork."

Behind him were three vidscreens, each two stories tall. While the outside screens were blank, the middle screen showed the speaker himself. His black silk toga hung from a tall and bulky body. He had white hair that made a sharp contrast with pale skin, flushed slightly pink. His voice was deep and commanding. Even without the presidency to cloak him with power, he was an intimidating man.

"Administration staff have reviewed all the debate requests and narrowed them down to two," the president continued. "As usual, each side will be represented once, with time allotted for counterpoints. I trust you have all read the overview for finer details."

Cambridge leaned over to whisper to Mok.

"With so many bills in each session," he explained, "senators rarely take time to read the reports. That's why what we say will be so important."

Mok nodded and swallowed, trying to work moisture into a mouth dry from nervousness.

"I now invite the honorable senator from Jersey North to come forward."

Cambridge whispered again as they watched a short, bald man walk with a cane toward the podium.

"Look to the right of the screens," Cambridge said. "You see that large black square with hundreds of small lights?"

"Yes," Mok whispered in return. Some were lit red, some green, and some white.

"A hundred years ago, before the World United assumed its role as the seat of world power, voting was done differently. Senators listened to endless arguments and only voted once. Now debate is limited by a preset time, and senators vote by pushing one of three buttons before them. They are free to change their votes as often as they want until time has run out. The count that stands then is considered the final vote. It has become something like the running scoreboard of a sporting match, and debaters play their arguments accordingly. You'll see that the board already shows some totals."

Mok gave no comment about the numbers on the board.

"I'm sorry," Cambridge said. "I forget you are handicapped by a lack of formal education. Don't be embarrassed that you cannot read. I'll simply explain."

The bald senator with a cane had almost reached the podium.

"The totals at this point reflect what we expected," Cambridge whispered. "There are seven hundred and three red lights, showing votes in favor of destroying Old Newyork, and seven hundred and two green lights against. The ninety-five white lights indicate the undecided senators."

The giant middle screen showed the senator's round-faced image, magnifying large eyebrows that seemed to hold all the hair missing from his scalp.

"Honorable Senators," he began, "my argument will be brief, simply because not much needs to be said. For decades, we have funneled criminals into Old Newyork. We send millions of gallons of pure water into the slums and in return receive less and less steel each day. Should we continue to take water away from our children and our law-abiding citizens? Should we continue to support lawless scum who murder each other and force the weak among them to work as slaves? The answer is no.

"Think of this as a war for survival, not unlike the great Water Wars. In each of your countries, millions died then. Should we let those millions of deaths mean nothing against the relatively few people in Old Newyork who take such a large amount of water? Should we give away water that was bought by the blood of your own people?"

The senator paused dramatically and spoke quietly, which made the entire audience lean forward. "In Old Newyork, they are not people but lawless animals. Erase them now and your voters will thank you by returning you to office next election."

He paused again. "Remember, it is not about what you feel, but about what your voters want. And you know voters care far more for their own water than for the scum who fill that island prison. So, ask yourself, do you each want to remain a World United senator?"

He stepped away from the podium and leaned on his cane as he hobbled back toward his seat. His slow, painful progress down the long aisle presented the picture of a noble man suffering for a righteous cause.

At first slowly, and then as fast as blinking eyes, green lights began to change to red. Before the senator had reached his seat again, the totals showed 53 undecided and 466 against. Nine hundred and eighty-one votes now favored total destruction of Old Newyork.

CHAPTER 87

THE PRESIDENT RETURNED to the podium. He consulted his notes. The giant screen showed that he held every muscle on his face motionless as he called for the next speaker.

"Countering the words of our honorable senator from Jersey North," the president said, "will be a common citizen named Johnson Cambridge."

Murmurs rose among the senators.

"Silence in the Assembly," the president ordered. "While this is unusual, Cambridge is speaking on behalf of African Senator Harper Chaim."

The president cleared his throat. The giant screen made it obvious that he was furrowing his eyebrows in disapproval. "I want the Assembly to note that Cambridge is from Benjamin Rufus Holdings, one of the world's largest single companies. I also think it fair to note that the Rufus company donates millions of dollars each year to Senator Chaim's region. You are thus forewarned of the obvious monetary reason for Senator Chaim to step aside, and you are welcome to vote accordingly."

Immediately, more of the green and white lights flicked to red.

As Cambridge and Mok stood, a ripple of boos greeted them. Cambridge spoke quietly to Mok as they walked the aisle to the podium. "That was an unfair introduction. Those millions are spent in helping Chaim's people develop farmland to feed themselves."

Mok was concentrating too hard on walking straight ahead to reply. He was afraid of tripping with all the eyes upon him.

Finally they reached the podium and, side by side, faced the entire Assembly. Cambridge was forced to wait until the scattered booing ended.

"If your argument is water," Cambridge said, "Old Newyork will *give* you water."

He braced himself on the podium with both hands and leaned forward. "Yes. You heard me correctly. Old Newyork will not take millions of gallons of water from Mainside; it will produce not only enough water for itself but also extra water to be shipped into Mainside."

Senators began flipping through the pages in their reports. This was an incredible piece of news.

"You will not find that proposal in your notes," Cambridge said. "It was not until yesterday that the owner of Benjamin Rufus Holdings signed an agreement to invest twenty billion dollars in large-scale water purification factories to be constructed in Old Newyork. These water converters—not steel scavenging, not slave factories—will be the basis of Old Newyork's new economy."

Red lights began to turn green. Within seconds, nearly the entire board glowed green.

The president strode forward and held up his hands for silence.

"Assembly," the president said, "that I am using my position to break into this debate shows the seriousness of my concerns. Some of you are swayed too easily by promises. I will pose questions of hard reality for our visitor. How do you expect to convince Mainside workers to enter the slum prison of Old Newyork? And once there, how would you expect to protect them against the ganglords who run the slave factories?"

Cambridge smiled a peaceful smile. "Your Worldship, it will be people within Old Newyork who work at the water purification converters. Not Mainsiders."

The president laughed. "Those people have no education. No law. They are animals that cannot be tamed, no matter how many soldiers you might send into the slums."

Green lights began turning back to red.

Cambridge's peaceful smile did not waver. "Your Worldship, I agree this is a bold plan. I believe that within a year, the people themselves will provide their own law and order, their own schooling."

The president snorted. "How do you expect this insane plan to work?"

"Christian principles," Cambridge said. "As simple as it seems, people in Old Newyork will

317

help one another, following in the footsteps of Jesus Christ of Nazareth."

"Christianity is outlawed!" the president said in a half-shout.

"With all due respect, Your Worldship, as you have pointed out, there are no laws in Old Newyork. There, then, the Mainside ban against Christianity does not apply."

More than a few faces in the large crowd grinned with appreciation at the truth in Cambridge's loophole. Yet no more of the lights changed to green; all attention was on the debate, not the voting.

Cambridge turned to appeal to the senators. "The Benjamin Rufus company has found someone who will unite an existing underground movement in the slums. This person will be granted the resources of Benjamin Rufus Holdings to deliver food, teachers, police, and whatever else is required to give the people of the slums a chance to save themselves."

Cambridge pointed to the giant screen on his left. "In moments, you will see that person. You will see scenes from cyberspace that tested him to the utmost. All I ask is that you watch and make your decision accordingly. Yes, I know you will have many questions about the details of the Rufus company plan. These will be answered in a full report to your administration. For now, honorable senators, all we ask is that you vote to delay the destruction of Old Newyork for two years. Give us that chance."

Cambridge nodded at a comtech. Seconds

later, images began appearing on the screen. First came an animated explanation of how cyberspace worked, how the candidate did not know he had been placed in cyberspace, and the purpose of each of the cybertests. Then, in full color, Mok saw the actions that were stamped in his memory as surely as if they had been real.

He watched the crucial moments of his time in ancient Egypt, with execution a threat. The Holy Land castle. The pirate ship. The Wild West. France and World War II in 1943.

Mok squirmed with embarrassment at all the attention. Yet when the cybersegments ended, many of the senators rose and applauded him.

In the silence that followed, Cambridge spoke again, more quietly.

"This young man before you is the same candidate you saw on the screen. His name is Mok, and he is from Old Newyork. He survived a quest that has prepared him to return to the slums and help his people, fully backed by the world's largest corporation. How then do you vote?"

Nearly all the red lights and nearly all the white lights disappeared in a blur of green.

"No!" It was the president's turn to speak. "Let the Assembly know that this man is lying. Think! Benjamin Rufus company is famous because its founder did not leave an heir. Have you forgotten it is run by a board of directors? When Cambridge said the owner has agreed to invest billions in Old Newyork, he was telling you something impossible.

And if that is impossible, we cannot believe the corporation is willing to put its resources into helping the people of the slums."

Lights began to flick back to red.

Cambridge nodded at Mok.

Mok put up his hand with some uncertainty. His movement directed the president's attention to him.

"Yes?" the president asked with a snarl.

Mok stepped directly behind the podium. "Honorable senators," Mok began. His voice croaked. He licked his lips and tried again. "Honorable senators, Cambridge did not lie. Yesterday, the owner of Benjamin Rufus Holdings did review plans for water purification. Yesterday, the owner did approve those plans."

Mok took a deep breath. "How do I know?"

He took another deep breath to speak. "I am that owner. I am the son of Benjamin Rufus. I have inherited his corporation."

CHAPTER 88

THE PRESIDENT thundered, "No! No! No!" Hundreds of excited, small discussions stopped among the senators. The president pointed at the vote board, lit with 1,328 green lights.

"Five minutes remain until the vote is frozen," said the president, slightly calmer. "By then, I expect a majority vote in favor of destroying Old Newyork."

If possible, the Assembly grew even quieter.

"As you know, the office of president allows for an override of majority if the president deems this an issue of global security," he continued. "I have received reports that the ganglords intend to break out of Old Newyork and begin war on Mainsiders. It is not something I wanted made public for fear of starting a panic. This, however, leaves me no choice. I command you to vote for the destruction of Old Newyork."

He, and his large image on the screen, glared out at the Assembly.

Slowly, the green lights began to switch to red. Within a minute, the vote board was as red as it had been green earlier.

"Thank you," the president said. He looked at

the clock. "Soon the vote will be official. After tomorrow, Old Newyork will exist no more. Now we can move on to less troublesome Assembly matters."

The president turned to Cambridge and Mok. "You are invited to leave."

"No," Cambridge said boldly for all the senators to hear. "You have lied. There is no plan for ganglords to break out."

"How dare you accuse me of lying?! What would I have to gain by that?! Guards—"

Without warning, the live image of the president wavered on the large center screen. It went blank. A new vidsegment appeared, showing two men on a bench in a park. As the camera closed in on the two men, audio broke through, interrupting the president's command. When the recorded voices echoed through the hall, the president snapped around to see what was happening on the screen.

It was his voice that reached the senators, his face clear on the giant screen.

"You want payment?" the president was saying to the other man. "Don't be ridiculous. Our deal was simple. Find a way to kill that miserable slum kid before he passed all their cybertests. But Mok is not dead. He is due to testify tomorrow before the Assembly of Senators. I will not pay you a thing."

"Yes, you will, Your Worldship." The camera closed in on the other man. Not Phillips, as Mok had expected, but the Committee member named Stimpson. *Stimpson?* Mok wanted to turn to Cambridge and ask about this unexpected sight, but Stimpson continued to speak and Mok didn't want to miss a word. "I have recorded many of our conversations. If you don't pay, I'll go public."

The president at the podium shouted at the comtechs. "Stop! Stop!"

The comtechs lifted their hands in bewilderment, as if they, too, were unable to understand how this vidsegment was overriding their controls.

The president ran to the screen. He tried to pull it down. It was a futile attempt, for the screen towered over him like a building.

"Blackmail?" the image of the president snorted on the vidscreen. "You fool. The men who have arranged to buy the land base of Old Newyork once it's destroyed are men with enormous power. Even I am afraid of what they might do to me if I do not get the World Senate to vote for the heat bombs. If you attempt to blackmail me, you will be dead within days, no matter where you try to hide."

On the vidscreen, the president rose from the park bench. "However, it will be less troublesome to throw you a bone than to risk inquiries that might result from your death. I will make billions for my part in this, and I am willing to toss you a few million. Send me all the recorded conversations, and my secretary will credit whatever bank account you prefer. Remember, though, if you ever attempt to blackmail me or even contact me again, you will be killed."

The screen went blank.

The president turned from his vain efforts to

pull down the screen. He faced the Assembly.

As one person, all the senators rose and began to boo.

The president fell to his knees.

Mok raised his voice to be heard as he spoke to Cambridge. "The other man on the Committee? Phillips? He was not the traitor?"

"Phillips agreed to take the blame," Cambridge said. "So that we could follow the real betrayer. Stimpson. It was brilliant on his part to arrange the plastic surgery for the assassin to look like him. We would have never suspected him without the ghost-site trap that gave him away."

"But in the meeting—" Mok began.

"We wanted Stimpson to feel safe enough to approach whoever had paid him to betray us," Cambridge explained. "Field ops followed him with long-range vidcams. We never dreamed we'd get a segment as good as we did. From there, it was simple to plug the vidsegment into the programming here."

The booing continued. But the senators were doing one other thing. Still standing, they reached down to their vote buttons.

For the final time, red lights began to change to green. When the time limit ended, not one light on the vote board showed red or white.

CHAPTER 89

A SMALL BREEZE riffled the Hudson River below an over-cast sky. Cambridge and Mok stood at the rails of a ferry, staring across at the skyline of Old Newyork.

"You know, of course, that a few years ago the Committee completed a tunnel beneath the river," Cambridge said.

"Over the years, that is how you have helped build the underground churches that wait for our arrival," Mok replied.

"You listen well. So now you might wonder why we are on this ferry instead."

Metal gates clanked behind them as the ferry left the dock.

"Sentimental reasons," Cambridge continued. "It was on a ferry like this that I last saw your father, some twenty years ago. He was doing much as you are, leaving behind the power and wealth of Benjamin Rufus Holdings to help those in Old Newyork. It just seems right that you also return by ferry."

"I wish I could remember him," Mok said. "And I wish I could remember my mother."

"I understand," Cambridge answered quietly. The ferry pushed against the river current. It was only a ten-minute ride, but the shores of each side were worlds apart. "All I can tell you about your mother is what I learned from Benjamin."

Cambridge paused. The ferry engines hummed in the background.

"Your father went into Old Newyork with a lung disease, only expecting to live for a few months," Cambridge explained. "He had a vidphone of course, which is how I stayed in contact with him. When your mother helped him escape from a ganglord named Zubluk, they spent enough time together to fall in love. I believe it was their love that kept him alive for two more years."

Cambridge paused.

"He was there to bring the New Testament news . . . ," Mok said, to encourage his friend to keep speaking.

"Yes. Imagine a generation of people cut off from any books or news. Benjamin wanted to give them hope, much as Jesus has done for people of all centuries. As long as he had strength to continue, we arranged for people being exiled to Old Newyork to smuggle audiobooks and other supplies to help him begin underground churches.

"For two years, he avoided Zubluk and the other ganglords. When it looked like the disease was certain to take him, he found a way to end the fight. With Zubluk gone, you and your mother were safe. The other ganglords battled each other to take Zubluk's territory. The confusion gave the Christian followers a much better chance of growing."

Cambridge turned to Mok and smiled. "Of course, Benjamin Rufus left behind more than that. You."

Mok nodded, feeling a mixture of sadness and joy.

"I'm not sure when or how your mother died," Cambridge said. "But I do know that she left you an audiobook so that you could learn without her. As for your father, he left—"

"One of the world's largest corporations," Mok said.

"More than that, Mok." Cambridge's smile turned the older man's face from intense to peaceful. "A tiny transmitter, implanted in the skin just below your ankle. He had a plan for you from the very beginning."

Mok raised his eyebrows.

"It was difficult for me," Cambridge said. "Many nights I lay awake wondering if I should take you from the slums and put you in your rightful place here on Mainside. But already the Committee was looking for a way to find a leader . . ."

"All along you knew where I was?" Mok asked.

"You were lonely," Cambridge said. "But not alone. Field ops watched over you all through your childhood. Several times, we had members of the underground churches try to talk to you, but you always ran away."

"I trusted no one in the slums," Mok said. "It seemed the only way to survive."

"Many were the times I wondered if we should just bring you to Mainside instead of leaving you alone in the slums," Cambridge said. "I regret I couldn't have made your childhood better."

Mok thought about it. "You shouldn't have. Even my quest in cyberspace was as a baby is born into life—with no choice but to go forward. It was the same way then in Old Newyork. All of us live the same way. Lonely but not alone. God was with me, and the home he promises is much greater than a corporation waiting on Mainside."

"Yes," Cambridge said simply. "Thank you."

They let some silence pass. The ferry was half-way across the river.

"There is something else you should know," Cambridge said, so quietly that Mok barely heard him above the splash of water against the ferry's hull. "You may hear of it in Old Newyork, and I want you to be prepared. It's about Benjamin Rufus."

"Tell me," Mok said.

"As a young man, he was sent to Old Newyork as a prisoner, for fraud. It was his idea to convert the slum dwellers into factory slaves. It was how he began his fortune, how he was able to raise enough money to bribe his way back to Mainside. Finally, after discovering wealth and power did not bring peace, he looked for the answers to life. And he began to follow Jesus, the Galilee Man. That was why he dedicated everything he had to bringing hope back to the slums. Now you can finish undoing his great wrong."

Mok would have replied, except an approaching passenger caught his eye. The sight stunned him.

"Voice-in-the-Wind," he whispered, more to himself than to Cambridge.

For it was. The pharaoh's daughter. The servant girl in the castle. The beautiful Pawnee of the western plains. Slim and tall with shoulder-length black hair, she walked closer, smiling at Mok.

Cambridge saw Mok's attention was elsewhere and turned to see.

"Oh," Cambridge said. "Mok, let me introduce you to Madeline. She and I were your cyberguides."

"She?" Mok sputtered. Cyberguides. They had shown up at different times in different places, telling him just enough to help, but not enough to let him know what was happening. *These two were the cyberguides?* "You?"

"As I recall," Cambridge said, "it was in ancient Egypt that you first insisted on the name Stinko for me."

"You? The dwarf?"

"It was one of the more fun aspects of your quests," Cambridge said. "Madeline and I got hooked up to other computers and traveled through cyberspace to deliver messages to you."

Mok just shook his head.

"Anyway," Cambridge went on, "Madeline will be helping us over the next years in Old Newyork. You may not have realized it, but this is our chance to prove that faith can change lives. If we can show the world what faith can do, I'm certain the day will come when Christianity will not be outlawed on Mainside."

"She . . . is . . . helping . . ." Mok had trouble speaking.

"Don't be so surprised," Cambridge said. "Madeline is my daughter."

She smiled at Mok. He wanted to be angry for how she had tormented him in cyberspace, but all he could think of was the time they had ahead—and that mysterious smile of hers.

The ferry changed course as it made final adjustments to connect with the farside dock, now only a hundred yards away.

"Nearly there, Mok," Cambridge said. "This is your last chance. If you stay on the ferry, you can return to Mainside and a corporation worth billions."

"No," Mok said firmly. "I saw Jesus allow soldiers to nail spikes into his flesh. Whatever sacrifice I make is nothing compared to that."

Cambridge clutched Mok's shoulders. "What? You saw soldiers nail . . ."

"At the cross. In cyberspace. You know, when you sent me to Jerusalem for Jesus to heal my gunshot wound."

Mok could not understand why Cambridge looked so surprised.

It took until the ferry banged against the dock for Cambridge to be able to reply.

"Mok," Cambridge said, his voice shaky, "some will say it was your own memory, reaching for fragments from the audiobook of your childhood. Others will say it truly was a miracle, that

Jesus did reach out and touch you in your moment of greatest need."

"What are you trying to tell me?" Mok asked.

"After you were shot in the cybersegment in Paris, we lost all cybercontact with you. We were certain you would die."

Comprehension and awed wonder flashed across Mok's face.

"Yes," Cambridge said with equal awe. "We did not program a cybersegment to put you at the cross of Jesus. Whatever happened there, happened without us."

Now Mok knew for certain. The man on the cross still lived.